Dear Reader:

All I can say is fasten your seatbelt because you are about to go on a breathtaking ride. Allison Hobbs is an author whose time has come. It is time for her to garner the attention that she deserves with this, her third novel. If you have not read *Pandora's Box* and *Insatiable*, you have been sleeping on one of the best novelists on the scene. It amazes me when so many authors or their publishers put them out there to be "hotter than Zane" or "in the tradition of Zane" and they write nothing like me, nor do they understand my market. I can honestly say that if there is any author in existence today who writes similar to me, but yet has her own controversial and erotic style, it would be Allison Hobbs.

I met Allison at the Baltimore Book Festival several years ago. She had self-published *Pandora's Box* and I approached her and asked her a ton of questions; all of which she answered with much enthusiasm and excitement. I purchased her book and was convinced it was going to be awesome before I cracked it open. Why? Because Allison was an author writing for all the right reasons. She was bubbling with creativity and believed in her product; much like myself from the onset of my writing career. I was right because the book was off the chain. I did not believe she could top *Pandora's Box* because it was so realistic, so sexy, and so engaging that I was ready to go hang out in a brothel. I was wrong because *Insatiable* was equally amazing. Now with *Dangerously in Love* Allison has yet again outdone herself. That is the mark of a great writer; one who is committed to growing with each offering.

I want to thank you in advance for reading this book. I guarantee you will love it. I gu

novels. If you have enjoyed my books, then you will go crazy over hers. The characters are conversation pieces all by themselves. The amazing storyline is the icing on the cake. This is an ideal book club selection because it can be discussed for hours among members. Some books are good for fifteen minutes of discussion and then it is time to eat and mingle. With Allison's books, you could talk and debate into the wee hours of the night. She keeps it real and serious readers cannot help but appreciate her dedication to her craft.

I want to thank those of you who have been gracious enough to support the dozens of authors I publish under Strebor Books International, a division of ATRIA/Simon and Schuster. While writing serves as a catalyst for me to release my personal creativity, publishing allows me the opportunity to share the talent of so many others. If you are interested in being an independent sales representative for Strebor Books International, please send a blank email to info@streborbooks.com

Peace and Blessings,

Zane

Publisher
Strebor Books International
www.streborbooks.com

ZANE PRESENTS

Dangerously In
Love

Allison Hobbs

SBI

STREBOR BOOKS

NEW YORK LONDON TORONTO SYDNEY

Published by

SBI

Strebor Books
P.O. Box 6505
Largo, MD 20792
http://www.streborbooks.com

ISBN-13 978-1-59309-188-0
ISBN-10   1-59309-188-5
LCCN 2005920188

First Strebor Books mass market paperback edition May 2007

10 9 8 7 6 5 4 3 2 1

Manufactured in the United States of America

For information regarding special discounts for bulk purchases,
please contact Simon & Schuster Special Sales at 1-800-456-6798
or business@simonandschuster.com

To All My Ex-Husbands
Former Boyfriends
Current & Future Lovers

I Thank You For Sharing Your Male Energy
For It Has Empowered Me

ACKNOWLEDGMENTS

I want to first thank the publisher of Strebor Books, *New York Times* Bestselling Author Zane, who has opened doors that were closed to me and continues to graciously share "her" spotlight with me.

Next, I want to thank my best friend, Karen Dempsey Hammond. Actually, calling you my best friend doesn't adequately describe the relationship. You are my *family* in every sense of the word. I don't know how I would make it through this adventure called life without you by my side. Thank you for holding my hand through the entire process of writing this book as well as *Insatiable*. Honestly, there isn't enough room on this page for me to adequately thank you for all you've done for me and mine.

Shari Reason: You've traveled up and down I-95 to book signings with me for the past two years and I deeply appreciate your loyalty, love, and support. Most important, I love you for loving my son. Hugs and kisses to my new family: Marquan Reason and Raekwaan Reason and my two little angels: Kha'ri Johnson and Kareem Johnson.

Kameron Hobbs and Keenan Hobbs. I probably don't say it enough, so here it is in print…I love you both from the bottom of my heart.

Kyndal Hobbs & Carl "Korky" Johnson: I love you, love you, love you.

To my Sister authors: Darrien Lee and Tina Brooks McKinney. You two are more than just fellow authors… I truly consider you both friends.

Rick and Charmaine Parker, Destiny Wood, Carlita Marsh, Dante Feenix, Shelley Halima, Harold L. Turley II, Keith Lee Johnson, Daaimah S. Poole, Nane Quartay, Rasheda Lewis, Reds and Wandan at the Delmar, Chanelle and Kendrick Sealy, Salima Jones, Frank Black, Kia Meyers, and Aletha Dempsey, I thank you all. Your sincere kindness has been a blessing in my life.

Bestselling Author Mary Monroe: We may be kindred spirits but I'll always be your biggest fan!

Nakea S. Murray of As The Page Turns Book Club in Philadelphia: Nakea and the book club members graciously invited me to their book club meeting in the park back when I was still a self-published author. I was scared to death to read a passage from *Pandora's Box*, but their warmth and encouragement made it a wonderful experience. I'm so proud that these intelligent and passionate readers are still holding it down in Philly.

Sunni K. Harley of The Princess Book Club: Thanks for the wonderful gifts and your support.

Special thanks to the best web designers on the planet: Cory and Heather Buford.

Thank you, Keith Saunders of Marion Designs for the banging book covers.

Finally…Dear Readers: Thank you for your support. I appreciate the time you've taken to come out to my book signings and I thank you for the emails you've sent letting me know how much you've enjoyed my work. I'm humbled by your words of praise and encouragement.

Much Love,
Allison Hobbs

Chapter 1

Dayna Reynolds stared at the test stick, took a deep breath, and waited for it to turn pink. Nothing happened. It was negative…again. Stabbed by the familiar pang of disappointment, she closed the lid of the cushy toilet seat and sank down onto it. Inconsolably sad, she dropped her head in her hands. Then, overtaken by a sudden hot anger, she hurled the test stick along with the empty home pregnancy kit into the wastebasket. Another fifteen dollars wasted. The hell with home pregnancy kits; she would not give the E.P.T. manufacturers another red cent.

She'd stopped taking the Pill a month after her marriage…and now, three years later, she still wasn't pregnant.

No longer able to skirt the issue, she had to face the fact that she and Reed had a problem. She wrinkled her brow in thought. Surely, *she* wasn't the cause; she was as fertile as they come. Two abortions during her college years attested to that fact.

Reed, on the other hand, had no children and had never been accused of fathering a child. He took pride in having been responsible when he was young, wild, and single, using condoms even when his partner swore up and down that she was taking the Pill. Most of his friends had been making child support payments since their early twenties. Teasingly, Reed often said that at the rate his buddies were still impregnating women, they'd be making child support payments well into their retirement years.

That line used to make her laugh, but today she found no humor in the fact that Reed's friends were procreating like jackrabbits. At thirty-four years old, her biological clock was ticking loud and fast. If she didn't conceive soon, she'd be at risk for all types of complications during pregnancy and while in labor. And if that wasn't bad enough, she'd read somewhere that a first-time pregnancy for women over the age of thirty-five was considered a *geriatric pregnancy*. Jeez!

Reed didn't seem the least bit concerned that they were childless.

Gloomily, she gazed around her beautiful mauve and gray bathroom. From the glitzy multi-colored shower curtains, plush bath mat, and thick towels and washcloths, to the soap trays and toothbrush rack—everything was expensive and perfectly matched. Great care was given to every room in her spacious Mount Airy home, yet her lovely home provided little joy.

She wanted, no, *needed* a baby. The pain and yearning was constant and felt quite physical.

Something had to be done and it had to be done soon.

First, Reed had to get tested. He needed to take a

sperm count test or something. But how could she bring up such a sensitive subject without bruising his ego? It was bad enough that she had a master's degree in special education and had been teaching for over ten years in the Philadelphia school district, earning a salary that more than doubled the money Reed made as an office manager at a telemarketing company.

He just wasn't ambitious enough.

After dating only six months, Dayna and Reed got married. Reed Reynolds, a product of the 'hood, was bilingual. He was articulate when necessary, but also fluent in hip street jargon and had convinced Dayna as well as her newly divorced parents that he had a plan to overcome his humble beginnings. That plan included obtaining an undergraduate degree from Penn's Wharton School. That prestigious degree would open many doors in corporate America, he'd said optimistically.

Dayna's father, Joshua Hinton, Esquire, typically overly cautious, was so easily won over by the charming future Wharton grad that he'd eagerly forked over twenty-five thousand dollars as a wedding gift to be used as a down payment on Dayna and Reed's Tudor-style home.

It was guilt money. Her father had left her mother after twenty-nine years of marriage. His new bride, or *that bitch* as Dayna's mother called her, seemed none too pleased about the wedding gift. Tough! Who cared what that home wrecker thought?

Though Dayna was a grown woman, the wound of

her father's abandonment had yet to heal and it didn't help that she was being further traumatized because her father and mother were having what could only be called an adulterous affair. Her father had somehow managed to turn his former wife into his mistress. It was a shameful disgrace and it hurt to the core to see her mother reduced to *other woman* status.

Sucking her teeth in disgust, Dayna directed her ponderings to her own marital problems. Unbeknownst to her parents, Reed had dropped out of school, deciding that higher education was a waste of a black man's time. He said he could accomplish more by becoming a member of the PBP, the Professional Brothers of Philadelphia, and networking with the members whom he referred to as his brothers. Dayna dreaded having to break that news to her parents and decided not to share this information with them unless they asked her outright.

Now he was rarely at home; he seemed more like a guest than an actual resident of the household. Reed spent long hours after work involved in PBP business. He often went away for weekends to secretive locations with his professional brothers. Wives were never welcome.

Aside from the innate desire to bear a child, Dayna also believed a baby could save her floundering marriage. No doubt, Reed would balk at being dragged to her gynecologist for testing, but perhaps he'd agree to see a male fertility specialist.

Buoyed by the idea of cajoling her husband into seeking help from a qualified physician, Dayna sprang up and trotted down the stairs to her fully equipped, ultra-modern kitchen. Preparing her husband's favorite meal might soften him up just enough so she could initiate the discussion of seeing a doctor.

And if it turned out that Reed had a low sperm, count or worse, if it turned out he was sterile, they'd at least know what they were dealing with and could make an informed decision on what to do. Artificial insemination, adoption, or perhaps there was some new miracle treatment for sterility? They'd never know if they didn't confront the problem.

☙❧☙

"You really put your foot in this potato salad," Reed said cheerfully as he forked up another heap that instantly disappeared into his mouth. Dayna accepted the compliment with a proud smile, though she'd merely added a little Dijon mustard and a couple teaspoons of relish to the ready-made container she'd purchased from the Farmer's Market in Chestnut Hill. The chicken he'd already devoured, however, was breaded and fried by her own hands.

"Try the green beans," she encouraged sweetly. The fresh green beans seasoned with minced garlic and basil was also her own creation.

"Don't worry; I'll get to those in a minute. Hey, how come you're not eating?" he asked when he realized Dayna was sipping tea and had not prepared a plate for herself.

"No appetite." She shrugged. "I guess I did too much taste-testing while I was cooking."

In three short years, she'd ballooned from a size eight to size fourteen and she realized if she didn't cut back, she'd be an absolute blimp during and after the anticipated pregnancy.

Reed nodded in understanding and continued wolfing down the potato salad.

She briefly gazed at him with pure adoration. He was so good looking, with his bright brown eyes, wavy hair, and gorgeous kissable lips. Reed was definitely considered a pretty boy! Together, they'd make a beautiful child.

Wondering if it was the right time to bring up the subject that weighed heavily on her mind, Dayna took another sip of tea, watching Reed like a hawk as she tried to gauge his mood.

Taking a chance, she cleared her throat. "How was work?" she asked, easing into the sensitive discussion.

"Same ol' shit." He looked up. "That's why I'm glad I joined the PBP. Those brothers are really about something.

"Yeah," he went on, "one of my brothers is hosting a meeting tonight at the Hilton Hotel on City Avenue. He's conducting a seminar for a new business venture that I'd love to get involved with while it's still on the ground floor. I'm gonna go check it out tonight."

"Tonight!" Dayna blurted. "I thought we'd spend a quiet evening together. You're hardly ever at home, Reed."

Reed pushed his unfinished plate away, shoved his chair away from the table, and stood up. "You're always complaining about my job...I don't make enough money... there's no potential for growth. I want to go to the meeting to get some information on a career where I might be able to make a decent income and call my own shots. Why are you trying to stop me?"

"That's not true, Reed. I don't complain about your job or any of your extracurricular activities. You know I'm one hundred percent supportive of— "

"Cut the crap. You're always bragging about your education and your salary." His face twisted with what appeared to be hatred. "I know your parents think you're slumming with me..."

Dayna stood up and calmly maneuvered around the oblong table and stood next to her husband. Determined to salvage the evening and keep her husband at home, she smoothed the hairs on his forearm comfortingly, and spoke softly. "My mother welcomed you with open arms and my dad certainly wouldn't have given us that down payment for this big house," Dayna waved her free hand extravagantly, "if he had any doubt about your earning potential."

Reed jerked his arm away. "Yeah, that's right. Your daddy gave us the down payment for the house. You know something? Accepting that money was a big mistake because every chance you get, you throw it up in my face." Reed flung the cloth napkin he'd been clutching onto the dining room table. He stomped into the living room, and grabbed his briefcase. "I'm out! Don't wait up for me!"

The slam of the front door, followed by the sound of Reed's car screeching out of the driveway, dashed all hopes of a civilized conversation that would lead to a visit to a qualified fertility specialist.

Dayna sagged into the chair Reed had just vacated. Feeling disoriented, she tried to sort out her thoughts and figure out what had just happened. What had she said to set him off like that? Absolutely nothing, she concluded. The numerous PBP meetings and even the alleged meeting at the Hilton was probably just a façade, convenient excuses to get out of the house.

He hated being around her; she was too fat. Oh God, why had she allowed herself to gain so much weight? Pondering the question, Dayna gobbled down the leftover potato salad on Reed's plate as well as the untouched green beans that were slathered with butter. Pushing away from the dining room table, she got up and ambled to the kitchen, where she stuck her hand inside a plastic container lined with napkins and helped herself to two fried chicken wings, a breast, and a thigh.

Filled to the gills, she felt worse than ever, but couldn't stop eating. With spoon in hand, she sought comfort inside a container of Ben & Jerry's ice cream. Then, shaking her head in bewilderment, she trudged up the elaborate winding staircase to relax and mentally prepare for another work day.

Chapter 2

Ignoring the 25-mile-an-hour speed limit on Lincoln Drive, Reed pushed the needle on the speedometer to seventy. Like a man possessed, he took the dangerous curves without a thought of decreasing his speed. The former Victorian hotel on the corner of Lincoln Drive and Gypsy Lane that now served as a police station became a quick blur as Reed defiantly zoomed past. Official Philadelphia police cars parked outside did not deter Reed. As far as he was concerned, the officers of the law that occupied the ancient-looking police barracks seemed more like park rangers than real cops. Fuck 'em. Those suckers were probably inside knocking off a couple boxes of Krispy Kreme donuts.

Reed gave a snort as he imagined his wife's reaction if she were sitting in the passenger's seat. He could just hear her: *Slow down, Reed*, she'd whine. *It's dangerous to speed on Lincoln Drive. You know what happened to that famous singer when we were kids—*

Then Reed would interject: *Chill out, Dayna. I can handle these curves without breaking my neck.*

He suffered a spinal cord injury, Dayna the Know-It-All would correct.

Neck, spine, whatever. Your face isn't buried in my lap, so I know I won't be going out like him.

Irked by Dayna's superior attitude, he'd feel compelled to drive even faster. Throughout her squeals of protest, her face contorted in fear, his wife would undoubtedly be holding on to the overhead handle while pressing her foot into an imaginary brake on the floor.

But thankfully, he didn't have to listen to her whine. Not tonight. Reed swerved to the left and headed for City Avenue. When he neared the Hilton Hotel, he accelerated instead of turning toward the parking lot entrance.

He checked the time. Six-thirty. Plenty of time to take care of what he had to do. Then, after a couple of hours of stress release, he'd head back to the Hilton to network for the last half-hour of the seminar. Yeah, a half-hour was all a brother needed to make some connections. Reed had little patience for sitting around listening to a bunch of speakers.

His car might as well have been on automatic pilot, for Reed had made no conscious decision to drive to Thirty-Eighth and Chestnut. He chuckled to himself and gave a shrug of indifference as he parked and then quickly ducked into the discreet entrance of Lizzard's, a strip joint in the heart of University City. The club featured a large selection of women with varying body types.

The few black chicks employed by Lizzard's were exceptionally pretty with perfect bodies. Indeed, some of the best black eye candy in the city was found swiveling down the pole at Lizzard's. Problem was, you could look but you couldn't touch unless you paid a crazy amount of money for a quick and unfulfilling couch dance. The stupid no-physical-contact rule irked the hell out of Reed. Still, just being in this tits and ass environment gave him a rush.

"Corona," he said to the bartender, knowing he'd get a scowl of incomprehension if he asked for a can of Old English, his preferred libation.

Sipping the weak beer, he winked at the dancer on stage. Heidi, a petite busty brunette, instantly sauntered over to Reed, trying to give him the impression that her performance was exclusively for him. But after licking her lips and rubbing her tits for over sixty seconds without a tip, she huffily moved on to the next lustful patron.

"Is Sensation dancing tonight?" he asked the bartender.

"Yup, she's up next," the bartender said, yawning pointedly as he looked down at his watch.

Reed gave the bartender a sneer; the guy had to be a fucking faggot to act like he was all bored and bothered by the never-ending parade of tits and ass featured at the strip club. His annoyance with the bartender, however, became a foggy memory the moment his favorite girl, Sensation, hit the stage in a flash of pink.

Coffee-colored with a drop of cream, Sensation looked good enough to eat in her glow-in-the-dark neon pink thong set. Curly blonde waist-length extensions swayed as she undulated to a slow song.

Sensation gave Reed a come-hither look, seducing him with pouting lips as she sensually rotated her hips, persuading him to dig deep into his pockets and pay for the special attention she was giving him. With a subtle pelvic thrust she urged him to be generous. *Pay me!* her body screamed.

Reed, however, interpreted her body language in an entirely different way. Her body was talking to him. Writhing with mounting desire, she was begging to get sexed up. Every gyration was a cry for release. Release that only he could provide.

Talk to me, baby! I know you want this dick. He almost shouted the words out loud, but restrained himself as he imagined himself and Sensation sweaty and naked, engaging in all the positions of the Kama Sutra.

With his eyes fixed on Sensation, his imagination running wild, Reed was at first unaware that many of the men in the club, also aroused by her display of oozing sexuality, had moved to the front of the stage and were showing their appreciation by flinging fives and tens onto the stage. These men, mostly suit-wearing Caucasians, seemed to be of one mind and had left Reed behind with their display of generosity.

Fighting for position was a wearisome reality at his place of employment. But he'd be damned if he'd allow himself to be chumped outside of the workplace and in front of a sister. Reed pulled out a neatly folded wad of one-dollar bills. He scowled at the money and stuffed it back into his pocket. Sensation deserved currency of a much higher denomination—a twenty at the least. From his back pocket, he extracted another wad and peeled off a twenty, changed his mind, put it back in his pocket, and pulled out a ten. Ten dollars was enough for the moment. He'd give her much more when they got together later at her place or at a hotel.

Quite suddenly, Sensation dropped to all fours and went into a sexy panther-like crawl, her hair sweeping the floor. Transfixed by this carnal exhibition, Reed forgot to throw his money on stage. Moments later, his reverie was broken by rude catcalls and whistles as a slew of drunken pink-faced college students rushed the stage. They made airplanes out of five-, ten-, and even twenty-dollar bills. Airborne money crash-landed on the stage. Caught up in schoolboy-ish frivolity, the men in suits decided to join in. As drunk now as the college kids, the suits absurdly attempted to transform their bills into airplanes, but having forgotten the technique, they quickly gave up and resorted to balling up the dollars and throwing them onstage.

Seemingly unaffected by the ever-increasing mounds of cash, Sensation eased into the next song. Climbing the pole like a slithering snake, she descended upside-down with only one leg wrapped around the pole. When both feet hit the stage, she stood stock still with her back turned to the crowd. Nothing moved except her perfectly round buttocks. One cheek at a time, her ass danced. The white guys howled in drunken delight, and threw more money at Sensation. Reed, an admitted ass-man, felt tortured as he watched Sensation's cheeks clap.

She moved quickly across the stage and jumped into a handstand. Working her ass muscles to the beat of the song, Sensation drove the crowd wild.

A hot current raced through Reed's loins, causing a swelling so painful, he prayed he wouldn't explode in his pants. He couldn't think straight. His dick was too hard. His mind was muddled and the only coherent thought running across his brain was that he had to get inside that pussy.

At this point, had he dwelled in a world without social constraints, Reed would have simply snatched Sensation off the stage, thrown her luscious body over his shoulders caveman style, and whisked her off to his private cave where he'd devote hours to ravishing her ass, her pussy, her mouth. What the hell, he'd fuck her tits, too. He'd fuck them until the skin was chafed and raw.

But sadly, he didn't abide in such a world. In his world, a man had to exercise great patience to get what he wanted. He had to put in the time to flatter, court, cajole, and ultimately pay for what should rightfully be his.

Paying for pussy seemed unfair, but Reed wanted

Sensation and he was willing to pay. Fuck getting her digits and bullshitting on the phone, fuck dinner and the movies. Plain and simple, he just wanted to fuck.

When the song ended, Sensation gathered and picked up the cornucopia of bills that were strewn around the stage in various shapes and denominations. She tossed the money inside a plastic bucket and sashayed off the stage. There had to be at least four hundred dollars in that bucket, Reed surmised. Not bad for fifteen minutes' worth of work.

Sensation had another set, but Reed had grown tired of this rock-hard-dick-inducing atmosphere that encouraged suckers to throw away their money, but offered no prospect of relief. He decided to go outside and chill in his whip…roll a Dutch and listen to some sounds until Sensation came out. It was now 8:03. Reed knew her four-hour shift ended at eight-thirty, so he had less than a half-hour wait. He hoped her price wasn't so steep he had to stop and tap an ATM machine.

When Sensation finally emerged from the club, Reed unconsciously began stroking himself. Looking like a chocolate milkshake poured into skin-tight jeans, Sensation slung a huge plastic Von Dutch bag over her shoulder and ambled toward the pizza parlor next door to the club.

Reed honked the horn. She stopped, turned in his direction. Recognizing him, she smiled and waved, but continued her purposeful trek.

Damn, now he had to wait for her to order a damn pizza!

He leaned back in his seat and got comfortable. Though there'd been no verbal communication between him and Sensation, and though no plans had been made to spend an evening together, Reed was convinced they shared the same carnal desire. That smile and the wave she just gave him was her way of asking him to wait a minute while she bought some grub. He knew she wanted some dick, but due to her line of work, she probably would expect to be compensated.

Hey, he couldn't blame her for mixing business with pleasure.

Swinging her hips, Sensation trotted past the pizza parlor, then slowed her stride and sauntered over to a parked gray Bentley. The driver, a young black man wearing a bright-colored do-rag, rolled down his tinted window. Sensation leaned in and gave the driver a kiss, and then dreamily glided around the car to the passenger side.

It was a startling revelation; Sensation was getting it on with Stone Allen, the star of the Philadelphia Seventy-Sixers! And if that wasn't Stone Allen, then he damn sure had a twin. Stunned, Reed didn't know how to feel. Damn! Stone was the man and everything, but goddamn, he could have any female on the planet, why'd he have to roll up and grip Sensation?

Defeated, Reed watched the Bentley as it ripped down Chestnut Street.

Chapter 3

Sensation had played him. That shit she had pulled was real greasy. Quietly seething, Reed entered the Apache, a strip joint on Masters Street in West Philly. Predictably, the club was dark, crowded, and funky. The Apache was a dive and any female who walked through the door could get hired. Fat, skinny, young, old—it didn't matter as long as the woman had a pussy, a set of tits, and an ass.

He scanned the pickings. It wasn't a pretty sight. Never in his life had he seen so many trifling-looking women parading around half naked. They were all drug addicts; they had to be because any woman who put herself on display looking that damn bad in a thong had to be on drugs. And even the women who had banging bodies and nice-looking faces were crazy—certifiably! He knew this to be true because he'd been intimately involved with enough dancers to know they all had issues.

Each woman who sidled up to him quickly scurried away. His scowl of disgust dissuaded even the most ambitious dancer from soliciting him for a lap dance.

The hell with a lap dance. The only thing on Reed's

mind was sex. He wanted to fuck. Straight up! No chitchat, no persuasive sweet talk, no haggling over the price. And the only girl who clearly understood his needs was Buttercup. He usually gave her forty dollars for a lap dance that quickly progressed to intercourse. So where the hell was she? Searching for Buttercup, Reed squeezed through the dark, musty, smoke-filled dive. He wished he were carrying Chuck's flashlight. Chuck managed the Apache and one of his responsibilities was to patrol the place, looking for any couple who appeared to be engaged in more than a lap dance. Chuck used his flashlight to illuminate the dirty dealings of any girl who was trickin' on the low. When caught, the girl had to give Chuck his cut. Any slick bitch with her thong pulled to the side who didn't pay up was instantly ejected and banned from the club permanently. Chuck didn't play those types of games.

"Hey, playa, you dancing?" asked a nutritionally challenged woman. Her practiced smile radiated confidence, but desperation shone in her eyes.

"You seen Buttercup?" Reed asked the woman.

The woman huffed up; her fake smile quickly twisted into a sneer. "Damn, nigga, why you gotta come off like that? I axed if you was dancing? Now, how you sound axin' me 'bout some other bitch?"

"My bad," Reed said, admitting to his bad manners. He pulled out two dollars. "I'm not dancing, sis, but here's a little something for your time." He took a deep breath to calm himself for he felt on the verge of strangling the little toothpick of a woman, an obvious smoker who was wasting his time and withholding important information.

Like a magician, the skinny dancer did a hand trick so swift, the two dollar bills went poof! The money disappeared somewhere inside her sagging costume. "My name is Flava, nigga—not *sis*," the dancer snarled once the money was safely tucked away.

"Yo, don't be comin' at me like that! I gave you a couple of dollars. Now, whassup? Is Buttercup here or not?"

"How the fuck should I know? Ax Chuck. He got the list; he oughta know whether or not she signed in tonight." Flava rolled her eyes at Reed and then weaved through the crowd, walking fast like she had just picked somebody's pocket.

Standing still, Reed scanned the dark room hoping to see the flicker of Chuck's flashlight. Or better yet, he hoped to catch a glimpse of Buttercup. He located neither. Feeling like a voyeur, he unwittingly observed couple after couple getting their freak on atop swiveling barstools, metal-folding chairs, and wooden benches. Some were standing up, copulating against the wall, their bodies twisted like contortionists as they got their freak on.

It wasn't his night, Reed angrily resolved. If he'd had a pistol he would have gladly unleashed his sinister side— the fiend that lurked within would have opened fire and, starting with that ugly little runt who called herself Flava, every hooker in the house would be dead.

✥✥✥✥✥

Someone approached from the shadows. "You dancin'?" The voice was low and lacked enthusiasm, as if she expected to be turned down.

A quick glance revealed a moon-faced, rather homely woman. The tire around her waistline spoke of too many late-night snacks and a long-expired membership at L.A. Fitness. Her appearance, coupled with a defeatist's attitude, assured Reed of getting what he wanted: a quick, cheap fuck. He nodded his head and allowed the dancer to lead him to an empty folding chair. Reed dragged the chair from the heavily populated area where it was positioned and took it to a more secluded area. "How much?" he wanted to know.

"Five dollars for a dance." The dancer quickly began to squat down into his lap. Reed caught a strong whiff of ass, which mercifully dissipated as the dancer began brushing her bare buttocks across his crotch.

Craning her neck, the dancer looked back at Reed and smiled. "My name's Unique," she offered when she felt the swollen lump that pressed urgently against her ass. "I'm giving out specials tonight—two dances for eight dollars."

He pressed his fingers into her shoulders, repositioning the woman so that she was sitting on top of his throbbing appendage. Her skin was damp—disgustingly clammy, but on nights like tonight when his sex drive was off the meter, a funky ass and sweaty skin would not deter him.

"How much to hit it?" he asked in a husky voice.

Unique stopped rotating her hips. She brushed copper-colored synthetic hair away from her face and looked over her shoulder at Reed. "You got a rubber?"

"Yeah, I got protection…how much?" Reed asked impatiently as he pulled her thong to the side.

"Um…fifty?"

"Fifty! Yo, that's too steep." He pushed her off his lap.

"Okay," she said, hastily wiggling back into position. "Thirty dollars; but I can't go no lower than that."

"Twenty," Reed insisted.

"Okay, but you gotta be quick because I'm not tryin' to break Chuck off when his nosy ass starts flickin' that damn flashlight over here," she grumbled.

Reed stuck the money in her hand. Seconds later he rolled on a condom.

"Ow," Unique complained when Reed tried to penetrate.

Reed smeared a generous amount of spit on his two middle fingers and inserted them, instantly moisturizing Unique's dry vagina. Fuck foreplay.

An adrenaline rush caused him to groan as he was overtaken by the incredible feeling of being inside wet pussy. Desiring even deeper penetration, he tightly gripped the dancer's flabby waist and pulled her closer.

Though Reed was hurting her, the dancer bit her bottom lip and bravely took the pain. Bouncing up and down with fake enthusiasm, she tried to hurry him along, hoping to get him off as quickly as possible.

While Unique pumped up and down in a seated position, Reed began to feel a familiar warm sensation followed by an increased heart rate. He was about to burst. Stealthily, he removed the condom. The music drowned out his savage cry.

Reed quickly stood up and zipped his pants. By the time Unique felt his hot cum running down her leg, Reed had vanished into the crowd.

Muttering curse words, such as "dirty," "slimy," "no-good bastard," Unique walked gap-legged into the restroom to clean herself up.

Finally satiated, Reed hopped in his car, revved his motor, and headed for home. The hell with the club meeting, he was too weary to put on the professional mask he wore around his pompous brothers.

Chapter 4

Happy Hour. Humph! Dayna was none too happy sitting at a bar munching on stale pretzels, but she'd been coerced by her friend Cecily to stop moping around dwelling on her marital problems. "Come on out and have a good time," Cecily had said. "Forget about Reed for a few hours. I don't know why you want to rush home; it's not like he's gonna be there with flowers, soft music, and a romantic meal. It's Friday, girl, and you know you won't be seeing him until well after midnight."

Dayna sighed in resignation. She gazed in the mirror behind the bar and wasn't too pleased with her image. Her attire was tailored and immaculate, and the cash she doled out to her beautician every week to keep her hair trimmed and stylish was money well spent, but Dayna lacked pizzazz. She had light brown skin and a roundish face. In the looks department, she was just ordinary. But at that moment, she felt so unattractive, so utterly unglamorous, she could have wept. No wonder she couldn't keep her husband at home.

Fifteen minutes into Happy Hour and she still wasn't

feeling very happy. In fact, she felt annoyed. Irritable. She shouldn't have allowed Cecily to drag her to this meat market for the thirty-something and over crowd. Back when she was single, she'd participated in all the singles' scenes; she knew the routine well. The more she thought about it, the more she regretted her decision to hang out in a club with a bunch of anxious-looking, desperate women.

She didn't belong here. She had what all the other sisters were looking for: a handsome husband and a beautiful home. Okay, her marriage was falling apart and her husband certainly wasn't the best in the world, but at least she had one. And she planned on keeping him. She just had to try something new. Lose weight, start wearing sexy lingerie. She'd think of some way to keep her marriage intact.

"Two Silk Panties," Cecily told the bartender with a wink.

"Silk Panties?" Dayna lifted a brow.

"Top-shelf vodka with a mixture of fruity liqueur. It's really good. Trust me, you're gonna love it."

The bartender returned with two pastel-colored drinks adorned with fruit on a plastic stick. "Drink slowly," Cecily advised. "It may look harmless, but it's potent. Two glasses will have you staggering up to Mr. Wrong, slurring your words while you're getting your flirt on."

"That won't be me." Dayna chuckled, waving her wedding band. She took a sip. "Mmm," she moaned in approval.

Cecily beamed with pride. "Do I know my drinks or what?"

"You got it going on, girl." Feeling less ornery, Dayna made a slight swivel on the barstool to observe her environment. It was early. Separated by an imaginary line, the men and women had not yet converged.

The women were clumped together in various groups sipping cocktails and bantering lightheartedly as if they didn't have a care in the world. But nervous adjustments to hemlines, stealthy glances in the mirror behind the bar, and quick hand pats to fresh hairdos implied that they weren't really feeling secure.

The men congregated together in various locations talking politics and sports. Enjoying each others company, they appeared confident and oblivious to the presence of the females.

As the evening progressed, echoes of high-pitched laughter intermingled with rich baritone mirth served as the musical prelude to the sensual drama that would soon unfold. The two genders had come to the club under the pretense of having the same goal: to kick back and unwind after a hard day's work. But each sex had a hidden agenda.

Most of the women in the club were single and desperate to catch an available man. They exuded carefree confidence but their motion detectors were on high alert to track a good-looking…well-dressed…successful man. It wouldn't be long, however, before they were hit with the realization that the pickings were slim. Then, after having indulged in one drink too many, most of the women would be willing to settle for a man who looked half-ass decent and could show evidence that he held down some type of steady job. Those who were most desperate would resignedly converse with the unattractive and even the "temporarily" unemployed while searching for any redeemable quality—a nice smile, a great sense of humor, or that he was just the right height.

The men, on the other hand, knew it was their world, which was why they remained aloof. Seemingly detached, the men appeared to have no desire for a woman's company.

An hour and a half into Happy Hour the mating dance commenced. A silent alarm must have sounded because the men began to slowly close in on the women, surrounding them like sharks circling prey. There were no offers to buy the women drinks. They didn't want to waste time or their good money on a deal that was being negotiated but had not been closed. The only thing a man needed to lure a helpless female was a good opening line and a seemingly earnest smile. Grateful to be chosen, the women smiled back with mouths that twitched slightly from intoxication. Fatigue. Resignation.

After listening to a pack of well-honed lies, the women typically left the club with the sharks. After engaging in meaningless sex, the women soon discovered, they'd lost their only bargaining chip. The next week, they'd return to Happy Hour determined to choose more carefully— to not make the same rash mistake.

Out of the corner of her eye, Dayna spotted a familiar-looking woman who was confidently feeding a good-looking hunk of a man the cherry from her drink. Dayna felt an instant and intense dislike for the woman before her mind could put a name with the face. Instincts alerted her that this person was not someone she'd want to encounter. Dayna swiveled back around, hoping she hadn't been recognized.

She quickly engaged Cecily in meaningless chatter, hoping to appear involved in a conversation so intense, a polite person wouldn't interrupt. But the woman who turned out to be Regina, a former classmate of Dayna's from Howard University, was obviously not a polite person. She tapped Dayna on her shoulder. Dayna turned around, manufactured a look of delighted surprise, and hugged Regina as if she were a long-lost friend.

With the hunk in tow, Regina said, "What a surprise. How are you, Dayna?" Both women shot glances at each other's ring finger.

"I'm great!" Dayna lied through her smiling teeth.

"I want you to meet my husband." She said the word *husband* with such pride, Dayna wanted to pimp slap both of them for bringing their happiness into her troubled corner of the world.

"Dayna, this is Roger, my husband and partner. We just opened our law practice on Eighteenth and Pine," Regina said, practically bursting with pride. Rent was not cheap in that tree-lined area of brownstones and expensive shops. "We're out celebrating." She turned to her handsome husband. "Roger, this is Dayna; we attended Howard together."

Dayna introduced Cecily to the couple, who resembled black Barbie and Ken dolls.

"I see you're married, Dayna," Regina said, shifting her gaze to Dayna's ring finger.

"Yes, three years," Dayna said with sunshine in her tone.

"Oh, how wonderful. You're a teacher, correct?"

Dayna nodded and tried to look proud of her career choice.

"What's your husband do?"

"He runs a brokerage firm. He's in Chicago. His job requires constant traveling, meeting with all their top clients—you know." Desperate not to appear pathetic, Dayna lied with ease.

Regina scowled. "Must put a strain on the marriage?"

"Quite the contrary. You know what they say…absence makes the heart grow fonder."

Not buying Dayna's fabricated happy life story, Regina scowled again.

"Any kids?"

Ouch! "No, not yet; too busy with our careers."

"Show her the twins, honey," the Ken doll piped in.

Regina dug into her purse and pulled out a photo of a beautiful boy and girl. "These are our children... Madison and Kyle. Aren't they perfect?"

And they were. Dayna could have cried with envy.

"We were so lucky to get one of each the first time. They're twenty-four months, but the term the terrible twos does not apply to our children...right, darling?" She looked up adoringly at her husband.

"Right, sweetie. They're as well behaved as they are beautiful."

"And smart!" Regina added gleefully. "They're learning to speak French. Can you imagine two-year-olds responding, '*oui, oui*'? It's so darn cute."

"The twins have Regina's beauty," Roger said with a goofy grin that instantly transformed him from a handsome attorney to a nerdy henpecked husband.

Regina bobbed her head in agreement, and then gushed, "And they have Roger's brains."

Dayna *hated, hated, hated* this Stepford couple; she could feel her forced smile begin to twitch as the verbal assault escalated.

"Look, it was really nice seeing you again, Regina. Nice meeting you, Roger," Dayna said, easing off the barstool. "I have to get to the ladies room. Too many of those." She nodded her head toward the half-filled glass of the vodka concoction.

Regina and Roger departed gracefully and Dayna dashed to the ladies room.

Her bladder did not demand immediate attention, but her bruised ego did. She pulled her cell out of her purse and speed-dialed Reed's cell.

"Hello," Reed said cheerfully.

"Where are you?"

"Home. Why?"

Dayna checked her watch. "Stay there; we need to have a serious discussion. I'll be home in a half-hour."

"Whoa! I've already made plans; I'm on my way out. Whatever you want to talk about can wait until later tonight."

"Later tonight? When? Three, four in the morning?"

"Dayna," Reed said calmly. "I've told you a million times to stop trying to keep tabs on me. We'll talk when I get back. If you're asleep, then we'll talk first thing in the morning."

Dayna's cell went dead. Her husband hadn't even asked where she was or if she was all right. Her marriage was such a sham. It was as if Reed used their home only as a place to shower and change clothes. He rarely even ate dinner at home. Too busy with his brothers…or his whores, as Dayna suspected.

Needing a shoulder to cry on, she flipped open her cell and called her mother.

It was only a little past eight in the evening, yet her mother answered with a sleepy "Hello?"

"Hey, Mom, did I wake you?"

"Um, I must have dozed off. Is something wrong?" her mom inquired in a whispery voice.

Dayna could tell the difference between a lustful voice and the voice of someone who had been awakened from sleep. Her mom was obviously in the middle of having sex.

"Get your rest, Mom. I'll talk to you tomorrow." Dayna snapped her phone closed. In deep thought, she leaned against the sink.

Dayna would have loved to be happy for her mom but all she felt for her was pity. That her mother had been demoted to the role of mistress was absolutely immoral.

Feeling lost and close to tears, Dayna returned to the bar with a prepared excuse. "I have to go, Cecily. My mom's having some type of crisis."

"Over your dad? She's still hasn't accepted the divorce, his marriage?" Cecily asked in amazement.

"After being married for thirty years; I imagine it's hard to move on," Dayna said with defensiveness in her tone.

She left the bar feeling confused and miserable. A daughter experiencing marital trouble should be able to go to her mother for emotional support, but her mother was in worse shape than she was, leaving Dayna without a soul she could turn to.

Chapter 5

T he bedroom was junky with second-hand furnish-
ings. There was a vast difference between this room
and his stylish bedroom at home.

In an act of decadent self-indulgence, Reed's eyes
roamed freely as he excitedly took in every nuance of his
surroundings. Sitting atop a dusty nightstand was a lip-
stick-stained glass containing murky brown liquid with a
cigarette butt floating inside. Crumbs and other uniden-
tifiable bits of debris dotted a worn carpet. His lustful eyes
rested on the unmade bed. The rumpled sheets spoke of
uninhibited passion. Hot, satisfying illicit sex.

In a squalid room such as this a man could reveal his
darkest secrets. He could act upon carnal desires that would
cause a wife to grimace and recoil in horror, and even
question his sanity.

A man could unleash the demons that allowed him no
peace.

Buttercup was in the bathroom and although Reed
could hear the sound of running water, he doubted that
she was actually taking a bath; most likely she was in
there getting high. He didn't mind. Buttercup became

more agreeable to his freakish requests when she was high. He smiled sardonically as he unzipped his pants, reached inside, and began to soothingly stroke the agitated beast while he waited for Buttercup.

Clutching the long red wig she'd had on earlier at Club Apache, Buttercup came out of the bathroom wrapped in a thin dingy towel. She looked entirely different than she did at work; she smelled different, too. Instead of emitting the scent of musk, which Reed was expecting, she smelled as fresh as morning rain.

Pissed off, Reed pointed an accusing finger at the moisture beads that rolled down her shoulders. "Who told you to take a fucking shower? Shit, if I wanted squeaky-clean sex, I could have gone home to my boring fucking wife and got off without spending a dime."

Buttercup paid him no mind and carelessly tossed the wig on the bureau; it landed on a tall can of oil sheen. Offering Reed a sidelong sexy glance, she began to peel off the towel.

But Reed didn't find her sexy at all. Without makeup, Buttercup's face looked blank, expressionless. Her natural hair was closely cropped, giving her the look of an adolescent boy. And what was even worse was the sight of her naked body—her cadaverously thin naked body. Her raisin-sized tits needed to be camouflaged with a provocative padded bra or a bustier. Without the adornment of glitzy apparel, Buttercup had zero sex appeal.

He was so disgusted by the drastic change in her appearance, his dick went limp.

Holding her in a smoldering gaze, he asked, "Why'd you take everything off?"

Buttercup looked at him like he was crazy. "So you can get your freak on and I can get paid." She extended an open palm.

Reed ignored the greedy gesture. "Stop acting stupid, you know how we do—you know what I like. I'm not with this shit."

Before speaking, Buttercup grimaced in confusion. "What the fuck did I do?"

"You went in the bathroom looking like a sexy female and came out looking like a skinny-ass dude," Reed responded, rolling his eyes.

"I'm standing here butt-ass naked, ain't that sexy enough?"

Scowling, Reed shook his head. "Go put on a thong set or one of those slinky costumes you rock when you're working at the club."

"Well, I'm not at the club," Buttercup grumbled under her breath as she began snatching garments from a bureau drawer. Grudgingly, she slipped into a black negligee. "You ready now?" she asked, brows arched, as she awaited his approval.

Reed shook his head again. "Put that wig back on." He preferred her face heavily made up, but didn't feel like waiting around for a full-face paint job. "Just put on some lipstick and some ho shoes."

"Why you trippin'?" She sucked her teeth and stomped to the bureau. Amidst the clutter, she miraculously retrieved a tube of lipstick and smeared it on without even glancing in the mirror.

What is wrong with this ho? Reed couldn't understand why Buttercup was being difficult. An experience that should have been as exciting as a roller coaster ride was threatening to become as boring as the sex he had at home.

The thought of Dayna and her damned biological clock caused his annoyance with Buttercup to escalate into full-blown rage. Yet strangely, at that moment, he could feel a hot flush as his manhood began to rise. By the time Buttercup located a pair of stilettos, Reed had stroked himself into a hard erection.

"It looks like you're doing all right by yourself. Sure you need me?" she teased.

Grunting as he swiftly worked his hand up and down, he gave her a look that was mixed with both loathing and lust.

"How come you still have your clothes on?" Buttercup wanted to know.

Reed detected exasperation in her tone. She sounded like she regretted having brought him home. But he knew she wasn't totally stupid. She realized the ball was in his court and if she expected to get paid, she'd have to play according to his rules.

"Need some help?" she asked, attempting to take the edge out of her voice. Reed ignored her; he didn't even look at her as he continued to manually stimulate himself.

Buttercup stepped into Reed's direct line of vision, forcing him to look at her. "What do you want? A blow job?" Frustration coated her words.

With his adrenaline pumping and acting on sheer instinct, he stopped masturbating, stood up, unbuckled his belt, and snatched it from around his waist.

Reed yanked Buttercup by her thin arm, flopped down on the bed, and promptly turned her over his knee.

"Let me go! Stop it!" She struggled to free herself from Reed's grip, but Reed pressed his forearm down hard on her back. "What's wrong with you—you crazy or something?" Buttercup raged.

Thwack! The strap landed across her bare buttocks. For a few seconds, her mouth fell open in silent shock. Then she let out a high-pitched wail that should have alerted a neighbor to call the police. In Buttercup's neighborhood, however, late-night screams were a common sound that competed with the background noise of gunshots and police sirens.

Reed raised his arm high; he held the leather belt as if it were a whip. He came down with another hard smack that delivered high-wattage pain. The pain was beyond anything Buttercup was familiar with. "Ow! Stop it! Oh my God, stop!" she screamed. "I'm not playing, you crazy muthafucker. Stop!"

Twisting around, she managed a flimsy grasp of the arm that was stretched high in preparation of bringing down another stinging assault.

Reed yanked away from her grasp and struck her again. This time he dispensed a flurry of hot lashes that landed in rapid succession.

Fearing for her life and having endured more than enough of this absurd flogging, Buttercup managed to fling herself off his lap and onto the floor where she swiftly slithered under the bed to a safe but dusty haven.

With Buttercup beyond his reach, Reed began to calm down and slowly returned to his rational state of mind. He was shocked by what he'd just done, and felt ashamed of himself. Confused, he sagged onto the bed and buried his head in his hands.

"Get the fuck outta here before I call the cops!" yelled Buttercup, who was still hiding under the bed.

Of course, Reed realized that her threat was empty. In her line of work—exotic dancer, hooker, and a booster, as well as having a drug habit—Buttercup would not bring unnecessary police attention to her own door. Still, he felt bad. He hadn't meant to hurt her; he didn't understand what had come over him.

Buttercup was an affordable and easy-going girl and

he definitely didn't want to lose her. She'd been a beacon of light for his carnal yearnings on many a dark night. He held his head in his hands, trying to figure out what the hell had made him go ballistic on Buttercup.

Trying to get his bearings, Reed stood up, tucked in his shirt. He gazed at the leather belt uncomprehendingly, as if it had come to life and acted in such a vicious manner on its on accord. Confused, he quickly threaded the belt through the loops on his pants.

"How much do I owe you, Butter?" He felt completely disgusted with himself, but he spoke in a casual tone. He sounded cheerful, actually, as if he were inquiring about her fee for giving him something as normal as a haircut.

"Yo, nigga, I don't want shit from you!" she shouted. "You better save your money 'cause after I let the police take pictures of the bruises on my ass, I'm gonna sue you for every cent you got!"

Reed sighed, more in response to his own insane behavior than to Buttercup's empty threats. He pulled out all the cash in his pockets. "Here you go, Butter. I have eighty-nine dollars, but I'll give you some more the next time I see you. All right?" He put the money on top of the junky dresser.

"Next time?" Buttercup blurted, still sequestered under the bed. "Ain't gon' be no next time, you sick muthafucker!"

"Take it easy, Butter. I'll see you later," he said, as he

playfully kicked the bed. Then with a lame smile plastered on his face, he put his hand on the doorknob and slowly pulled it open, but before he closed the door behind him, he gave the bed that sheltered Buttercup one last regretful look.

Chapter 6

Chanelle Lawson was not a prostitute. Using the name Sensation, she danced exotically, gave half-hearted couch dances, but was steadfast in her refusal to engage in sex with any of her customers. Her benefactors paid for her company at dinner, the movies, or whatever, but she always let them know in advance that she was not a prostitute.

The club owners and girls she worked with were aware of her moral standards, and thus only invited her to gigs outside of Lizzard's that were of the highest caliber—events where she'd never be expected to perform sexual favors for pay.

So when Lexi, a willowy blonde co-worker with big fake breasts invited her to dance at a bachelor party that paid two hundred and fifty dollars an hour plus tips, Chanelle didn't hesitate. Well, she did hesitate for a few seconds because she had a date with her so-called boy-friend, Malik.

But Malik wasn't really her boyfriend; she just allowed him to think he was. He was Stone Allen's cousin. However, they looked so much alike people thought they were brothers. Malik was in the Allen inner circle, which included perks such as access to Stone's cars, great seats at Sixers games, and VIP passes to just about everything that was anything in the city as long as Stone didn't want to go. And the fact that Malik never knew if he could get tickets to high-profile events until the last minute was the exact reason why she didn't consider him her real boyfriend. He was just fill-in; someone to fool around with until the real thing came along.

The man she would eventually marry wasn't going to be pushing someone else's whip; he'd have his own Bentley, Porsche, Hummer, or whatever.

Chanelle rode to the bachelor party with Mandy, another bosomy blonde. Mandy pulled onto a tree-lined street somewhere on the Main Line—Narberth or Bryn Mawr, she wasn't sure. Chanelle had only recently become acquainted with the ritzy Main Line through Malik, who often took her to his cousin's sprawling estate.

Sadly, her visits to the celebrated NBA player's lair were not formal invitations. In fact, she'd never even met Stone Allen. When the Allen family went on trips or vacations, Malik was delegated the task of housesitting the mansion. Chanelle didn't mind helping Malik look after the fabulous estate. It was fun to pretend to live in a mansion and practice the lifestyle she envisioned for herself in the future.

Unlike most exotic dancers, Chanelle did not have her

head in the clouds with aspirations of becoming a celebrity. She didn't expect exotic dancing to land her a cover on *Playboy* or catapult her to stardom.

But she did expect to snag a husband—a very rich and handsome husband.

Mandy squinted at the address when they approached a gorgeous stone Colonial- style house. "Yup, this is the place. Pretty snazzy, huh?"

Chanelle ogled the beautiful home and indulged in a quick fantasy. Her wealthy future husband was right inside waiting to share with her all his worldly goods.

"What did you say these guys do for a living?" Chanelle asked, coming out of her daydream.

"Investment brokers…I think. I'm not sure. I know they have a lot of money," Mandy said as she parked her BMW at the end of the long driveway that was crammed with expensive cars.

Chanelle surveyed the impressive territory and noticed a gleaming Escalade parked at the curb near the house. There was a detached two-car garage with the doors left open revealing two Benzes: one black, the other white.

"Oh! I forgot to mention something," Mandy said. "The two guys paying for this little soiree are expecting to see a two-girl show at some point tonight."

"A two-girl what?" Chanelle snapped her head away from the sea of luxury vehicles. "Count me out," she said, shaking her head adamantly. "You can just turn this car around and take me back to Philly because you know I'm not into girl-on-girl shows."

"I know. I know," Mandy soothed. "Relax, Sensation. The guys specifically requested to see two girls dance together. All we have to do is dance provocatively. We can fake it—you know, just give the illusion of the lesbian stuff."

Chanelle rolled her eyes. "Why don't you and Lexi pretend to be lesbians? And while we're on the subject." She glanced at Mandy. "Why the hell did she forget to mention this important detail when she asked if I would work this party?"

"Beats me." Mandy shook her head and shrugged.

Chanelle sucked her teeth in disgust. "Every time I accept a gig outside the job, I always end up regretting it. There's always some small-print shit that no one bothered to tell me." Chanelle glared at Mandy. "So, why the hell did you wait until we were way out here in east jeblip before you decided to tell me the whole story?"

"I…um, I thought Lexi had already told you. I was just reminding you." Mandy threw her hands up as if Chanelle were making a big deal over nothing. "Look, I'll do all the work, you just dance. It'll be fine. Okay?"

"It's not okay. I should curse Lexi out for even putting me in this position." Chanelle shook her head angrily. Instead of mentally gearing up for the possibility of making a couple thousand for the night, Chanelle was now pondering the colossal waste of time she'd spent coordinating costumes, shoes, jewelry, hair, and makeup. It was all for nothing.

Feeling vengeful, she decided she'd put zero effort into her performance and made peace with the fact that she'd probably earn only the minimum pay, two hundred and fifty dollars an hour. A lousy five hundred bucks. Oh well!

She gazed at the clock on the dashboard. "It's nine o'clock, and I'm dancing for two hours and that's it! So don't have me waiting around when the party's over; I want to get out of there by eleven sharp. Understand?"

Mandy responded with a noncommittal sigh.

Inside the elegant house, well-groomed white men with good skin and even, white teeth quietly milled about. Some had drinks in their hands, but Chanelle doubted they had yet to feel the effects of the alcohol. They were too calm. No one seemed anxious to see the girlie show.

Small groups of men clustered in sections of the main room, the dining room, the kitchen, and other parts of the house. They bantered among themselves, seemingly intent on sending out the message that the arrival of the strippers was no big deal.

Fuck those uppity assholes. Chanelle then gazed around and caught sight of Lexi.

Fully clad in white Dolce & Gabbana everything—jeans, shoes, and a tight T-shirt with a sequined number 20 glittering across her implanted breasts—Lexi drank champagne from a crystal flute while she schmoozed it up with a few of the guests. She glanced at Chanelle and Mandy and nodded toward the staircase. "You girls can change in the first bedroom at the top of the stairs." Her tone was crisp and authoritative, as if she were the lady of the house and Chanelle and Mandy were nothing more than pesky but necessary scullery maids.

Mandy smiled obligingly and made her way toward the stairs. Chanelle, however, stood stock still, arched a defiant brow, and cocked her head to the side. "Can I speak to you? In private!" Chanelle demanded.

Lexi smiled helplessly at the male guests and promised to be right back.

"Mandy said you expect me to—" Chanelle stated loudly with a hand on her hip.

"We'll talk upstairs," Lexi whispered, cutting Chanelle off. She quickly threw the party attendees a look that said, "I've got everything under control" and then trotted up the stairs.

Under normal circumstances, Chanelle would have been impressed by the designated dressing room, but not tonight. She was too angry to enjoy the richly decorated bedroom, furnished completely in sturdy mahogany furniture. The bed was so high off the floor it seemed one would need a ladder to climb on it. Fuchsia-colored curtains of a light fabric adorned the windows, and a gorgeous Persian rug lay in the middle of the room. There was also a working fireplace with brass andirons, as well as a full-sized bathroom. Three steps in one corner of the room led down to a smaller dressing room, which was the area to which Lexi walked Chanelle to have their little tête-à-tête.

Mandy followed and instantly dropped her workbag on the floor when she spotted four delicate crystal flutes and a bottle of champagne that sat on ice inside a silver bucket. She snatched the champagne out of the bucket, ripped off the shiny wrapping, and began anxiously working on the cork until it finally popped. She filled one of the flutes and then sank down into a cushy small sofa situated very close to the bubbly. She had a ringside seat to watch Chanelle and Lexi go at it.

"Jesus," Lexi snapped at Chanelle. "Did you have to get so loud and boisterous in front of the fellas?"

"Jesus," Chanelle mimicked. "Did you have to lie to get me here?"

Lexi's face turned crimson. "I didn't lie. I'm paying you two-fifty an hour."

"To do what?"

"Dance. And to…you know…keep the guys entertained."

"I'm not a prostitute," Chanelle reminded her.

"We know!" Lexi and Mandy shouted in sarcastic unison.

"So, why did you book me to do a lesbo show when you know I'm not into that type of party?"

"Why are you twisting an innocent, sensual dance with Mandy into a full-scale lesbian exhibition?"

Chanelle paused as she considered Lexi's words, then

she raised her head. "If it's such an innocent dance, why aren't you doing it? And come to think about it, how come you were sitting downstairs acting all chummy with the men?" Chanelle looked Lexi over. "You're still wearing your street clothes; aren't you gonna change into your stripper gear, too?"

Indignant fingers fluttered to Lexi's chest. "Not that it's any of your business, but I'm coordinating this event and I'm the person who's going to pay you. I never told you I was planning to participate. Besides, you shouldn't concern yourself with what I do."

Enraged, Chanelle got so close to Lexi she imagined she could hear Lexi's heart beating through her plastic tits. "Bitch, I know you must have bumped your head talking to *me* like that." Acting confrontational, Chanelle pressed her shoulder into Lexi's arm. "Don't think because I'm the only black person out here in whitey's world that I won't pull off my jewelry and proceed to whippin' your ass."

Lexi gave Mandy a frantic look and took a step backward; Chanelle took two steps forward.

"Why do you have to resort to violence?" Mandy interjected on Lexi's behalf. "That's so not cool."

"I'll resort to whatever I have to because I don't appreciate being used. Mandy, I guess you'll be dancing by yourself since Miss Diva is too good to strip tonight." Chanelle looked heavenward. "Fuck this. I'm out!" She snapped her cell phone off her belt loop, flipped it open, and pushed 411. "Can you connect me with a cab company. I don't care which one. Just get me a cab that will take me to Philly," she barked into her cell phone.

The operator asked for Chanelle's location.

"Where the hell are we? What's the fucking address?" Chanelle asked in a high voice, twisting her head toward Mandy.

Intent on defusing the situation, Lexi stepped forward. "Okay, listen. I'll pay you an extra fifty dollars if you stay—that's three hundred an hour and all you have to do is dance."

"You just insulted me. Do I look like my name is Kizzy? Fuck off! I said I'm out!" Chanelle put the phone back to her ear but got dead air; the operator had hung up. She let out a huge sigh, but before she could push redial, Mandy popped out of her seat and quickly poured Chanelle a glass of champagne.

"Please don't leave the guys hanging like this; they're trying to give their buddy a nice send-off," Mandy cajoled. "Here, have a drink and just sit tight for a minute while we try to figure something out." Encouraging Chanelle to have a seat, Mandy inclined her head toward the sofa.

Breathing like a dragon while grumbling that slavery was over, Chanelle surprisingly complied and plopped down on the sofa. Mandy exhaled with relief and then turned to Lexi with a steely look that said, "I've done the immediate damage control; now, you have to clinch the deal."

On queue, Lexi scooted over to the sofa and sat next to Chanelle. "I'm so sorry for forgetting to tell you about the girl-girl thing. Don't give it another thought. I'll dance with Mandy. And look, I don't usually pay up front, but here's your money." Lexi flicked open the buckle of her white leather Dolce & Gabbana purse and pulled out a wad of cash. She counted out the money. "That's six hundred for two hours," she said, pressing the bills into Chanelle's hand. "Just do your usual routine, okay? You brought your music, right?"

Mellowed by the champagne and the sweet smell of currency, Chanelle wore a wary expression, but nodded in agreement, rooted around in her bag, and handed Lexi a CD.

"I can sense the natives are getting restless, so I'm gonna go back downstairs and smooth things over. You girls go ahead and get dressed. By the way, you're up first Mandy. Sensation can work the crowd before her set. After Sensation's set, Mandy and I will do the hot grand finale," Lexi said excitedly, as if being demoted from hostess to sleazy lesbo stripper was the best news of the day.

Lexi poured herself a drink, a reward of sorts for winning Chanelle over. She checked her watch and floated back downstairs to announce that the show was about to begin.

Chapter 7

Chanelle slipped her foot into a red strappy stiletto. She was wearing a red fringed fishnet gown with long slits on both sides, matching thong, and an underwire bra that pushed her natural D-cups up to the rafters.

She strapped on the other shoe and then gazed in the full-length mirror. Lingerie and heels—a combination that had become as familiar as her own skin. But not for long! Once she hooked a husband, she would never again put on anything shimmering, slinky, or see-through. She'd be sleeping in flannel pajamas and padding around her dream home in fuzzy slippers.

Hanging up her G-string for good was her favorite fantasy.

"Toxic" by Britney Spears, which was Mandy's corny theme song, broke into Chanelle's reverie. As much as she disliked the tune, oddly, she felt a strong desire to dance. Suddenly parched, she rotated her hips to the beat as she danced over to the bubbly and poured herself another glass. She took a few swallows of the extra dry champagne that delighted her taste buds. It may have been her imagination, but the second glass seemed to taste even better than the first.

Less than a half-hour ago, Chanelle had to restrain herself from putting her fist in Lexi's mouth, but now she felt, well…fabulous! *This is weird!*

One last cursory glance in the mirror confirmed her belief: she looked hotter than ever. In fact, she was the finest mocha chocolate mama on the planet and those uptight white boys downstairs had better act like they know and have her money ready. Chanelle no longer had the feeling of being an outsider. Giggling and bouncing rhythmically, she descended the staircase.

It was time to shake her moneymaker.

Still garbed in Dolce & Gabbana instead of stripper wear, Lexi gave Chanelle a warm smile. How strange. Considering that Chanelle was late and should have been downstairs attending to the men fifteen minutes ago, she expected Lexi to give her a scowl of disapproval or to mouth off some type of chastisement, but Lexi maintained a pleasant expression.

Yes, the mood in the room had definitely changed. Not only was Lexi more relaxed, the men also seemed less uptight. They were more animated and actually looked entertained as Mandy slithered around on a leopard sheet, gyrating to Britney's awful song.

Chanelle leaned over to Lexi. "Where's the groom? I want to congratulate him and uh, you know, give him a special dance before I start my routine. Oh, yeah, where's the best man—is he tipping for the groom?"

Lexi scanned the crowd and then shrugged. "The groom was here a few minutes ago. I'm sure he'll be right back. In the meantime, why don't you go make nice with Brad over there?" She nodded toward a muscular young man who was watching Mandy's performance from the back of the room. "Brad and the best man are paying…" Lexi paused; her head swiveled around until she located the best man. The best man had his head buried so deep in Mandy's bosom it was impossible to get a clear view of his face. Lexi chuckled as if the best man's behavior was the cutest thing she'd ever seen. "They're paying for this shindig. I told them not to worry about the groom. His dances are free—part of the cost."

Free dances! Now, Lexi knows she's wrong. However, for some reason Chanelle decided to let it fly. Though it was her nature to gripe and bitch endlessly when she believed someone was trying to exploit her, Chanelle merely shrugged and said, "Okay, I'll hook the groom up. What's his name?"

"Trevor."

"Okay, let me know when Trevor's ready. I'm gonna give him a bangin' send-off."

Lexi smiled. "Okay, but look…Brad is the one who specifically requested a black chick," Lexi added.

Chanelle wasn't aware that anyone had *specifically* requested a black girl. The request seemed racist, but she was feeling too good to let it bother her. Determined to put a smile on Brad's face and some extra cash inside her purse, she sexily wound her way to the back of the room.

Dressed down in jeans and a T-shirt, Brad was tall and muscular. He looked more like an Eagles linebacker than an investment broker. He was the only man in the room not wearing professional attire. With a brooding look, he stood slouched against a wall chugging down a Heineken. His eyes kept darting worriedly in the direction of the kitchen where the whizzing sound of a blender could he heard.

Then his green eyes landed on Chanelle. He broke into a huge, appreciative grin and seemed instantly to forget whatever was going on in the kitchen that seemed to trouble him.

"Hey, handsome. Havin' fun?" Chanelle asked as she moistened her outlined and glossed full lips.

"I am now." He looked and gave a bashful smile. "You must be Sensation?"

"That's what they tell me," she said sassily. She stared into his eyes; the shade of green reminded her of the pictures she had seen of the ocean in the Cayman Islands. His eyes were so pretty, she wondered if he was wearing contact lenses.

Mandy's next song came on—something by Hilary Duff. Though Chanelle was definitely not into white girl music, she found herself inexplicably locked into the bass line of the song.

And another weird thing was happening to her. The sporadic movement of Brad's Adam's apple had her mesmerized. For some reason, Chanelle was intensely, yet pleasantly aware of everything! It was so weird, but in a good way.

She was ready to start dancing. Hell, as good as she felt, she'd dance for free. That strange admission put an amused smile on her face. Poking out her chest and rotating her hips, she rubbed up against Brad. And for the second time, he blushed.

Not being under the roving, ever-watchful glare of the bouncer at Lizzard's, the attendees at the private bachelor party took many liberties with the dancers. Brad, smiling sheepishly like a shy little boy, was no exception. His naughty intentions became apparent when he suddenly thrust one hand beneath Chanelle's gown and cupped a breast with his other hand.

Chanelle gasped in surprise. Seemingly ambidextrous, Brad simultaneously squeezed her right butt cheek and her left tit. In the grip of some mystifying euphoria, she wasn't resistant; she didn't jerk away. Instead, she moved dreamily from side to side. With her eyes closed blissfully, Chanelle gave in to the enjoyable feeling of Brad's self-assured hands.

As unthinkable as it was, Chanelle, now enraptured,

forgot about collecting tips. She concentrated completely on her own pleasure. Brad worked his hand under her bra and began to circle her nipple with an index finger. The friction of his fingertip was powerfully stimulating, causing her to utter a small moan.

Taking that sound as a green light to proceed to uncharted territory, he slid his hand to the front of her thong, caressed her mons pubis through the fabric, and then boldly slipped his hand inside.

He raked his fingers through the abundance of crinkly hair. The crackling sound of fingernails against pubic hair sounded melodic, sensual, and stirred her passion. Chanelle inched closer to Brad's musical fingers and breathed out contentedly.

"It's your turn, Sensation," Lexi called, breaking up the sexually charged moment.

Chanelle was at first unable to tear away from Brad's skillful fingers, but when she heard the first few bars of her theme song, she felt an overpowering urge to dance.

"Be right back," she assured Brad, and blew him a kiss.

Welcoming her with whistles and a cacophony of whooping sounds, the male audience had become much more energized. Chanelle assumed the stiff jerks were finally feeling the effects of alcohol.

Chanelle strutted to the front of the room. The moist stickiness between her legs made her very much aware of her sensuality; she felt eager to give a dazzling display of her erotic dance moves.

With great pride, she watched the faces of her audience as she swiveled, undulated, and twisted to the pulsating rhythm. Unlike Mandy, Chanelle was not standing before them merely shaking her ass, fondling her breasts, and swinging her hair. No, she was giving the men something neither Mandy nor Lexi could give: uninhibited dancing from the soul of a sexy black woman.

They gaped at her with awe as if she were some rare exotic creature they could only dream of capturing. Gazing at her audience with narrowed, seductive eyes, she lowered one thin strap of her gown and then slowly lowered the other. The men gasped as if baring a shoulder was the equivalent of parting her vaginal lips and inviting them all to explore the mysteries of her dark and forbidden womanhood.

Feeling extremely powerful, Chanelle unhurriedly removed the fringed dress, exposing her beautiful blackness as she stripped down to just a slinged thong and a push-up bra. The uptight bunch of brokers went wild, blanketing the floor with cash. A pelvic thrust as she cupped and caressed her crotch sent the crowd into a frenzy that inspired another shower of greenbacks.

Strangely, she was falling head over heels in love with a profession she thought she despised. She couldn't imagine why she had considered the privilege of displaying her beauty and talent as something unwholesome and demeaning.

As a finale, Chanelle whipped around and worked the

muscles of each buttock. In other words, she gave the audience her spectacular ass—to kiss.

After stashing her cash, Chanelle rushed to the rear to continue the sex play with Brad. She found him in the kitchen having a heated argument with a short and rather scrawny man who was holding a pitcher of a pastel-colored daiquiri he'd concocted in the blender.

The drink looked delicious. With her mouth feeling as dry as the Sahara desert, she was about to ask the short man to give her a glass of the exotic-looking drink. But there was something in the icy look the man gave her that made her change her mind. That look and the tone of the quarrel between the two men made Chanelle raise a puzzled brow. She left the kitchen to look for another male playmate.

Someone placed a single chair in the middle of the dance area. Lexi pointed to the chair and announced gaily, "And now, it's time for Trevor to have his last hurrah!"

"Trevor, Trevor, Trevor," the intoxicated attendees began to chant as they craned their necks in search of the guest of honor. Chanelle stopped working the crowd long enough to catch a glimpse of the elusive Trevor.

Annoyed, Trevor emerged from the kitchen, gave the drunken crowd an impatient look, and said, "Give me a second." He disappeared back into the kitchen.

Chanelle couldn't have been more surprised that the disgruntled "Daiquiri Dan" was Trevor, the guest of honor. She took a few seconds to ponder what was going on in the kitchen and decided that Trevor and Brad were probably having a dispute over the thing people argue about most—money.

"Sensation," Lexi called. "I don't know what's wrong with Trevor, but the boys are getting restless. Would you be a dear and give another performance?"

"No problem," Chanelle replied, feeling uplifted and unusually happy.

"Mandy's gonna join you," Lexi quickly added.

"Okay." Chanelle smiled brightly. All was well in her world.

It was hard to catch a groove dancing to Mandy's ridiculous music, but Chanelle rode the bass line and then started moving as if she owned the song.

In fact, she forgot Mandy was a part of the performance until Mandy sidled up to her and attempted to match the swings and sways of Chanelle's womanly hips. It was an impossible task. Mandy quickly gave up and got the attention of the spectators by brazenly stroking Chanelle's private parts.

Revved up and sexually aroused, the guys started sticking five-dollar bills in Mandy's G-string, encouraging her to escalate the sex play. Taking a surprisingly willing Chanelle by the hand, Mandy took a seat in the designated bachelor's chair and invited Chanelle to join her. Chanelle bent over and pushed her ample derriere between Mandy's thin white thighs.

It was a totally new feeling. Feminine softness replaced

the hard dick Chanelle was accustomed to feeling against her butt. Moreover, the sheer decadence of the routine was a turn-on. As Chanelle grinded her ass into Mandy's crotch, Mandy groped around and unhooked Chanelle's bra, exposing her breasts. The contrast of Mandy's white hands fondling Chanelle's dark breasts drove the men even wilder.

"Let's see some chick-lick! Chick-lick!" the audience chorused. Ever obliging, Mandy leaned forward, reached over Chanelle, and took a bottle of Heineken from one of the guys. She dribbled beer over Chanelle's breasts, then turned her around and began licking the brew off.

One of the drunken spectators decided to get into the act. He nudged Mandy out of the way and boldly poured beer over Chanelle's shoulders. Beer ran down her chest and arms. And that's when things started to get out of hand.

The oversexed group of men went into their bizarre chant again: "Chick-lick! Chick-lick!" Looking perplexed, Mandy froze and moved away from Chanelle. Lexi tried to enforce crowd control, but couldn't.

In a matter of seconds, the bawdy men had drenched Chanelle from head to toe with beer, vodka, and gin, and shouted for Mandy to lick Chanelle.

Shocked out of her euphoric state, Chanelle screamed for them to stop. Her yelling did not deter one ambitious attendee from pouring the entire contents of the daiquiri pitcher over her head, coating Chanelle's face and body with the cold, mushy mixture.

Temporarily blinded by the combination of alcoholic beverages, Chanelle stumbled toward the stairs. Neither Mandy nor Lexi came to her rescue with a towel or even comforting words. As if she weren't humiliated enough, she heard titters of feminine laughter as she stumbled up the stairs.

Chanelle stopped mid-climb, struck suddenly by the knowledge that those two bitches had put something in her drink. It was probably Ecstasy—what else would cause her to act as wanton as she had? There was no other explanation for her behaving like such a happy hooker.

It took every bit of restraint not to run back down the stairs and kick some white ass—Mandy's and Lexi's as well as those of the bastards who'd disrespected her by dousing her with their drinks. But the desire to clean herself up had a more powerful pull. She'd deal with those two bitches later.

Oh God, she thought as she rushed up the stairs, besides allowing Mandy to slurp beer from her breasts, she'd even let that pumped-up muscular dude put his nasty fingers all up inside her pussy. She felt her heart pumping with rage. Damn, she wanted to fight everybody, but her biggest concerns at the moment were to take a shower, put on some clothes, and get the hell out of there.

Wiping muck from her hair and her face, she groped for the door handle of the changing room. But to her surprise, she quickly realized that she was in the wrong room, and was even more surprised to see that two men were together in bed! Her eyes blinked rapidly in disbelief.

The groom was wearing one of her prized costumes, a sheer one-piece micro-mini dress. He was lying on his back with both legs held up by the crook of his arms. "You like black bitches?" she heard the groom demand in a mean, raspy voice.

Sitting on his haunches, with his dick rubbing against Trevor's ass, Brad hissed, "Shut up, Trevor; I was only fucking around. You're the cheat who's actually getting married. I can't believe you're gonna marry a goddamn cunt." Brad's final words were accompanied by a violent anal thrust, which caused Trevor to groan in what sounded more like pain than passion.

Chanelle shuddered at the sight of such debauchery. The male lovers seemed not to notice her standing there. She scurried from the raunchy scene and rushed into the dressing room where she snatched up her belongings. Fuck the sullied micro-mini. That bitch Trevor could have it as a wedding gift.

Chapter 8

"What have I ever done to deserve such callous treatment?" Pamela Hinton asked her daughter through mournful sobs.

Before answering, Dayna took a moment to think about the situation. It was Mother's Day; her father had invited her mother to brunch at the Four Seasons and then cancelled at the last minute. Dayna switched the phone to her other ear and then cleared her throat as she searched for a tactful response. "Well…Mom, you know… maybe it's time to let go," she advised meekly. "You've been divorced for years, yet you and Dad are still carrying on…I mean…it couldn't be healthy to have to sneak around with your ex-husband."

"I don't consider myself sneaking around with the man I was married to for thirty years," Pamela added petulantly.

Dayna's parents didn't seem to realize that it was very difficult for her to come to terms with their divorce and current torrid affair. She couldn't quite define her own personal feelings, but if pressed to come up with a word to express how she felt, she'd have to admit she felt… *abused*.

Her parents had raised her with a strong set of values, stressing that she must always conduct herself in a manner that would never cause them embarrassment. But their mid-life, socially unacceptable behavior seriously clashed with the morals they'd instilled in her. They were both hypocrites and having to view them through adult eyes was extremely painful.

"Mom," Dayna said in a tone as gentle as she could manage considering her own conflicted emotions, "Dad's remarried—"

"Oh, Dayna, please stop stating the obvious," her mother cut in. "If you don't have anything positive to add to this discussion, I might as well just hang up and wallow in my sorrow alone."

Ugh! Dayna hated when her mother did the guilt-trip thing. As much as she tried not to, she always caved in. "Okay, Mom. I have an idea! Why don't I take you to brunch?"

Her mother stopped sniffling for a moment as she silently considered her daughter's offer. When the sniffling resumed Dayna concluded that her mother had found the idea unappealing.

"Come on, Mom," she persisted. "We'll have a good time. Do you want to try that new place in Manayunk?"

"What new place? There's always some new restaurant opening in Manayunk. You know I'm not impressed with those trendy places," Pamela Hinton said curtly. "Your father was taking me to the Four Seasons. We always go to the Four Seasons on Mother's Day. I can't believe he would just stand me up like this."

"He didn't actually stand you up, Mom; he called and cancelled, right?" Dayna felt compelled to defend her father despite being annoyed with him for causing her mother such grief. In fact, she was annoyed with both parents and irked as hell by her forced participation in their illicit liaison.

"He made those reservations for Mother's Day brunch months ago," Pamela Hinton fumed. "*I'm* the mother of his *only* child and he'd rather spend Mother's Day with that bitch!" Anger and indignation strengthened her mother's voice. "If I find out he took her to The Four Seasons on *my* day, I'm going to—" Her mother paused abruptly.

Curious, Dayna waited for her mother to finish the sentence. Divorcing her father was no longer an option, so what would she do? What *could* she do? Absolutely nothing!

Her mother gave a huge sigh when the futility of her threat sank in. In a choked and anguished tone, she said, "Honey, I know you're trying to help, but honestly, I don't feel like going out. I'd rather stay home."

"Mom, please don't sit home alone on Mother's Day. Let's go out and have some fun."

A tense silence hung in the air. "No thanks, baby," her

mother finally said. "I know you're trying to help and I apologize for bothering you with my problems."

"You're not bothering me," Dayna began to protest. "I don't mind—"

"It's just so hard to accept that the man I spent my life with could turn out to be such a liar." Her mother spat out the words as she revved up for another tirade. "I know that bitch is responsible for this. She knows we spend every Mother's Day together. Why wouldn't we?" Pamela Hinton asked, incredulously. "Your father is just despicable. Such a lying, spineless, and poor excuse of a man."

Ow! It hurt to hear her father so badly maligned. However, her father's mistreatment of her mother also hurt. They were both breaking Dayna's heart.

The uncomfortable lull in the conversation pulled Dayna away from her thoughts. She quickly shifted into pacifier mode. "I know you're going to get hungry later on; I can bring something over. How about your favorite? Do you want some seafood lasagna?" Dayna spoke gaily, with a forced upbeat lilt in her voice.

"Honey, I don't have an appetite. I'm gonna hang up now; I'll talk to you later."

"I'm here if you need me, Mom."

"Thanks, sweetheart. I'll be all right." Her mother's words caught in her throat, a clear warning to Dayna that she would not be all right.

The click on the line terminated the conversation.

Dayna's face crumpled into a frown as she tried to think of a solution. However, there was none. Wasn't it painful enough that her parents had divorced? The agony of the day her father dropped the bomb on her mother, telling her that he was leaving her after thirty years, was still a strong memory. Dayna had shared her mother's emotions; they both felt frightened, abandoned, and betrayed.

Her father tried to convince Dayna that the divorce had nothing to do with his love for her. His words were not comforting. She still felt unloved.

Rushing into marriage with Reed had been a distraction from the pain—a bandage over her lacerated heart. The bandage, however, had slipped off, exposing her marriage as a sham. Dayna cupped her face with both hands and solemnly shook her head. Reed didn't love her either; she realized that now.

Finally seeing the light, Dayna realized that she had tried to get from Reed the love her father had abruptly withdrawn. How sick was that? Still, she had treated Reed with warmth and all the love she was able to give and had received nothing in return.

As badly as she wanted to have a child with her husband, she had to face the reality that bringing a child into an unhappy marriage was not the answer. She had to take the advice she'd offered her mother only a few moments ago: *It's time to let go.*

Dayna drew in a deep breath as if preparing herself for

the lifestyle change that would soon occur. She actually felt good and wanted to tell her mother. Then, she realized that her mother would not be happy to learn that her daughter's marriage had failed. There was a strong possibility that her mother might even take Dayna's failed marriage personally—as if she'd passed on to Dayna some mutant gene.

So Dayna decided to handle her situation privately—in her own way and in her own good time.

Chapter 9

I'm out with Cecily. Be home around nine. Reed snatched the Post-it off the refrigerator, crumpled it, and pitched it into the waste can. Narrowed eyes fixed upon the gleaming chrome stove, where not a pot or pan was in sight. He quickly shifted his gaze to the microwave, approached it with suspicion, and snapped the door open. The sparkling clean oven was empty. There was no dinner plate waiting to be zapped. No Post-it with further instructions on where to find his dinner. Nothing! Bewildered, he wondered what was going on with Dayna. Where the hell was his dinner?

He scowled in thought. Unwilling to believe his wife would behave so irresponsibly, he backtracked to the double-door refrigerator. Smiling in anticipation, he opened one of the doors. But to his dismay, there was no carefully covered plate filled with heaping portions of his favorite foods. There was nothing for him. The only thing in the refrigerator was rabbit food: carrots, cucumbers, mushrooms, tomatoes, and three bags of shredded lettuce.

He slammed the refrigerator door and opened the

freezer. Maybe she decided to freeze his plate. Again, there was nothing for him, just boxes of more diet shit. Reed perused the labels on the boxes: Weight Watchers, Lean Cuisine, Healthy Choice. Nothing in there but a bunch of inedible bullshit.

Reed felt a storm rising inside, but subdued by hunger and with no available target, he calmed himself and scanned the frozen choices again. Just about everything in the freezer boasted *low calorie, low carbs, low fat, low sugar*, so he begrudgingly selected a small box of frozen turkey with a miniscule portion of stuffing and gravy. He ripped open the cardboard top and stuck the meager meal into the microwave.

Muttering obscenities, he abruptly changed his mind, yanked open the micro-wave oven door, and tossed the frozen dinner in the trash. He'd stop and get something more filling and more appealing while he was on his way to the PBP meeting.

He made a mental note to have a serious discussion with Dayna later that night regarding his dinner expectations. Then he let out a crude chortle. Shit, Dayna didn't have the resolve to stick to a diet; she'd be back to frying chicken and pork chops in no time. Knowing her, she'd probably already admitted diet defeat and more than likely was chillin' with Cecily at The Olive Garden stuffing her fat face at that very moment.

Starvin' like Marvin, with his stomach on dead E, Reed

did not enjoy the mental image of Dayna sitting up in a restaurant somewhere sticking her fork into an enormous platter of colorfully arranged, aromatic, steaming cuisine. Seething, he raced up the stairs. Without caring where it landed, he flung his leather briefcase, which was more for show than necessity, and changed from his monkey suit into casual gear.

❧❧❧❧

"You're kidding?" Cecily turned her drink up to her lips and took a quick swig.

"No, I'm very serious. I'm going to ask Reed for a divorce." Dayna let the statement hang in the air for a few seconds. "The house, however, is in both our names; I'm sure that's going to present a problem." Dayna swallowed. "I should have listened to my mother; she warned me not to include his name on the deed. But I was so in love. I never dreamed it would come to this."

"What happened? How do you go from marital bliss to divorce court in a couple of days? Last I heard, you were talking to your travel agent about a cruise."

Dayna laughed sardonically. "Yeah, I thought a cruise would rekindle the old flame. But how can you rekindle something that was never there?"

"Oh, Dayna, I'm so sorry," Cecily said, getting out of her seat to give Dayna a hug.

"Girl, please." Dayna motioned for her friend to sit back down. "I'm fine. I swear... I'm fine." She gazed out into the moonlit night and briefly enjoyed the view. She and Cecily were sitting outside at a small table on the upper deck at one of Dayna's favorite restaurants. Cecily was having the Finlandia vodka special as Dayna sipped water that cost seven dollars a bottle. The bottle was tall and beautiful with an unusual shape; it looked like hand-blown glass. Dayna decided to get her money's worth by taking the bottle home to use as a vase.

She turned back to Cecily, prepared to tell her friend that observing her parents' dysfunctional relationship had opened her eyes, but out of respect for her mother, she changed her mind. Her mother would be mortified to know that Dayna was airing the family's dirty laundry. She said instead, "Reed's been getting a free ride throughout our marriage. His only responsibility is the monthly note on his Lexus and his car insurance."

"You deal with the mortgage payments by yourself?"

Dayna nodded. "And everything else."

"Well, how did you allow things to get so..." Cecily searched for the right word. "So inequitable?"

"I don't know. There's something in a black woman's nature that makes us try to be the champion of our men. Reed could never get ahead on his job, which of course, he blamed on everyone but himself. He didn't make enough money to drive the Lexus and help with household expenses. I tried to be understanding. I thought I was helping him to maintain his self-respect. Now I realize that trying to help him caused me to lose my self-esteem." Dayna gave Cecily a sad smile. "Anyway, it's over now. I just have to figure out how to get him out of the house and get his name off the deed."

"Have you seen an attorney?"

"Not yet."

"What are you waiting for? You can't figure this legal mess out on your own. You need to let your father know you're in trouble; he can solve this problem quickly."

Dayna ignored the mention of her father. "It's going to be a bitter battle and I'm just not up for it yet." Dayna sighed and then suddenly brightened. Changing the subject, Dayna said, "In case you haven't noticed, I've lost three pounds."

Cecily, who'd been a size six her entire adult life and couldn't fathom being encumbered by a weight problem, gave Dayna a blank look. "Good for you," she said with a shrug and then leaned in close. "Walk to the restroom with me; I want to check out that hottie sitting at the bar."

Dayna turned her head in the direction of the bar.

"Don't be obvious!" Cecily scolded as she slid out of her seat. "Come on, you can get a look at him on the way to the restroom."

Somewhere along the walk from their table to the restroom, Cecily trailed off into another direction without giving Dayna any warning. Dayna spotted Cecily smiling into the face of the hottie. Cecily didn't play when she was on a manhunt. Social amenities went out the window. Dayna shrugged and went to the restroom alone.

She left the stall and peered into the lighted mirror as she washed her hands. Her face looked smaller. The three-pound loss really made a difference. All the green salads she'd consumed and the gallons of water she'd drunk during the past two weeks was finally paying off.

Dayna left the bathroom beaming, walking with the confidence she'd had when she was a size eight. She cut her eye toward the bar looking for Cecily.

Now seated on the bar stool next to Mr. Hottie, Cecily was in full-flirtation mode, chatting enthusiastically, fingers fluttering to her exposed cleavage and lashes batting away like crazy. Dayna smiled and shook her head. Cecily was seriously putting her thing down.

Despite all the light-hearted fun she seemed to be having, Dayna knew Cecily was desperate for a committed relationship. She hoped this encounter worked out for her.

As she approached the bar with the intention of discreetly telling Cecily she was going to head on home, Dayna had the distinct impression that someone was watching her. Her eyes darted away from Cecily and locked on to the hazel eyes of a brown-skinned man standing behind the bar. Whoa! She felt herself flush.

Bronze-colored skin contrasted with hazel-colored eyes was an unusual, and well…lethal combination.

Beautiful locks brushed his shoulders and added to his physical attractiveness. Dayna felt slightly woozy and gripped the side of the bar as she quickly averted her gaze. She inched up to Cecily, who didn't see her coming, and placed a hand on her shoulder.

"Sorry to interrupt," Dayna said breathlessly.

"Hey," Cecily said, twirling around on the barstool. "I want you to meet my new friend, Kendrick. Dayna, this is Kendrick."

"Hi. Nice meeting you, Kendrick," Dayna said politely, and then addressed Cecily. "Look, I'm going to head home; I totally forgot I have to grade some papers. Oh, and I have to work on an IEP for one of my students. It feels like our workload has doubled since the state took over the school district, don't you think?" Dayna rambled. The handsome bartender had rattled her nerves and she couldn't understand why she felt the urge to run away. It wasn't as if he'd spoken to her. They'd simply shared a moment; eye contact, that's all.

Unable to figure out why Dayna was going on and on about nothing in the midst of her love connection, Cecily began a series of rapid head nods, nonverbally communicating, *Dag, can't you see I'm busy? Go ahead, leave! Roll out!*

Flustered by the eye contact with the bartender, Dayna didn't pick up Cecily's signal; she continued to ramble until she caught a glimpse of Cecily's strained smile. She bade Cecily and Kendrick a speedy good-bye, gave Cecily two quick air kisses, and fled the restaurant as well as the penetrating eyes of the devastatingly handsome bartender.

She immediately spotted her Chrysler in the well-lit parking lot, disarmed it, and slid inside. As she mentally reviewed the highly intense connection with the bartender, Dayna could feel a bright shade of pink rising from beneath her honey-toned skin. With all those pretty, slender chicks surrounding him, she wondered how he even noticed her. Maybe she just imagined the whole thing. It didn't matter anyway. Ending her marriage to Reed was going to deplete all her energy; it would be a long time before she had the strength to get back into the dating game.

Dayna started her car and then remembered the pretty bottle of water she'd left at the table. She shook her head at her forgetfulness, but after locking eyes with a black Adonis, it's a wonder she remembered her own name.

Chapter 10

Reed ate dinner at Champagne's Restaurant on Chelten Avenue. The combination seafood platter, three beers, plus the tip he gave the waitress had depleted his cash. He swung by the Sunoco station to gas up and to tap the ATM machine inside. After jabbing in the secret code, the message on the screen asked if he wanted to withdraw funds from checking or savings. He and Dayna had joint accounts, but she paid the household bills from the checking account and kept a running tally of the funds in that account. Reed chose to dip into their savings account to get some fun money for the evening.

Fifty bucks would have been a sufficient amount to indulge his leisure pursuits for one night, but Reed withdrew the entire daily limit—six hundred dollars—just for spite. If his dinner had been ready, he reasoned, he wouldn't have had to dig into his pocket for a damn meal. It was all Dayna's fault; she only had herself to blame.

There was no official PBP meeting at the hall on Broad Street, but he stopped by anyway just to bust it up with his brothers.

"Yo, what's up, Reed?" Chris Miller, a member of the PBP, greeted him. Reed didn't like Chris; he hated the brother's self-assured smile.

"Give any more thought to that business deal I told you about? Man, I'm telling you, you don't want to miss out on this venture. Now, I'm trying to put you down with some serious money." Smiling confidently, Chris shook his head like Reed was an imbecile for not writing a check on the spot.

"I'm on it, man. I just need a couple more weeks," Reed said, stalling.

According to Chris Miller, the city of Chester, though just a small town, was brimming with financial possibilities. There was talk that casino gambling was coming to Chester in the next five years and Chris had already started buying dirt-cheap property. At only thirty-two years old, Chris had inherited twelve rental properties from his deceased parents and apparently had inherited their real estate acumen as well.

According to Chris, the deal he offered was not a get-rich-quick scheme. It was a well-planned, fail-proof business maneuver with guaranteed mega bucks for those fortunate enough to get in on the ground floor. Chris envisioned Chester as the next Atlantic City and spoke with the confidence of Donald Trump. Chris's next goal was to buy entire blocks of boarded-up and abandoned houses. It was a chance of a lifetime and Reed wanted in, even if it meant five more years of Dayna's emasculating control. The problem was, Chris expected him to come up with twenty thousand dollars as soon as possible and Reed didn't have access to that kind of cash.

Reed's expensive car and the home he and Dayna were buying made him appear prosperous, but it agitated him to no end that it was all just a front. He'd thought about asking Dayna to dip into her retirement fund, but he knew she wouldn't go for it.

His best bet was to try to hit Dayna's father up for a loan. But then again, accepting her father's money would give Dayna co-ownership; she'd start acting like she was Ivana Trump in the Chester casino venture and Reed was certain she'd attempt to reduce him to the role of an aspiring apprentice.

Reed suddenly felt uncomfortable and out of place. Most of the PBP members were flourishing in their chosen professions. It seemed as if every one except him had the magic formula to success. After being accepted into the group, he had expected an instant lifestyle change. So far, all he had gained was invitations to expensive events, membership fees, endless requests to perform civic duties, and now the impossible task of coming up with twenty grand just so he could feel like he was a true player in the game.

"Yeah, I'm going to sit down with my accountant in a couple of days; I'll get back with you," Reed told Chris, his voice filled with manufactured confidence and self-importance. Then, with a tremendous amount of resentment toward Chris and all his so-called brothers, Reed straightened his slumped shoulders and exited the suffocating atmosphere.

With music blasting and tires squealing, Reed roared down Broad Street. He felt powerful behind the wheel of his black Lexus SC430. So powerful, he felt like he deserved some female appreciation.

There was no point in looking for Buttercup; he knew she still had an attitude. He couldn't blame her. He shook his head in remorse as he thought about his inexcusably bad behavior that night. Then, remembering the money in his pockets, his eyes lit up. Money was a powerful persuader that Buttercup wouldn't be able to resist.

It was Tuesday. Where would she be on a Tuesday night? It was hard to keep up with Buttercup. She was a smoker, addicted to crack. She wasn't disciplined enough to follow a schedule or stick to the rules and regulations of most strip clubs, so she just floated around, getting in wherever she could fit in. When there was nowhere to fit in, she worked the streets.

Not knowing where to begin, Reed decided to try Smitty's Lounge, a small dive on Fortieth and Ludlow Streets that featured lap dancing in a small room upstairs on Tuesday nights.

Reed paid the five-dollar admittance fee at the door

and rushed past the bar without even nodding to the bartender or any of the patrons. The excitement of knowing there would be a smorgasbord of bare-assed women milling about and competing with each other to ride his dick made his heart race as he bounded up the stairs.

There was an additional bar in the back of the darkened room upstairs. Reed went straight to the bartender and ordered an Old English. Taking a swig, he turned around and leaned against the bar as he scanned the small room looking for Buttercup. She wasn't there, he quickly assessed. Disappointed, he guzzled the entire bottle and immediately ordered another.

Feeling dejected, Reed slumped against the bar, but instantly perked up when the MC introduced Aziza. A few feet above floor level were planks of wood that had been hammered together to form a makeshift stage. Carrying a cloth satchel, Aziza, fully covered in a long black satin and lace negligee, took center stage.

Aw, shit! Fuck Buttercup; it's on now, Reed thought to himself as he waited for Aziza's set to begin. Aziza was a veteran; she'd been dancing for over twenty years and Reed had been thinking about getting with her for quite a while. He'd felt a little intimidated because she was an experienced pro, but fuck that. Tonight, he'd make a move.

A mature and big-boned woman, amazingly Aziza was still sexy as hell. She didn't bullshit around on stage like the young dancers did. The young girls were impatient to get back on the floor to collect the ten dollars per lap dance and usually gave lackluster performances onstage.

Aziza wasn't like that. She was a pro and gave a man his money's worth on and off stage.

Reed could feel his member coming to life the moment Aziza swayed into action. Getting comfortable and trying to take some of the pressure off his swollen dick, he took a seat on the barstool.

Her routine began with gentle hip sways as her hands caressed her fleshy body, and her fingers ran against her large sagging breasts. She closed her eyes dreamily as if in a state of ecstasy created by her own touch.

"Dancin'?" A soft voice asked, distracting Reed from the show. With the word *no* already formed on his lips, he turned in the direction of the voice. To his surprise, a toffee-colored, slim cutie was trying to push up on him. Acknowledging her attractiveness, a slow smile played at the corners of his lips.

Taking the smile as consent, the dancer backed into Reed, gyrating as she quickly wedged herself between his legs.

"Yo, Shorty. I'm not dancing right now."

"Why not?" The dancer asked as she reluctantly pulled away from his crotch.

"I'm watching the show."

"Why you wanna look at her tired ass?" she asked, facing him now and blocking his view.

"Hey, Aziza's well seasoned. She's got it going on; you young girls need to take some lessons."

"That fat old bitch can't teach me shit. What she gonna do—show me how to make a coupla dollars by showin' a worn-out coochie and a bunch of gray pussy hairs?"

Reed chuckled as he gently nudged the young dancer out of his line of vision. "Go 'head, shorty. Stop back by a little later. All right?"

"Whatever," she muttered as she moved toward the next man seated at the bar.

Reed leaned forward anxiously, eyes fastened to the stage. At some point, while the young woman had been in his face, Aziza had lit a candle and placed it in the back corner of the stage.

In time with the music, she slowly raised her gown. Inch by inch, she displayed thick legs and well-cushioned thighs. When her gown climbed to her crotch, Reed noticed the shiny red fabric of her thong.

It was showtime! Reed and a throng of spectators moved in and began flinging one-dollar bills. They stood as close to the stage as Joe, the bouncer who also acted as MC, would allow.

With her gown hitched up and gathered around her waist, Aziza now revealed the entire thong. Like railroad tracks with a destination to the Promised Land, there was a black zipper running up the middle of the red thong.

Reed felt his nature rise and bulge against his pants.

He took another generous swig from the bottle of malt liquor and wiped his mouth with the back of his hand.

Now using her chin to secure the black negligee, Aziza began to unzip. She pulled the head of the metal zipper, slowly splitting the red fabric by unzipping one track at a time. Beneath the paunch of her abdomen, which was streaked with stretch marks, wiry dark pubic hair came into view. The excess flesh on her body did not detract from her allure. Her imperfections enhanced the lewdness of the act and brought out the freakiness in all the men, prompting them to unclench their tight fists and to start tipping generously.

Aziza dropped the black negligee and then reached beneath the gown. She tugged, pulled down, and stepped out of the red zippered thong. Then she lifted the gown again and proudly presented her womanhood.

The crowd gasped in perverted fascination as Aziza revealed her extraordinary vagina. Her inner labia—dark and thick with deep wrinkles—jutted out at least four inches past her hairy mound. With long red fingernails, she tugged on her pussy lips; causing them to droop until they hung so low, they touched the top of her thighs.

She dropped the gown again and gave the men a look that promised more. Then, walking like a proud black goddess, she sashayed to the back of the stage. She stuck the thong inside her satchel and pulled out a beach-sized towel, strutted back, and spread it on the homemade stage.

The men crept closer as Aziza lay on the towel. In an unhurried manner, she pulled up the satin and lace and then slowly, teasingly spread her thighs.

The moment the crowd roared, the bartender, who'd seen Aziza perform at least a thousand times, rushed from behind the bar to catch the best part of the show.

She pinched the tips of her elongated pussy lips and pulled them apart—spreading them like the giant wings of a Monarch butterfly.

The look of Aziza's well-fucked, well-sucked pussy made Reed's dick so stiff, it throbbed with pain. If he didn't get some type of relief, he was going to lose his mind.

Undeniably, Aziza had a pussy with a past. And Reed was confident that he had enough money to slide his dick up in that wonderfully worn historical landmark.

Joe brought Aziza the burning candle from the back of the stage. Without the slightest hesitation, she poured hot candle wax down each thigh, and then, as if in the throes of red-hot passion, she moaned loudly as she humped and bucked, thrusting upward as if she were being stud-fucked. Completing her act, she emitted orgasmic groans and shuddered until she appeared spent. Congealed in a stream running down her thighs, the wax resembled dried cum.

Joe picked up Aziza's money from the floor as she collected herself and gathered her candle and towel.

Reed stepped forward and flashed a fifty-dollar bill.

Aziza nodded and hurried to the restroom, which the dancers used as a dressing room.

There was no reason for Reed to prolong his stay and endure the endless harassment from the prowling shadowy figures of women who sought to give him a dry fuck at best. He tipped the bartender and brushed past the money-hungry, stupid little girls. His dick had an appointment with a pro.

Sitting in the Lexus blasting his sounds, Reed waited patiently for Aziza to take him to her place where he'd get a private showing of her beautiful black butterfly.

Chapter 11

B rowsing through the racks at City Blue in the
Gallery Mall, Chanelle pondered the consequences
of doing bodily harm to Mandy and Lexi. It wasn't
that she'd punked out or anything, but when she came to
the realization that whipping their white asses would
cause her more grief than satisfaction, she had to accept
that her plan for revenge was nothing more than a mali-
cious fantasy.

She meandered over to a table with neat colorful
stacks of tops designed by Apple Bottom. Chanelle loved
glittery garb and felt an instant rush when she picked up
a bright pink top with a rhinestone apple in the center.
Momentarily forgetting her troubles, she grabbed six
tops of various colors and designs.

"You look very nice today," said the gleaming-eyed
Middle Eastern salesman. Knowing Chanelle always
spent at least five hundred dollars whenever she set foot
in the store, he stayed close to her, pointing out new
arrivals and offering to knock ten percent off the price of
anything she purchased.

Loaded down with three pairs of sneakers, jeans, and

tops by Enyce, Baby Phat, Von Dutch, and Apple Bottoms, she finally left the store. She wanted to stop at the Sunglass Hut for a new pair of designer shades, but she was carrying too many bags to trudge all the way to the opposite end of the Gallery.

On the cab ride home, her thoughts turned back to the dilemma with her co-workers. There was no doubt in her mind that if she laid a hand on those two slimy bitches, they'd press charges and have her ass hauled off to jail. Just thinking about being handcuffed gave Chanelle the shivers; she wasn't even going to pretend that she was built like that.

However, knowing that a snide comment or a sidelong glance from either of the two might set her off, Chanelle decided it was best to change her shift. But damn, she liked working from four-thirty to eight-thirty. Working those hours gave her the opportunity to shop during the day and party at night.

It was times like this that really made her wish she was married to someone wealthy. As thorough as she was, she shouldn't have to deal with these types of issues. She should have a rich husband who had her back, making it possible for her to tell all parties involved to kiss her pretty black ass.

With her looks, it made no sense for her to be living in the 'hood. She should be in a phat-ass crib like they show on MTV's *Cribs*. Just the other night, she'd seen Shaquille

O'Neal and his family on the show. First of all, she didn't even know Shaq was married, so she had to deal with the pain of the loss of him as a potential husband. Second, his wife was all right and everything—kind of cute—but she wasn't all that. She wasn't a thoroughbred like Chanelle. Some people thought it was a compliment to tell Chanelle that she looked just like Foxy Brown, but Chanelle was quick to retort: "Excuse me—I don't think so. I look waaay better than Foxy Brown." Chanelle did not consider herself conceited; she just believed in keeping it real.

The cab dropped Chanelle in front of her apartment at two o' clock, two and a half hours before she was scheduled to start work, which gave her more than enough time to call her job and request a shift change.

Once inside her apartment, she tossed her bags on the sofa, called Lizzard's, and asked to speak to Vic, the manager.

When Vic got on the phone, Chanelle started running down a bullshit story about needing to change her hours because her grandfather was terminally ill and the entire family was pitching in, taking turns to give him around-the-clock care. She amazed herself with the sincerity in her voice as she weaved her little fable.

"Uh, this wouldn't happen to have anything to do with Lexi, would it?"

Huh? Where the hell did that come from? She hadn't written that dialogue into the script. "What?" Her voice was deliberately tinged with both annoyance and confusion.

"Look, Sensation," Vic said with a sigh. "Do us both a favor and cut the shit, okay?"

"Okay," she said, wondering how the incident at the bachelor party had reached Vic, and what the hell did he care about stuff that had happened after work and outside of the work environment?

"You worked last Friday, right?"

"Yeah," she said suspiciously.

"You were in the VIP lounge, right?"

"Yeah...and?" Chanelle said challengingly. She didn't have a clue where the conversation was going.

"Lexi told me you spent about twenty minutes with Big Bernie."

"So what!" Big Bernie was one of Chanelle's best tippers; she always spent quality time with him. "Vic." Chanelle was pissed, but managed to speak in a respectful tone. "I'm not sure where you're coming from. What's wrong with spending time with Big Bernie as long as he's tipping?"

"Lexi accused you of going a lot further than an innocent little couch dance. She said when you finished the dance, she saw Big Bernie put his pecker back in his pants."

"That's a fucking lie."

"Cut the shit, Sensation. I talked to Big Bernie and he confirmed it."

"They're both lying!" Chanelle couldn't believe sweet Big Bernie would lie on her like that. This was some kind of conspiracy that Lexi and Mandy had created to ward off the ass-kicking they knew they had coming.

"He said he paid you extra to rub his cock against your ass. Now, he's suspended from the club for a week. But you…well…I hate to do it, but I can't risk getting the club shut down. Sorry, Sensation…you're fired."

Time stood still. Then her heart started thumping ten times its normal rate. She felt hot flashes followed by freezing cold chills. She wiped perspiration from her forehead while her teeth chattered uncontrollably as she listened to Vic's parting words.

"Lexi cleaned out your locker; we're only gonna hold your personal items for two days, so if you want your stuff you need to get it as soon as possible."

Snapped back to reality, Chanelle yelled, "Fuck whatever's in that locker and fuck you, too, Vic! Lexi set me up and I'm—" The blare of the dial tone cut off her words.

She was fucking FIRED. She couldn't believe it. She had a love/hate relationship with Lizzard's but it was her second home. She'd never worked at any of the other strip clubs and from the horror stories she'd heard, she didn't want to.

Okay, okay. I have to calm down. What should I do? All answers eluded her; her mind was blank. Her eyes darted around in thought, and landed on the City Blue bags. In one fell swoop, she knocked the bags off the sofa and then kicked them across the room.

I need a fucking husband; I'm only eighteen years old and I'm so fucking tired. I can't do this shit by myself. Her bottom lip began to quiver, and then she burst into tears.

Chapter 12

D ressed for work, Dayna looked in the bedroom
mirror, then leaned in close as she outlined her
lips and applied lip gloss. She could see the
reflection of Reed's form in their bed. He was completely
covered from head to toe—cocooned inside the sheets
and comforter as if blocking out the world. He stirred.
Dayna cleared her throat. "Are you awake?" she said to
his form.

"I am now." Aggravation coated his words.

"We need to talk," Dayna said calmly.

Reed popped out of the cocoon. He looked fearsome.
As attractive as Dayna found her husband, she had to
admit, he was an awful sight first thing in the morning.

"You wanna talk about what?" he asked irritably. "Look,
I know I came home a little late last night, but you have
to understand, I don't have control over the length of
those meetings." His eyes were dark and scowling.

Dayna was not intimidated. She gazed at him with
interest, as if truly seeing him for the first time. "I just
said we needed to talk; I didn't say a word about last
night." It was such a relief to honestly not care where

he'd been or what he'd been doing. She gave a little snort. "Reed, your nocturnal activities don't interest me in the least."

"Then what's this about?" He threw off the covers that were gathered around his waist, got out of bed, and charged to the bathroom, inconsiderately leaving the bathroom door open.

The sound of his long pee stream was loud and annoying. Dayna sucked her teeth in disgust. How had she deluded herself into thinking she'd ever loved this self-indulgent creep? It was as if she'd been under some crazy spell that had rendered her love-dazed and retarded. Thankfully the spell had been broken and she was seeing Reed with unclouded, twenty-twenty vision.

Trudging back into the bedroom, Reed plopped down on the bed, sighing heavily as if preparing for a major altercation. "So what's up? You want a baby…your biological clock's still ticking?" He shot Dayna a condescending smile. "That's what you want to talk about, right? Well, I've been doing some thinking and until my financial situation is more secure, we're going to have to put this baby business on hold."

"Baby business?" she mimicked with a sneer. "It's good to know your point of view on a topic that should be spoken of with reverence. Bringing a child into the world is sacred, it's not *business*. However, that's not what I want to talk about."

"Then talk. Dammit! You have my undivided attention for the next…" He paused to look at the bedside clock. "You have exactly ten minutes because I have to get ready for work."

"Oh, I don't need ten minutes," she said coolly, feeling the power of her new-found self-worth and confidence streaming through her.

Reed frowned.

"I want a divorce." There, she'd said it, and she hoped her words had the impact of a head-on collision.

Reed gawked at her in amazement and then dropped his head like he'd been hit with a sledgehammer. His reaction gave Dayna deep satisfaction. After a few moments, he looked up. "A divorce? Here you go with the drama."

"I'm not being dramatic. Listen, this marriage isn't working and I'm not willing to waste my time staying in this miserable situation a second longer than I have to." Dayna's expression was serious; her tone was stern and adamant.

"I stay out a little late and just like that—" He snapped his fingers to punctuate his statement. "You decide you want a divorce."

She tossed the lip gloss and a compact into her purse and snapped it shut. "My decision was not sudden. But it is final and I don't intend to argue with you. I'm going to see a divorce attorney today; I suggest you do the same."

She checked her watch. "Oh! Look at the time. Shouldn't you be getting ready for work?" Dayna threw her husband a coy smile and calmly strolled out the room.

❧❧❧

At three-thirty, Cecily rushed into Dayna's classroom. "Whew. Glad I caught you before you left. Can I get a ride home?" she asked breathlessly.

"Where's your car?"

"It's in the repair shop. Getting the works: wheel alignment, brake pads, oil change, the whole nine. My mechanic promised to have it ready for me when I got off work; I just called and he's not finished. He said it won't be ready until five."

"Oh, okay. I can give you a ride."

As the two women walked to the school's parking lot, Dayna confided, "I asked Reed for a divorce."

"What? You're kidding." Cecily's eyes twinkled in delighted astonishment.

"Actually, I didn't ask. I demanded," Dayna corrected. She hit the switch that unlocked the doors to her Chrysler.

"I'm shocked."

"So was he."

"What did he say?" Cecily said, strapping on the seatbelt.

"After getting over his initial shock, he tried to suggest

that I was being overly dramatic because he stayed out past midnight—as usual."

"I don't know what to say. I think *I'm* in shock. I mean despite the fact that Reed is an asshole, I thought you were hopelessly in love with him."

"Not anymore."

"How can you just stop loving your husband overnight?"

"I had an awakening," Dayna said in a matter-of-fact tone. "Anyway, I spoke to an attorney over the phone; she said if Reed cooperates, we can terminate the marriage in ninety days. I have an appointment to see her next week."

"Will you have to sell the house?"

"I hope not." Dayna sighed deeply and rubbed her forehead, then backed out of the lot. "My mother tried to talk me out of allowing Reed to be a co-buyer, but I wouldn't listen. Blame it on stupidity, but the house is in both our names. That's the only thing that will prevent the divorce from moving along smoothly."

"Well, your dad's an attorney; talk to him. Find out what you can do to get Reed's name off the deed."

"I don't think it can be done. Besides, I don't want to involve my parents at the moment. I'll be giving them information on a need-to-know basis." Dayna pursed her lips together in a manner that let Cecily know she did not intend to discuss her parents any further.

"Men! You give them the best part of yourself and all they do is trample on your heart and feelings until you can't take it anymore," Cecily declared, wisely taking the focus off the taboo topic of Dayna's parents.

"The odd thing is I feel like I've been playing some sort of role that really isn't me. I can't believe I allowed myself to behave like such a wimp. And I could kick myself for putting on all this weight. But believe me, these excess pounds are coming off."

"I can see a difference already," Cecily complimented.

"You're kidding. I've only been dieting for a few weeks," Dayna said, blushing with pride. She'd dropped another two pounds and was thrilled that Cecily could see the difference.

"I don't know...your face looks smaller. And..." She scrutinized Dayna. "Something's going on around your collarbone area. Have you been sneaking to the gym?"

"Nope. Just working out with a yoga DVD at home."

"Yoga? Isn't that boring?"

"No, I like it. It's relaxing and you don't work up a sweat. You know how I am about my hair; I can't be sweating out my 'do." Dayna laughed heartily. "I don't expect to see changes overnight, but I'm trying to get into a lifestyle change as I purge myself of Reed."

Dayna stopped for a red light and turned toward Cecily. "Reed is good looking; that's all he has going for himself. He's totally self-absorbed and honestly, there's almost something evil about him. Every word he speaks seems to be a lie and if he's not lying, then he's criticizing something about me. He's just not a very nice person and I feel like the wool has been suddenly ripped away from my eyes—like I'm seeing him for the first time." She paused and looked at Cecily intently. "And I'm repulsed by what I see."

"Damn. It's that deep?"

"Yes, it is. I don't want him sleeping next to me anymore; he actually gives me the creeps." Dayna shook her head and accelerated when the light turned green.

"How are you gonna kick him out of the bedroom?"

"I don't know, but I have no intention of ever again sharing the same bed with that man."

"Let me ask you something?"

"Go ahead."

"Is Reed…um…does he get physical with you? Is he violent?"

Dayna laughed. "No," she said, shaking her head for emphasis.

"Well, I don't understand the comment about him being evil."

"I can't explain it. It's just a feeling." Dayna shrugged.

"For your information, the police will kick Reed out of the house if he puts his hands on you."

"Girl, I'm not trying to go there."

"I'm just putting it out there."

Dayna pulled up in front of Cecily's house. "So, how are you going to get your car?"

"The mechanic's gonna pick me up."

"Oh yeah? Do I detect some hanky-panky?"

"Oh, hell no. I don't do greasy mechanics. I like my men to look good, smell good, and have clean fingernails."

Both women laughed.

"Dayna! I forgot to tell you. Remember Kendrick?"

"Who?"

"Kendrick. The fine brother I met at that club in Manayunk last week?"

"Oh, yeah. I didn't know you two had kept in touch."

"We exchanged numbers, but I didn't call him and he just got around to calling me last night. He invited me to an art exhibit—at his home. Apparently he lives in a big house in north Philly and leases space for various events."

"Sounds interesting, but with my marital problems, this isn't a good time for me to purchase art or anything else."

"I'm not buying anything. I'm just going to have a good time and get to know Kendrick better. I get the impression that we won't be attending a typical exhibit. He mentioned something about a jazz combo, a caterer who'll be serving fried catfish, collard greens, candied yams, a whole smorgasbord of soul food."

"Sounds good. When's the exhibit?"

"Friday night at seven. Wanna go?"

"Sure. Why not? I guess I can tolerate the artsy crowd," Dayna said, laughing. Then she groaned, "Aw!"

"What's wrong?"

"My diet! I've been doing so well, but I might have to let it go for some fried catfish."

"I know that's right," Cecily said as she exited the car and trotted up the steps to her house.

Dayna watched Cecily enter her house before pulling off. She shook her head, envying the simplicity of Cecily's life. Dayna knew she wouldn't be attending the art exhibit with Cecily, but had played along because Cecily would have held her hostage in her own car until she agreed to go.

Her emotions for her husband had suddenly gone from adulation to revulsion and just that morning she had dropped a serious bomb on him—the marriage was over and she wanted out. Something told her that Reed was none too pleased about her announcement and would soon be declaring war. And winning a war against Reed was not going to be easy.

Chapter 13

Deanna's Den was billed as a gentleman's club. It was considered the top strip club in the city—the chill spot for sports figures, entertainers, and all the major players with tons of money to throw around. Since Chanelle was in the market for a man with mucho mullah, she figured Deanna's Den was where she needed to be. Supposedly, the dancers at Deanna's Den made ten times what she made at Lizzard's, so she considered getting kicked out of Lizzard's a blessing in disguise.

There had been complaints, however, that Deanna's Den was worse than Lizzard's with respect to hiring black girls, so Chanelle decided to pay the club an impromptu visit instead of calling in advance. She wanted them to see her pretty black face in person before they even thought about making a prejudiced determination.

Chanelle took a cab and arrived at the strip club bright and early before the club officially opened for business. Certain that her unexpected presence would be perceived by the owner or whoever did the hiring as a gift from above, she boldly rang the bell.

"Yeah?" a male voice crackled over the intercom.

"I'm here to audition," she said proudly.

There was no response.

"Hello." She patted her foot in annoyance.

"Do you have an appointment?" the voice asked.

"No, but—"

"Wait a minute."

Chanelle patted her foot for an entire ten minutes before she was buzzed in. Once inside she was hustled to a small room by a swarthy muscular guy who was carrying a clipboard. His T-shirt was extremely tight. So tight, Chanelle expected him to burst out of it like the Hulk.

He ushered her to the dressing room, sat her at a dressing table, and handed her the clipboard. "Here you go. You have to fill out this employment application."

"Are you serious?" she asked.

"That's the procedure," the overly pumped-up man replied. He shook his head and smiled grimly. "The manager will review your application and if she's interested, she'll give you a call back to audition."

"How will she know if she's interested if she doesn't even know what I look like?"

"I'll tell her." There was nothing in his voice that indicated his impression of Chanelle's appearance.

Taking a deep breath, Chanelle peered down at the two-page application. Filling out a long-ass application was definitely not a part of her game plan, but if she wanted to keep her apartment and continue her frenzied shopping sprees, she'd need to have a reliable income.

As she labored over the never-ending employment

application, the emaciated dancers who worked there began to stream in. They regarded her with bemusement as they began readying themselves for the first shift.

"You're applying for a job *here?*" one of the stick figures asked.

"Uh-huh," Chanelle responded absently as she thought about her response to a portion of the application that asked her to disclose something about herself that no one else knew. *What the hell kind of question is that?* She looked up and caught a glimpse in the mirror of two women exchanging catty smiles. Realizing that they were amused by her, as if she shouldn't be taken seriously, Chanelle glared at the women and went back to the application. *Hmmm. Something about myself that no one knows?*

Then, hit with a burst of inspiration, she began scrawling: *I'd like to settle down one day and have two or three children… maybe a beautiful set of twins—girls of course—and one little boy. But not until I'm married to a man who can provide a nice comfortable lifestyle for all of us.* She reviewed her words and felt satisfied that what she'd written was impressive. Without spelling it out, she was letting the employer know that she wasn't about to turn up pregnant. No, her life was well planned and they could depend on her until she was ready to settle down.

Every now and then, Chanelle would gaze up from the application and check out the competition. Never in her life had she seen such scarily skinny women prancing around like they were the shit.

Chanelle was appalled when they wiggled out of their street clothes and were stripped down to their underwear. They were all just skin and bones. Skeletal frames with crazy big tits, high cheekbones, puffed-out lips, and an occasional extra padding in the ass. Fake, fake, fake! Sure, most of the white girls at Lizzard's had breast implants, but this shit was ridiculous. A pack of stick-thin women with synthetic body parts. She wondered how they could even move on stage without all that silicone and collagen—or whatever—shifting out of place.

No one said another word to her; and she didn't say shit to any of them. When she finally finished filling out the application, she left the dressing room to search for the Hulk.

She heard snickers when she closed the door. It took all her strength not to yank off her earrings, barge back into the dressing room, and bust somebody in the mouth. But the thought of her knuckles being covered with that nasty mess that was injected in their lips gave her a change of heart.

Three days later when she still hadn't heard a word from Deanna's Den, she called the club to find out what was up. The Hulk came to the phone.

"Hey, how ya doin'?"

"How I'm doing depends on what kind of news you have for me."

"Well…I'm not gonna jerk you around. The schedule's

full right now, but look...I have your number and as soon as there's an opening, I'll give you a call."

"In other words, don't call us; we'll call you?" she said sarcastically.

The Hulk gave an uncomfortable snort. "Yeah, something like that."

"Yeah, well fuck you, too," she said, and then slammed down the phone.

Fuck all those honky muthafuckers. Humph! Deanna's Den and Lizzard's weren't the only jumpin' spots in the area. Shit, she'd heard there were plenty of upscale places in Jersey. But damn...How the fuck was she gonna get to Jersey every night? She damn sure couldn't rely on Malik.

Thinking about Malik made her furious. Where the hell had he been for the past week, anyway? She'd left a zillion urgent messages on his cell, but he hadn't called her back. It was as if the nigga had his antennae up, knew she was in need of some financial support, and had deliberately gotten ghost. What a punk!

But it was all good. She wouldn't be down long, and once she was back up, she was definitely going to give Malik her ass to kiss. He couldn't do shit for her anyway. She needed somebody with their own dough.

And dammit, she couldn't find her future husband moping around the house. She had to get off her ass, get glamorous, and find herself a gig.

Chapter 14

The money Reed had spent on Aziza was worth every dime, but after the bomb Dayna dropped on him; he knew he'd have to tighten up on his spending until he could figure out if she seriously wanted a divorce or was just trying to mess with his head.

Aziza had whipped it on him good. She did things with her pussy that no other woman had ever done. Aziza definitely knew what she was doing. Even though he could usually control his orgasms, Aziza let him know that her pussy was in charge.

She'd wait until he had his dick deep inside her and after he'd caught a good groove, the kind of rhythm he could ride on for hours, she'd whisper in his ear: "Slow down, baby, what's the rush; we got all night." Then after obligingly stopping his thrust for just a second or two so he could downshift to second gear, Aziza took her big pussy lips and tied them into a knot—a tight knot around his dick—locking him in and making him ejaculate against his will. Yeah, Aziza had a powerful pussy. Expensive, too!

He shook his head mournfully as he reminisced about their night together. He would not be seeing Aziza again anytime soon. With Dayna's recent unpredictable behavior, he wasn't sure if she'd cut off the funds he used for recreation. He had to spend his money more wisely. The two hundred dollars Aziza charged was now out of his price range.

He needed an affordable hole to dip his dick into. It was time to mend his relationship with Buttercup. To show his contrition, he decided to pay her sixty bucks instead of the forty he usually paid. He figured sixty bucks was more than enough to kiss and make up.

Reed checked the dashboard clock. Six o'clock. Too early for Buttercup to be out at any of the clubs, but knowing her as he did, he assumed her lazy ass was still lying in bed. He parked his Lexus and dashed to the front steps of her rundown apartment building on Pearl Street. He knew the doorbell didn't work so he pounded on the front door.

When the door finally opened he found himself staring into the inquisitive and paint-specked face of a sweaty man wearing painter's garb. True, it was rather warm for May, but the man was perspiring like it was high noon in the middle of August.

"You looking for Darlene?" The question had an accusatory tone.

Reed assumed Darlene was Buttercup's real name. "Uh, yeah," Reed admitted uncomfortably. "Does she still live here?" He asked, not knowing whether the man owned the place or was just hired to paint it.

"Nope, not no more; I had to put her out."

Reed wondered if Buttercup had left a forwarding address.

"She kept crazy hours—played her TV real loud 'til all hours of the night and couldn't none of my other tenants get no sleep," the landlord complained. Reed shook his head sympathetically, which encouraged the man to go on.

"She was a terrible tenant and she played too many games with the rent. Always giving me the rent money in dribs and drabs. Every time I came around to collect my money on the first of the month, I had to hear one of her sob stories." The landlord screwed up his lips in disgust. "Man, I got sick of her mess. She acts like I ain't got bills to pay, too." He wiped his brow with the back of a paint-splattered hand. "If I had known how bad she had torn this place up, I would have put her out a long time ago."

The only thing that kept Reed from hurrying away from the long-winded malcontented landlord was the modicum of hope he held that the man might know Buttercup's current whereabouts.

"How do you know Darlene? You seem like a decent young fella, not like the drug addicts and winos she brings around here." He paused and surveyed the meticulously groomed and well-dressed Reed. "By the way, young fella, you wouldn't happen to be looking for a place, would you? 'Cause I'm not renting to no more riffraff."

Reed furrowed his brow, pretending to weigh whether

or not he was in the market for an apartment. "No, I don't need a place, but I have a cousin who may be interested."

"He got a job? 'Cause like I said…no more riffraff."

"Oh yeah, he's working. Recently divorced…you know. My man's trying to rebuild, get his life back together."

The landlord looked hopeful. "I'm gonna jot my number down. Tell him to call me and leave a message with my wife if I'm not there."

The landlord searched his pockets and withdrew a crumpled business card. He ran a line through the imprinted telephone number and scribbled in his current number. "Tell your cousin to give me a call. I should have this place ready to show in a couple of days."

"Okay, I'll do that. Oh, yeah, you wouldn't happen to know where Darlene's staying, would you?"

"Don't tell me she owes you money, too?" the landlord asked suspiciously.

Figuring it would work to his benefit to portray himself as a victim, Reed nodded solemnly. "Yes, sir, she sure does. She's related to my wife," Reed quickly lied. "My wife's real soft-hearted and tried to help Darlene." Reed shook his head. "I let my wife talk me into loaning that girl some money; would you believe she said she needed it to pay her rent?"

"Ha! That girl ain't paid me nothing," the landlord exploded. "So, if y'all related, then you know her great-grandmother over on Delancy Street."

"No, she's just an in-law. She's related to my wife on her father's side," Reed lied quickly. "I don't know that side of the family too well."

"Okay, well, I heard she's living over there with Dottie, her great-grandmother, and that's a damn shame because all Darlene's gonna do is spend up the little bit of social security money the poor woman gets. Dottie ain't right in the head no more. She lives right on the corner of Fifty-Fourth and Delancy—directly across from the barbershop."

Reed thanked the man and abruptly headed for his car.

"Don't forget to tell your cousin about the place," the man shouted as Reed got in his car and took off.

❧❧❧❧

Dottie's Hair Salon. The faded old-fashioned lettering on the ragged board hanging off the side of the ramshackle storefront property indicated that Buttercup's great-grandmother resided in a former hair salon. Reed looked around for a doorbell, finding none; he peered through a smudged triangular window pane, but couldn't see inside. Impatient, he pounded on the heavy wooden door.

The door slowly creaked open, startling him. A wrinkled, gnarled hand with jagged, yellowed fingernails held the partially open door in place while a pair of opaque-colored, obviously confused eyes appraised him.

Reed cleared his throat. "Is Butter...I mean, is Darlene here?"

"Who?" the voice croaked.

"Darlene?" he repeated. "Do you have a great-grand-daughter named Darlene?" Reed spoke in a raised voice. He assumed the old woman was hard of hearing.

"Who's Darlene?" Matching Reed's tone, the old woman took her volume up several notches.

With increasing impatience, Reed took a deep breath, but before he had to repeat himself for the third time, he heard Buttercup's voice and it was music to his ears.

"Did you call me, Grandma?"

"Who you callin' Grandma?" the old woman demanded, furious. She let go of the door and turned angrily toward the stairs that Buttercup was running down.

Reed gasped. He couldn't help it. With the door opened a little wider, he was provided a closer look at the old woman and what he saw was beyond ghastly. The old woman was wearing makeup. Hideous, thick pancake makeup—two shades lighter than her chestnut-colored skin. Garish red lipstick was smeared across her cheeks. The same red lipstick was used as a substitute for eye shadow, but she chose a black eye pencil to draw a big round beauty mark just above the edge of her sunken upper lip.

"Why you got the door open, Grandma? You want somebody to come in here and rob us?" Buttercup chastised. She pulled at her great-grandmother's arm, but the old woman jerked away. "Get off me, girl. Can't you see I got me some male company?"

Buttercup pulled the door completely open, took a look at Reed, and tried to slam the door in his face, but Reed stopped the door with his foot and used his shoulder to push it open.

"What the fuck you doing here?" she demanded when Reed pushed his way inside. "You stalking me now?" She glared at Reed through narrowed, poisonous eyes.

Looking humble and repentant, Reed said, "Yo, Butter… I came to apologize." She was wearing baggy pajamas, no make-up, and her hair was pulled back into a short ponytail. Reed knew he had no right to hold her appearance against her, but he couldn't help wishing she looked more glamorous.

"Apologize! Nigga, you trippin'. I'm not fuckin' with your sick ass no more."

"Aw, come on Butter; don't be like that. How long have you been knowing me? You know that's not how I get down. I had too much to drink that night. I think somebody slipped something in my drink because I was rammin'. I just lost control, baby. Why don't you let me make it up to you?" He pulled a roll of bills out of his pocket. "I got something for you. I want to make amends. All right?"

Trying to assess the amount he offered, Buttercup studied the knot he held. "How much?" she finally asked.

"Yeah, how much?" her great-grandmother asked, as she stepped out of the shadows.

Reed drew back reflexively. Buttercup's great-grand-mother was wearing a knee-length dirty cotton robe; dried food covered the front. She had on a pair of those black old folk's shoes with the Velcro straps. Topping off her macabre appearance, there was a silky black ponytail pinned to the top of the woman's short, gray knotty afro. If this kooky old woman was Dottie, the former owner of the hair salon, Reed would bet good money that she had fucked up many heads of hair in her day.

"Go sit down, Grandma."

"I'm not gon' sit down so you can make all the money." She let out a snort and rolled her eyes. "I got the same thing she got, mister," Dottie shouted. "Only mine is mo' better," she added boastfully.

"Come on in while I try to get her upstairs," Buttercup said to Reed. "Come on, Grandma; it's time for you to get some rest." Buttercup tried to steer her resistant great-grandmother toward the stairs.

"Have a seat," Buttercup told Reed as she struggled with her grandmother.

Reed didn't want to risk offending Buttercup, but there was no way he was sitting down. The place had the musky smell of piss and liniment. The old-fashioned sectional sofa was covered with hard, torn plastic. Reed strongly suspected that Grandma had peed all over everything.

"I'm straight," he responded, standing erect with his hands clasped in front of him. His eyes did a quick, disgusted sweep. Cobwebs clung to corners near the ceiling; faded wallpaper was peeling off every wall; yellowed and curled newspaper photos of both President Kennedy and Martin Luther King hung crooked on the walls in dusty old frames.

In the kitchen area, he saw a mouse shoot across the floor and after experiencing a quick case of the willies, he abruptly shifted his focus back to his own reflection in his polished and shined shoes.

Buttercup tugged on her great-grandmother's arm, but the old woman escaped from her grasp. With unusual speed, she raced toward Reed and quickly tore off her robe to show off her goods. Rolls upon rolls of slackened flesh drooped from her body. A flap of flesh hung over big bloomer-sized panties. Her shriveled bare breasts hung like two used teabags.

Reed recoiled. "Damn, Butter. Come get your grandmother."

"Leave him alone, Grandma. Come on, now. Why you always gotta act up?"

But her grandmother flatly refused to leave Reed alone. Grinning toothlessly, she rotated her pelvis enticingly as she tottered toward Reed.

Staggered by revulsion, Reed took an unsteady step backward. "Yo, Butter. Take your grandmother upstairs."

"I'm trying," Buttercup said as she draped her grandmother's robe across her shoulders. "You shouldn't have pulled out that money in front of her."

"Why not?" Feeling repelled, he really didn't want to know the answer.

"My grandma used to trick."

"That old lady used to turn tricks?" He asked with an expression of astonishment.

"Uh-huh. A long time ago, before she went legit and opened her hair salon. My grandma used to be real pretty. She stayed wearing fly gear, and always kept her hair laying. She was something! I can show you pictures…"

Reed found that very hard to believe, but declined seeing the photographs.

"But now she got this dementia and something else called sundowners."

Perplexed, Reed screwed up his face.

"Sometimes she don't know nobody; she even forgets her own name," Buttercup explained. "Then when the sun goes down; she really starts to trip. She starts thinking she's still back in the 1950s when she used to live in Chester. Back then, she used to work in a whorehouse owned by some lady named Miss Addie Mae. She called herself a sportin' girl," Buttercup said with a giggle.

"I *am* a Sportin' Girl!" Dottie insisted. "And Miss Addie Mae don't like a whole buncha talk with the customers before they hand over the money," Dottie continued with her horribly painted lips poked out. She struggled some more and tried to pull away from Buttercup's strong grip.

"See what I mean?" Buttercup said, laughing. Then, turning serious, she said, "It's so hard to control her. I have to hide my lingerie and shit because she'll start messing in my stuff when she thinks it's time to start trickin'. But mostly she's all right in the morning and afternoon. She can be real sweet and pleasant." Buttercup smiled warmly at her great-grandmother.

The old woman didn't return Buttercup's smile; she rolled her eyes and muttered, "Bitch!"

Reed just shook his head. He was ready to get out of there. Everything in the house was old and dusty; he wanted Buttercup to hurry the hell up. The creepy dusty house was causing him to itch. A few more minutes in this hellhole and he was going to start coughing and sneezing and carrying on.

"Look, why don't you just leave her for a little while. I gotta get some air. You wanna go out and take a ride with me?"

"Where to?"

"I don't know, anywhere. Just hurry up," he snapped, no longer feeling the need to be polite.

"Okay, just let me get her upstairs. If I don't lock her door, she'll start rampaging around this house like you wouldn't believe. Come on, Grandma," Buttercup coerced sweetly and placed a comforting arm around her great-grandmother.

"Okay," the old woman replied, suddenly docile. Looking weary, she began to shuffle toward the stairs. Then, in mid-step, she changed gear and dramatically threw off the robe. Reminiscent of an old James Brown move, Dottie slid across the floor, wiggling and shimmying her way back to Reed.

Taken off guard, Reed threw up both hands defensively.

Buttercup grappled with her grandmother and dragged her to the stairs.

Having seen and heard more than enough, Reed hollered, "I'll be outside in the car!"

"Okay, but I have to get myself together before I come out. I don't want to get you worked up and acting crazy, so I'm gonna put on some makeup and grab one of my wigs."

"Yeah, all right. Get yourself together, but please... hurry up."

He waited patiently for a few minutes, but feeling antsy, he decided to pass some time by patching things up with his wife.

There wasn't a chance in hell he was going to let Dayna drag him through a divorce. He knew how to handle her. All he had to do was serve her up some good dick, talk some shit about starting a family, and she'd be walking around on cloud nine, buying baby clothes and changing one of the spare bedrooms into a nursery. And most important, she'd cut out all that diet bullshit and start cooking some real food.

He pulled out his cell and cleared his throat. It was time to sweet-talk his bitch of a wife.

Chapter 15

Dayna didn't have high hopes that Reed would do the honorable thing and vacate their bedroom. So instead of allowing him to deplete her energy with an emotionally charged argument, she decided it would be less stressful if she made the move herself.

By quarter to seven that night, however, she was still plowing through her clothing and personal items. Progress was being made very slowly and it appeared that it was going to take a few more days to transfer all her things to the spare bedroom.

The spare room wasn't nearly as large as the master bedroom and it didn't have a private bathroom. What she liked about the room was the canopy bed, which was draped with sheer white fabric. Beyond that, having her own private space more than made up for the lack of extra perks.

Dayna filled a large plastic container with shoes and dragged the container into her new bedroom and left it sitting in the middle of the room. At seven o'clock, famished and exhausted, she decided she'd done enough for one night. She'd start fresh tomorrow after work. Hopefully, she'd be asleep by the time Reed got in. She'd left the master bedroom in shambles. Her new bedroom was in a state of chaos and disarray as well, but she was too tired to finish straightening up. She decided to eat a quick meal, put in the yoga DVD, do some stretches for about a half-hour, spend another hour or so grading papers, and then call it a night.

She padded down to the kitchen and stuck a Lean Cuisine in the microwave. As she waited for the quick meal to heat, she reminded herself to take a sleeping pill before she retired to ensure a deep and undisturbed sleep. She was not in the mood to listen to Reed rant about the mess she'd made.

Dayna sagged into a kitchen chair, emotionally drained. She'd invested so much into her marriage; it hurt to have to accept that she'd been wrong about Reed. He was not the man he appeared to be.

It was Reed who had wanted to rush into the marriage. That should have raised a red flag, but instead she chose to be flattered. Even though she had wanted to delay the ceremony for a little while longer so she could plan a really extravagant and unforgettable wedding day, he told her he couldn't wait. He was too much in love. Looking back, she realized that planning a wedding was a pleasant distraction from the pain of her parents' breakup.

While she thought she was being swept off her feet, she was actually being hustled by a fast-talking smooth operator who needed the legitimacy of marriage to get the things he wanted in life. Marriage to the daughter of a prominent attorney was definitely a step up for Reed.

But their marriage was based on lies. Dayna now knew that Reed had never been accepted to Wharton's business school. Emotionally blinded by their own rocky relationship, her parents were charmed by Reed and it was easy for him to persuade them that he was the right choice for their daughter.

My husband never loved me. Those words had become a mantra she had to keep repeating in order to stay focused. Deep in thought, she chewed the food without tasting it. Reed, with his self-serving behavior, fit the profile of a sociopath. She'd studied personality disorders in college and had taken a refresher course a couple years ago. At that time, she didn't recognize any of Reed's characteristics because she was focusing on the students she taught. Teaching emotionally disturbed children was challenging. The refresher course provided her with a deeper understanding of the numerous wounded children she was responsible for educating.

Dayna recalled how she recognized sociopathic characteristics of a sociopath in one of her students of whom she was quite fond, an eight-year-old named Preston. He was a beautiful child who came to school tardy and unkempt. He was being raised by a grandmother since his own mother was in prison. Getting teased by his classmates was a daily occurrence in Preston's life, causing him to routinely lash out and fight his classmates. Dayna always rallied to his support like a mother lioness, offering him comfort and chastising his tormentors.

One day Preston arrived at school crying inconsolably. Through his racking sobs, Dayna was able to determine that he'd had a birthday the day before and no one in his family had acknowledged it.

Determined to spare the child further damage to his self-esteem, Dayna ran out during her lunch break and bought a sheet cake. It was decorated with a toy truck and the words *Happy Birthday Preston* were written in blue icing. Giving Preston an impromptu birthday party, Dayna bought ice cream and party hats for him and his classmates to wear. Her heart swelled with pride as she watched the scorned child enjoy being the center of attention. For that one day, instead of being the butt of every joke, Preston was a hero.

"Can I take the rest of the cake home to my grandmother?" Preston asked at the end of the day.

"Of course," Dayna readily agreed. What a sweet child to want to share his cake with the grandmother who had ignored his special day. Tears stung her eyes as she watched Preston leaving the classroom proudly carrying what seemed to be his very first birthday cake.

A few days later as she was going through Preston's records, she noticed his date of birth: July 6, 1996. How could that be? He'd just celebrated his birthday two days before. Mystified, Dayna scratched her head. Thinking it a mistake, she had the secretary check his birth date on the computer. Sure enough, Preston was born July 6.

Dayna was stunned and as soon as Preston arrived to school the next day, she pulled him aside to privately ask him why he'd lied about his birthday. To her utter astonishment, Preston jerked away from her. "Don't be pullin' on me. Get your fuckin' hands off me, you stupid bitch," he snarled, his face twisted in rage. "Fuck that cake; I'm not kissing your ass over no dumb birthday cake."

Later, when she hauled him off to the principal's office and insisted he be seen by the school psychologist, it was determined that Preston hadn't been invited to a cousin's birthday party and needed to feel some type of satisfaction. Had Dayna never caught on to his scheme, Preston would have continued to show her his sweet side only.

It had been a chilling experience for her and throughout the duration of the school year, Preston had continued to waver between being an absolute angel when he wanted something and the worst demon from hell whenever he was disappointed. When Preston chose to be an angel, Dayna found him nearly impossible to resist.

She now realized that Reed suffered from the same disorder. He was incapable of giving or receiving love and incapable of feeling remorse. He was an emotional shell and emulated feelings only when it benefited him.

If Reed's personality defect was influenced by genetics, she could only thank the Lord that she hadn't conceived a child with him. The mere thought of giving life to his unholy spawn sent a shiver down her spine.

The telephone rang. She looked at the caller ID. It was Reed calling from his cell phone. "Hello," Dayna said in a tone that would let him know his call was not welcome.

"Hey, sweetheart. How ya feeling?"

Dayna didn't bother to respond.

"Oh, so you're still upset with me? Okay, well, look I know I haven't been the best husband, I've been putting the PBP before you but all that's about to change. I don't want to lose you. You hear me? Nothing is more important than our relationship and I'm willing to take full responsibility for everything that's going wrong in our marriage." He spoke with warmth in his voice. Dayna hadn't heard him speak in that tone in months. If she were the same idiot she'd been in the past, she would have instantly believed him.

With her guard up and bolted in place, she responded, "To answer your first question, I'm fine. Nothing has changed; my mind is made up. I don't want to talk about what you could have done in the past. Our marriage didn't work, I'm really sick of it, and judging by your frequent absence here, I can only assume that you want out of this marriage as much as I do."

Reed winced and then spoke in the same soothing tone.

"I'm confused. I never said I wanted to end our marriage. I'm cool. Look, it must be that time of the month or close to it. You know how you get," he said with an uncomfortable chuckle.

"Don't go there—blaming my hormones as if I'm emotionally unstable." She switched the phone to her other ear. "Reed, listen to me. I want a divorce and my decision is final."

"Damn, Dayna. What the hell is wrong with you? You can't just suddenly disrupt my life and expect me to go along with it."

"It's not all about you, Reed," she said calmly. "This is also about me. I don't love you, you obviously don't love me either, and this horrible marriage is like an anchor weighing me down."

Reed gritted his teeth to control his mounting anger. He forced himself to speak in a calm tone. "I know your parents spoiled you. Gave you everything money could buy. But you're a big girl now and you should know that in the real world, people don't always get everything they want." The threat behind his words was unsettling, but Dayna stood her ground.

"Your lack of cooperation won't stop this divorce."

"But I can delay it, and in the meantime I'm going to make sure your life is a living hell," he announced menacingly, and then clicked off.

Dayna held the phone briefly and then hung up. Somewhat shaken, she thought perhaps she'd have to involve her parents after all. Reed sounded really vicious, as if he were gearing himself up for some vindictive action. She'd be damned if she was going to sit back and allow him to wreak havoc upon her life. She'd call her dad first thing in the morning to let him know that Reed had threatened her. Her dad would know what legal options were available to her.

Chapter 16

Oddly, the unpleasant exchange with Dayna had aroused Reed. It was as if his hatred for his wife had materialized into a hot hand that now caressed his groin. He jerked his neck toward Dottie's Hair Salon and leaned on the horn. *What was taking that whore so long?*

The door finally swung open. Buttercup popped outside wearing a red wig, tight low-rider jeans, and a skimpy red top. Liking what he saw, Reed nodded in approval.

She climbed inside the Lexus. As she bent slightly to place her purse on the floor, Reed caught a glimpse of a red thong sticking out of her jeans. His aggravation began to subside until thoughts of Aziza entered his mind. The smell of Aziza still filled his nostrils; the acrid taste of her vaginal juices remained on his tongue; he felt a yearning so strong he had to restrain himself from pushing Buttercup out of his whip. He felt like roaring away from Delancy Street and screeching to a stop in front of the nearest ATM machine to get the two hundred dollars Aziza charged.

But he couldn't. Thanks to Dayna's temper tantrum

and hollow threats, his cash flow would be limited for a while. He had to exercise control. However, he knew it would be hard to find satisfaction in an ordinary pussy. He felt like doing something freakish and wondered what kind of debased act he could talk Buttercup into.

"Where are we going, Joe?" Buttercup asked. Reed had told her his name was Joe when he'd first met her and had never bothered to tell the foolish girl otherwise.

Reed shrugged. "I guess we can rent a room at that spot on Fortieth Street. They charge by the hour, but I think we might need more time than that."

"How long you think we're gonna need?" Buttercup looked apprehensive.

"I'm just saying I know you want to get high. That's gonna take some time."

"No I don't. I'm clean," Buttercup exclaimed with pride.

"Since when?"

"Two weeks, nigga," she said playfully.

"Aw, that's nothing. You'll be back doing your thing the minute you get your hands on some money."

"That's a lie. I got money. I get my grandma's SSI check."

"Oh yeah? How much is that?"

"Come on now…mind your bizness," she said with a wink.

"I hope that Social Security check is worth moving out to your own place. I can't understand how you can bear to live in that ancient ruin. No disrespect, Butter, but damn...your great-grandmother's house doesn't seem fit to live in. I'm surprised the people from the city haven't kicked y'all out and boarded it up. That place is a health hazard."

"Stop trippin'. It ain't all that bad. Besides, I gotta reason for staying there."

Reed rubbed his jaw in thought. "Oh yeah, what's the reason?"

"Like I said, mind your bizness, nigga. Now how much you plan on spending tonight? 'Cause if you ain't talkin' what I want to hear, you can just drop me off at the Apache."

"Naw, I gotchu, I gotchu," Reed promised.

Buttercup stuck out her open palm. "Then stop talkin' shit and let me hold something."

Reed chuckled and turned onto Market Street. He pulled up in front of the Wine and Spirits shop. "I know you didn't stop drinking," he said as he turned off the ignition. "What do you want? A bottle of gin?"

"I swear to God." Buttercup raised her right hand. "I quit doing all substances." She sounded weak and unconvincing.

"Who do you think you're kidding? You know you still get your drink on. What are you saying...if you have a drink, you'll start smoking that shit again? I know you're not that weak."

Buttercup grappled briefly with the dilemma, then

shrugged. "Okay, get me a bottle of Hpnotiq." She figured if she broke down and took a drink, she might as well let him treat her to something that cost more than eight dollars a bottle.

Reed came out with a chilled bottle of Hpnotiq and handed it to Buttercup. He sped to Fortieth Street and parked in front of a rooming house. "Wait while I take care of the room," he instructed. "Oh yeah, I have cups in there." He pointed to the glove compartment.

After making the arrangements, he came outside and beckoned Buttercup. She trotted across the street, tightly clutching the Hpnotiq as it were a four-thousand-dollar bottle of Hennessy Timeless cognac.

The no-frills room was practically bare. No bureau, no chair, not even a closet. There was a hook on the back of the door, a bed with a lumpy mattress, and a chipped wooden nightstand. The single window was covered with a grayish-colored shade.

Reed took the bottle from Buttercup, cracked open the top, and poured her a drink.

"Ain't you drinking, too?" she asked when she noticed he'd filled only one plastic cup.

"Naw, this shit is for women; it gives me a headache. But go ahead, drink up."

"Don't be trying to get me drunk so you can take advantage of my womanhood," she said jokingly. Then turning serious, she said, "Now look…I might laugh and joke but I get serious when it comes to money." She stuck out an open palm.

Reed looked stung. "After all this time we've been dealing with each other, you still don't trust me? You think I'd run out without paying you. Damn, Butter, I thought we were better than that."

"Whatever," she said, taking a swig from the cup.

Reed reluctantly withdrew three twenties and handed them over. "Are we straight now?"

"Hell no, nigga. Not after that shit you put me through. There were welts on my ass for days."

Reed peeled off another twenty.

Buttercup nodded in consent." Now we're straight." She stuck the money in the pocket of her jeans. "But this money don't give you permission to start beatin' on me."

"I told you somebody slipped something in my drink. I'm cool now." Reed started pulling off his pants. "You miss Big Daddy?" he asked her as he stroked his expanding manhood, which had started to throb with a dull ache.

Buttercup took two big gulps of the blue elixir to help get into her role. "Uh-huh, I missed you," she said unconvincingly, then downed the entire cup and helped herself to more.

"Then why are you ignoring him?" Reed complained. "Look at him." He pointed his generously sized member in Buttercup's direction. "Give my man some attention, baby."

Buttercup walked over to Reed holding the cup of Hpnotiq in her hand. She bent down on one knee and guided his penis into the cold blue liquid.

"Aw shit," Reed moaned. He squeezed his eyes tight and leaned back, ready to enjoy whatever freaky thrill Buttercup had in mind.

She licked the dripping liquid from his dick, moaning and making slurping sounds as she licked him dry. Then she took in just the head of his dick, encircling it with the tip of her tongue teasingly. She began to suck on it, pulling in an inch at a time. She stopped suddenly and took another swig and inserted his dick inside her fluid-filled mouth.

If her juicy mouth hadn't felt so cold, Reed would have felt like his dick was inside a vagina filled with cum. After a few moments the liquor felt warm and Reed's thrusts became so hard and violent, the liquid began to seep out the corners of Buttercup's mouth.

Feeling like she was about to choke, she pulled back, swallowed the Hpnotiq and allowed his penis to slip out.

"What's wrong, baby? Why'd you stop?" Trying to push himself back inside Buttercup's mouth, Reed wore the expression of a desperate man.

"You act like you tryin' to push your jawn all the way down my throat; I'm not gonna allow you to choke me to death. Damn, I thought you wanted your money's worth, but seeing as though you're in a rush, then come on and get it over with."

"Okay, okay. My bad," he admitted as he tried to calm down. "Damn, you had me so excited, I just got carried away. How come you never did that shit before?"

"You ain't never bought me no Hpnotiq before," she said with a hint of arrogance. "You ready?" she asked with a seductive tilt to her head.

"I don't know," he responded with a chuckle.

Buttercup threw her head back and emptied the cup into her mouth. She crooked her index finger and beckoned him.

Reed slowly entered the watery abyss. With each thrust, he heard a splashing sound that was driving him mad. And like the tide of the ocean, the waves began to recede. Buttercup was slowly swallowing the Hpnotiq, but she left just enough in her mouth to keep it moist enough for his dick to slip in and out with ease. Suddenly, she put a suction hold on his stiff member, holding him captive, rendering him helpless as he succumbed to a heart-pounding, body-shaking, powerful orgasm.

When his heart stopped pounding and he could finally catch his breath, Reed glared at Buttercup. "I wasn't ready to bust a nut. Damn, Butter!" he complained.

"Humph," Buttercup muttered in response after spitting his cum into one of the plastic cups. She quickly gulped down more Hpnotiq. The bottle was now only half-filled.

He checked his watch. "We've only been here for about twenty minutes. I paid for two hours," he lied.

"Nigga, I ain't staying up in here for no damn two hours. I got shit to do."

"Well, just give me another ten or fifteen minutes. Damn, baby, I haven't seen you in a while. Why you wanna rush me?"

Buttercup sighed and poured herself another drink. "I hope you don't expect me to sit here all night while you try to get it up again. Anyway, I'm not giving out no free head."

"Free!" He balked. "I just gave you eighty dollars. You think you can make more than that at the club?"

"Probably," she said skeptically. "I know one thing…I can't make another dime if I'm sitting up in here." She shifted around impatiently.

"All right. Here's another twenty."

Buttercup greedily snatched the money and tucked it inside her pocket with the rest of the cash.

She leaned over unenthusiastically and lifted his flaccid dick. Reed moved her hand away. "Yo, stop rushing. He ain't ready yet." Seeming relieved, she sat up and quietly sipped the Hpnotiq.

"Take those jeans and shit off. That might help," Reed barked while tugging on his dick. He looked over at Buttercup. She put the cup down and propped up a pillow and huddled against it; her eyes had a drowsy intoxicated look. She was finally feeling the liquor. Good. He liked her better when she was high. And vulnerable.

Reed helped her out of her jeans and top and let them drop to the filthy floor. Skinny as she was, she looked real sexy in the red bra and thong. He squeezed one of her small breasts and then got up and hung his clothes on the back of the door. When he rejoined her, he put his arm around her, allowing her head to rest on his chest.

"Baby, why do you keep making me pay for it when you know how much I dig you? I think of you as my girl."

"Stop lying," she muttered in a sluggish voice.

"For real. Can't nobody please me the way you do. Don't you think if I didn't have real feelings for you, I would have left your ass alone a long time ago? I could get my dick sucked by any one of those jawns at the strip clubs or I could pick up somebody out there hustling on the streets. But they're not *you*. Now, I admit it; I'm not going to lie…it was just sex in the beginning. But then I started catching real feelings for you, but I wouldn't let myself express how I felt knowing you were out there tricking with anybody for twenty dollars. And the more I think about it, I'm coming to realize why I acted like a madman the last time we were together."

She looked at him with curiosity.

"It was jealousy, baby. I can't bear the thought of you sucking on any dick except mine."

"For real?" A ray of light shone in her eyes.

"I dig you, girl. But how can I consider you *my* girl if you're out there doing whatever with whomever."

She pulled her head away from his chest, sat up straight, and looked in his eyes. "What am I supposed to do for money?"

"I can help you out, baby. It's not like you got a lot of bills. How much do you need to get through a week?"

Buttercup searched the stained and chipped ceiling for an answer. "I guess a couple hundred."

"All right," he said nodding. "Well, how much are you getting from your grandma?"

"Not much. She only gets a few hundred from Social Security every month. I'm working on some paperwork she needs to get her ex-husband's SSI. After I get through that process, we'll get a lump sum, retroactive from the time we applied."

"That sounds pretty good. How much do you think you'll get?"

"About four or five thousand, I think. That money will help out, but that's not the money I'm really interested in."

Suddenly interested, Reed shifted his position. "Oh yeah?"

"Right. When I was a little girl, my grandma used to brag about this money she had hidden somewhere in the house."

Reed sucked his teeth. "Humph. That sounds like something a kook would say. If you moved into that rat-infested place based on something your nutty grandma told you, then you're not dealing with a full deck your damn self."

"For real! My hand to God, I'm not lying. Back when she was in her right frame of mind she showed me a whole lot of money. Rolls and rolls of money. My grandma's old school. She don't trust no banks. She had that money rolled tight with a rubber band wrapped around each roll."

"And how much was in each roll?"

"I don't know. I was just a kid, but I don't remember any small bills—just fifties and twenties, maybe even hundred-dollar bills. Her stash filled up two coffee cans. She told me she was going to pay my college tuition with that money."

Reed let out a loud guffaw. "College tuition! Okay, well you blew that dream, so I guess the money's all spent by now."

"Yeah, that's what I thought until one day she was feenin' for some snuff—"

"What the hell is snuff?" he asked with a grimace.

"Chewing tobacco. It comes in a pouch. Anyway, like I said, she was feenin' and I ain't have no money to get that shit for her. She went upstairs and the next thing I know, she done came back down with this old-ass fifty-dollar bill, talking about I better bring her back all her change 'cause snuff don't cost nothin' but fifteen cents."

The potential for a sudden windfall of badly needed cash gave Reed a sudden adrenaline rush, but he kept a stoic expression. "And you think the money came from her stash?"

"It had to. Even the man at the corner store acted like

I had gave him a bar of gold. He was talkin' some shit about old bills being worth something and he was gonna check to see how much he could get for it."

Reed could no longer contain his excitement. "And you just gave that muthafucker a piece of currency that may be worth thousands?"

"What else could I do? My grandmother wanted her shit and I ain't have no money. I don't know if that fifty was really worth something or not. I'm just trying to point out that she still got that stash and I plan on finding it."

Reed regained his composure, but his mind was working overtime on how to benefit from the windfall, if such a thing truly existed. "Well, look here, Butter. I don't care about that money and I really don't even think it exists. Dream on if you want to. In the meantime, if you're gonna be my girl, you're going to have to stop tricking. You hear me?"

Buttercup blushed with pride. "Whatchu sayin'? You don't want me dancing no more, either?"

"You can dance, but no more selling pussy. That pussy belongs to me."

"All right, Joe." She giggled. "So…we're like…goin' together now? I can consider you as my man?"

He nodded. "And I'm gonna be checking on you at the strip joints to make sure you're not cheating on me. I want you to go to work, dance, get your money, and be out. Look, it's gonna be hard enough watching you let dudes push up on you, so don't allow them to get all up in your face, talking shit and wasting your time. You hear me? And another thing," Reed said sternly. "I don't want you out all hours of the night. You should start dancing at the Honey Club; that joint opens early. You can start dancing there at two in the afternoon."

"I know, but it don't be no money up in there that early," Buttercup whined. "I hate sittin' around waitin' for money to come through the door. I get frustrated quick and that's when I start tricking."

Reed shot her an evil look.

"I'm just saying… I mean, it's not like I'm gonna still turn tricks. I'm just explaining why I think two o' clock is too early to try to make some dough."

"Okay," Reed conceded. "How about if you start around four or five and then finish up by about ten. When I swing by the club to pick you up; I don't want to hear any excuses. When I say it's time to go; you better be ready to roll."

Buttercup nodded. Judging by the look of sheer pleasure that lit up her face, the mack daddy routine Reed was putting down was going over quite well.

Crack-head hoes need love, too, Reed supposed, laughing to himself.

"That's weird, though," Buttercup said with a nervous little titter.

"What's weird, baby?" he said with tenderness.

Buttercup blushed. "It's weird that I don't even know your full name and you don't know mine."

"Joseph. My name's Joseph Moss," Reed Reynolds said without hesitation, borrowing the name of a childhood friend. "And your name is Darlene…uh…what's your last name, baby?"

"Hayward," she replied happily and then leaned over and pressed her lips against his. His impulse was to pull away, but he gave in and kissed her hard. He even opened his mouth and offered his tongue.

He wanted his kiss to feel sincere, as if he were offering her his heart. When enough time had elapsed, he broke the kiss without alerting her of his revulsion. He slowly pulled his lips away, and then allowed her to nestle her head against his chest. He murmured in her ear, mumbling meaningless sounds, imitating raspy murmurs of endearment. Amidst the mumbling, ever so often he'd speak the word *love*—making sure it came out crystal clear.

Women were such suckers for love.

He laid her down on her back and pulled off her thong. Next, he propped her legs up. He bent and parted her thighs as if he were a gynecologist trained to explore this sensitive region. Buttercup trembled and closed her eyes as Reed carefully spread her vulva.

He inhaled and exhaled in rapid bursts of excitement. Her inner lips were pink and plump, but small. Too small, and without any elasticity. Nothing like Aziza's. Deeply disappointed, Reed let out a low groan. With the tips of both thumbs and index fingers, Reed gently pulled her inner lips, trying to stretch them, enlarge them.

Buttercup moaned and became moist. Reed tugged harder and twisted each vaginal lip between his fingers. She arched her back, her juices oozing, thick and slippery.

"You like that, baby?" There was a guttural sound to his voice.

"I love…Oh God," she moaned. Desire caused her words to catch in her throat. "I love it."

Then, stretching the glistening lips as far apart as possible, Reed could no longer fight the primal desire. His organ felt like it was on fire as he slowly began to penetrate. Excited, he forced himself deep within, then increased his speed, proclaiming with each thrust that he owned Buttercup's pussy. And Buttercup passionately agreed.

Unsatisfied, Reed asked mid-thrust, "How come your pussy doesn't look like it belongs to me?"

Buttercup wrinkled her face in a combination of passion and confusion.

"If that pussy was really mine, it wouldn't be this tight. Would it?" he asked with a hard thrust.

"No," she whimpered.

"Are you gonna let me open that shit up?"

"Yes," she whispered.

"Are you gonna let me wear your pussy out?"

"Yes!" she screamed louder.

Finally aroused to the point of delirium, Reed gave a raspy cry of release. On the edges of his mind was the knowledge that it was going to take a tremendous amount of effort to get Buttercup's pussy up to par. He was going to have to fuck her pussy nonstop to make it look beat-up and raggedy like Aziza's.

Chapter 17

For three days Chanelle had combed the city, going from one supposedly upscale strip club to the next, filling out applications and leaving her telephone number with the club managers, yet no one had called with an offer of employment. It was as if she'd been black-balled.

Sulking in the backseat of a cab headed for Thirteenth and Arch, Philadelphia's red-light district, she realized there was nothing left to do except swallow her pride and psych herself up to go shake her tail at one of the low-class titty bars that had a clientele consisting mostly of grubby blue-collar workers. This was not a good career move and she was braced for an evening of degradation. The scruffy patrons, she'd heard, were permitted to touch the girls everywhere. Ugh. They were allowed to pat their asses, squeeze their tits, touch them just about everywhere except beneath the wisp of fabric that concealed the vulva.

Until she could figure out another strategy, she'd have to suffer through the humiliation. One thing was certain… she wasn't going to meet her future husband in a hole-in-the-wall bar on Thirteenth Street.

Chanelle paid the cab driver and hopped out on the corner. Here it was the end of May and the sun was blazing, hot as a bitch. She checked her watch: three o'clock. Her appointment wasn't until three-thirty. Damn. She hoped there was somebody inside the club because she would surely perish if she had to stand around outside in the scorching heat.

She looked around for a cool place to take shelter and saw nothing except office buildings and an adult entertainment establishment with a neon-lit arrow pointing to the rear and advertising that a live-girl peep show was taking place inside.

Chanelle shook her head and sucked her teeth. If money ever got so tight she had to put herself on display behind a cum-stained glass mirror, she hoped somebody would put her out of her misery and put a bullet through her head.

She started walking. A few doors down, she reached her destination: Phat Philly Girlz. With a sense of martyrdom, she reminded herself to be nice to the cheap-ass, blue-collar men she would now have to rely on to pay her rent. Resignedly, she pulled the handle of the door.

Harsh sunlight streamed into the darkened club as Chanelle entered. The big bald dude who stood guard at the door blocked his face with an arm, grimaced, and slammed the door as if he was a vampire and the rays of the sun might set him aflame. "Can I help you?" he asked in an unfriendly tone that suggested he did not intend to be helpful.

"Yeah. Um, how ya doing?" Chanelle asked.

The big guy grunted a response.

Chanelle blinked rapidly as she tried to adjust her vision inside the dark room. "My name's Sensation. I spoke to Reggie earlier. He said if I came in, I could start working today." Her eyes wandered around her new place of employment, hoping to find some redeeming quality. Except for the bartender, the place was empty. No girls. No customers. "What time do you open?"

"We open at six, but um…who did you say told you to come in?" the bald guy inquired. His lips looked like they were curving into the beginning of a smile. An unkind, taunting smile.

"Some dude named Reggie. He said he was the manager."

Unable to contain himself any longer, the big guy started laughing and then bellowed to the bartender, "Yo, Black… Reggie told this jawn he was the manager."

Amused, the bartender added a deep baritone chuckle to the unnaturally high-pitched squawks coming from the big bald guy.

Chanelle was steaming mad; she didn't appreciate being referred to as a "jawn" and she didn't find one thing funny about being duped into believing she had a job. Damn, her shit had gone from bad to worse.

"Yo, dig. Reggie ain't no manager. He don't do nothin' but clean up around here."

Chanelle drew in a deep breath to keep herself from

throwing a fit. She actually wanted to fall out and start kicking and screaming while pounding the floor with balled fists. But she restrained herself.

"So, who should I speak to?" she asked coolly, hoisting her heavy work bag onto her other shoulder.

"You gotta talk to Mike, but he ain't here."

She sucked her teeth and shifted her feet. "So, why do y'all allow the cleaning man to pick up the phone and pretend like he's the manager? Dude told me I could start work tonight. That's messed up."

The bald guy screwed up his lips, threw up his palms, and lifted his shoulders in a dramatic shrug that indicated that he didn't have an answer and he truly didn't give a damn.

Determined to have not wasted her time, Chanelle pressed on. "So, where can I find Mike?"

"Mike's at the other club on Twelfth Street."

"Where on Twelfth Street?"

"Right across from the Reading Terminal. It's called Silky & Sweet."

"Thanks." She whirled around and exited Phat Philly Girlz.

Standing outside the club in the suffocating heat, she tried to get her bearings. The concrete burned the bottom of her thin-soled, delicately jeweled sandals making it feel as if she were standing in bare feet on flaming hot coals. This was bullshit. She couldn't ever recall spring weather feeling like this. She felt like she had stepped inside an incinerator.

It was probably ridiculous to try to catch a cab for the short ride around the corner, but that was exactly what Chanelle intended to do as she looked up and down Thirteenth Street. But there wasn't a cab in sight and it was too hot to just stand around hoping a taxi would come cruising by, so she turned and reluctantly started moving toward Juniper Street.

After taking a few torturous steps, a metallic gray BMW honked the horn and pulled up beside her. Behind tinted windows, she made out the form of a woman. Chanelle's first thought was that the woman was the jealous wife of one of her customers. She felt no fear; in fact, she felt invigorated as she stopped, dropped her bag, and assumed a combative stance. *Bring it, bitch, because I'm mad as hell and ain't got shit to lose.*

The woman lowered the window. Chanelle reflexively balled her fists and approached the car.

"Is that where you work?" asked a slender, dark-brown-skinned woman who looked to be in her early twenties, maybe a little older because she appeared extremely self-assured and sophisticated. And the whip she was driving was the truth.

Chanelle had to force herself not say, "What's it to you?" It was her nature to be defensive, but there was something about this chick that made her hold her tongue.

For starters, she was pushing a phat ride, her hair and French-manicured nails were hooked up, and a pair of fly-ass shades were pushed up on top of her hair gleaming like they cost a stack. Although the chick was young, she was very much on point, which impressed Chanelle into curious silence—at least long enough to find out what the woman wanted.

"No, I don't work there, I thought I was going to start dancing there tonight, but um…somebody gave me some wrong information. I'm on my way to see the manager over on Twelfth Street." Now why the hell was she spillin' like this to a total stranger? *Must be the heat*, she thought.

"Girl, you're too cute to work in that hell hole," the woman said, including her head toward Phat Philly Girlz.

Chanelle absolutely agreed, but given her options and dwindling savings, she didn't have much choice. She needed to go see this Mike guy so she could start making some money. Shit, her rent was due. "I used to work at Lizzard's, but I got fired. I can't seem to get my foot in the door at any of the other top spots. Anyway, why'd you roll up on me? What's up?" Chanelle asked impatiently.

"Get in; I'll explain while I drive you to the club on Twelfth Street."

The humidity alone was causing beads of perspiration to trickle down the sides of Chanelle's face, threatening to ruin her makeup and hair. She wiped the sweat away and then without giving it another thought, she yanked the door open and slid into the cool sanctuary of the air-conditioned car. "It's right across the street from the Reading Terminal," she offered, hoping the red lights and slow-walking pedestrians prolonged her stay in this heaven-sent, air-conditioned chariot. "It's called Silky & Sweet."

The woman gave her a sidelong glance. "Silky & Sweet? Okay, so you're walking around in this hellish weather, dragging that heavy bag to go beg for a job at another dive? Do you really think that's a step in the right direction? I mean, after working at Lizzard's I'm sure you got used to decent working conditions and leaving with a thick knot in your purse every night."

"Yeah, working at Lizzard's was sweet but right now I need a job." Chanelle looked out the window to see how close they were to the other strip club. This know-it-all hoochie was starting to get on her nerves.

Undeterred by Chanelle's annoyance, the woman continued. "I know the club owner at Lizzard's didn't let the customers grope all over y'all. Am I right or wrong?" The woman asked with a knowing smile.

Chanelle ignored the pesky woman, though she was enjoying being inside the cool BMW.

"Did you know that if you get the job at Phat Philly Girlz, you're gonna have to change in a funky bathroom with about twelve other women? That's twelve women with twelve big-ass bags, costumes, wigs and hairspray, makeup, and all the rest of their shit spread everywhere in one tight-ass room with one tiny mirror over the sink and no fuckin' air. That's right. They don't have air conditioning in the bathroom. I bet y'all had a nice dressing room at Lizzard's—plenty of room and big bright-ass, full-length mirrors."

Since Chanelle didn't know where the conversation was leading, she simply nodded and decided to sit back, relax, and wait for Miss Thang to start giving up some tapes. There had to be a reason why she'd rescued Chanelle from the unforgiving heat. Chanelle appraised her from the corner of her eye.

The woman wasn't as cute as Chanelle, but she was iced out—earrings, necklace, bracelet—and her gear looked straight up out of *Vogue* magazine. She definitely wasn't rocking anything from City Blue or Sneaker Villa—two of Chanelle's favorite shopping haunts.

The young woman cruised to a stop in front of Silky & Sweet. She flipped open a pink leather clutch bag, rooted around, and pulled out a card, which she handed to Chanelle with a smug expression.

In the center of the high-quality beige card was the embossed logo of a set of chocolate lips. Dark brown script stated: Hershey's Smooches: a delectable array of delicious milk-chocolate beauties. On call for your private pleasure twenty-four/ seven. There was a phone number at the bottom of the card. The message was short and sweet and straight to the point.

"You work for an outcall service?" Chanelle inquired.

"No, baby. I own it. I'm Hershey," she said proudly, extending her hand.

"Well, if you're offering me a job, let me set the record straight. I'm a dancer, not a ho."

"Look," Hershey said, swiveling in Chanelle's direction. "I own a full-service agency. We do it all: Escorts, Bachelor Parties, Super Bowl parties, one-on-one, whatever the guy holding the credit card is in the mood for... and he's usually in the mood for sex. Sex is what it's all about. The kind of money you make climbing up and down a sweaty pole for tips ain't shit. Why would you want to limit your cash flow like that?"

"I do all right," Chanelle said defensively and then wrapped her arms around herself and ran her hands up and down her upper arms.

"You cold?" Hershey reached to turn down the air conditioning.

Chanelle shook her head and dropped her arms. "That's just a habit—something I do when I'm trying to get my thoughts together." She looked directly at Hershey. Chanelle's eyes were filled with such sorrow, Hershey dropped her gaze. "I don't trick because of a promise I made to my mother." Chanelle began softly. "She got sick while I was in high school. She had cancer." Chanelle's eyes became misty. "I was only sixteen and in my junior year at high school. I dropped out so I could try to take care of her because we didn't have any other family. Her job stopped paying her and we didn't have any money and I had to do something to help out."

Hershey patted Chanelle's shoulder.

"My mom knew what I was out there doing and she knew why. But she made me promise never to sell my body and to quit as soon as I found a decent man to take care of me. She knew she was gonna pass soon and she said she wouldn't rest in peace if I didn't have somebody looking out for me." Chanelle's voice cracked. Sitting in a car with a total stranger, she gave in to the tears that had not fallen since the day she'd put her mother into the ground. She'd been too busy trying to survive to afford the luxury of tears.

Chanelle wiped her eyes and cast a clouded glance at Silky & Sweet. She was so tired of the sex industry; she just wanted to be able to quit. Game over. Surrender. Lead a normal life. But she didn't even know where to begin.

Hershey opened her glove compartment and handed Chanelle a tissue. "I've been in your position," Hershey said softly. "I know what it's like to work for other people and have them controlling how much money you make. First of all, let me school you about the strip clubs. The Italians got all those jawns on lock. They even got a grip on the so-called black clubs. Believe me, they may put a brotha up front, but there's a dago somewhere behind the scenes collecting that dough. So what I'm trying to say is, if somebody has a beef with you, you're not gonna dance nowhere in Philly, or any of the nicer spots in Jersey either. By the way, who do you think owns Phat Philly Girlz *and* Silky & Sweet?"

Chanelle shrugged.

"Italians. The dude you're gonna go see—Mike, right? He's Italian. And he likes his women skinny like me, but he likes 'em light-skinned. You don't fit the mold, baby. That's probably why his sidekicks sent you trotting outta there. Shit, if you were high yella, they would have hired you right on the spot—wouldn't have needed Mike's approval." Hershey tapped her finger on the steering wheel. "Go ahead in there." She nodded toward Silky & Sweet. "If shit doesn't work out, you have my card. Give me a call, but you're gonna have to reevaluate your sexual hang-ups."

Chanelle squirmed against the plush leather upholstery. "I don't have sexual hang-ups; I just don't think I need to be a prostitute in order to survive."

"Okay. Then, let me back up and rephrase my statement." She turned and leaned in close, looking Chanelle straight in the eye. Hershey's piercing look made it difficult for Chanelle to maintain her gaze. "You think it's cool to let muthafuckers dry fuck you for a couple of dollars?"

Chanelle opened her mouth to protest, but Hershey held up a hand. "Let me finish. In my business, dude busts inside a rubber; in your world he leaves cum stains on your ass. So, tell me…what's the difference?"

Chanelle grimaced. "Eew. Cum stains. That's gross!"

"Girl, stop frontin'; you know I'm telling the truth. Those muthafuckers that pay for a lap dance be tryin' their best to bust a nut before the song ends and you know damn well lots of them have succeeded. So tell me how you feel when you get up and feel that nasty shit smeared all over your ass?"

Chanelle took a deep breath. "Furious," she admitted.

"I bet you demand extra money from those trifling perverts, don't you?"

"Damn right."

"Well, you can prettify it any way you want, but a ho is a ho. I pay top dollar, depending on the gig. You don't have to work on a schedule, you work when you want to. Oh! And you ain't gotta worry about none of my customers asking for a white girl or a light-skinned chick. If you checked out my card, it's pretty clear that Hershey's Smooches come in all shades of chocolate. If they got a taste for something else, then they gotta take their business somewhere else. And girl…you'd be amazed at how many rich muthafuckers got an addiction to chocolate."

The way she'd been scrambling around for over a week trying to get a job was maddening and nothing had materialized. Hershey's offer was starting to sound appealing. Chanelle's head popped up. Squinting suspiciously, she asked, "So, why'd you roll up on me back there? What do you do—prowl around waiting for girls to come out of the club?"

Hershey chuckled. "No, baby. I don't have to make those types of moves. You should see how the chicks start strutting and prancing around when I roll up in the clubs. They all know I pay my girls top dollar and I only select the best. I was gonna slip in before Philly's opened and find out if they'd broke down and hired any brown-skin dime pieces. Then I saw you struggling with your bag and was spared the trouble of having to drive around to search for a place to park. Parking's a bitch in this area."

Hershey pushed the gear into drive. "You still gonna pay Mike a visit?"

"I don't think so," Chanelle said, shaking her head. "So what can I expect to make if I work for you?"

"Depends on how often you're willing to work. You can make a couple stacks a week or even more if you want to. I have this one chick who works a couple gigs a night, five days a week. No lie, she's pulling in about ten stacks."

"Ten thousand dollars a week!" Chanelle couldn't believe it.

"Uh-huh. But she's a greedy bitch. I call her the Terminator 'cause she don't nevah wanna quit. She'd work seven days if I let her, but I keep her ass in check. I can't have sis making so much money she thinks she can compete with my lifestyle. Oh, hell no," Hershey said, laughing. "So look, give me a call when you're ready to start and I can have you working immediately. Cool?"

Chanelle nodded, reluctantly opened the door, and got out. Standing back outside in the blazing heat, she watched the silver chariot rip through a yellow light and roar away from the congested red-light district.

Chapter 18

Reed arrived home in a good mood and feeling confident he could persuade Dayna to reconsider seeing a divorce attorney. He proudly held a stunning display of orange and red flowers purchased from an outdoor vendor. The flowers were attractively wrapped in cellophane and tied with a big red bow.

He was mildly troubled that the lights were out and the house was quiet. Dayna always kept at least one light on. But when he thought about the way she'd been flipping lately, nothing she did surprised him.

She was probably on the rag. Every month like clockwork when her period came on, she started acting like a nut. Reed believed that being the emotional female his wife tended to be, Dayna irrationally blamed him for her inability to conceive.

Shrugging off his irritation, Reed clicked on the light in the living room and broke the silence as he raced up the stairs cheerfully calling his wife's name. She didn't answer. He was irked anew, but instantly placed a practiced smile on his face when he reached the top of the winding stairs.

Her silence indicated that she unwilling to communicate, but he knew he could disarm her with the flowers. And as she began to melt, he'd kiss her, cuddle…hell, if it turned out that she wasn't on the rag, he'd fuck her if necessary. And while he was putting his thing down, he'd be sure to remind her of the beautiful baby they were conceiving at that very moment.

Reed couldn't suppress the sarcastic smile tugging at his lips. The hell with the flowers, he could have saved his money. Just pretending that he wanted to make a baby would be enough to solidify the marriage and halt any further mention of the word, *divorce*.

He supposed he'd just have to start making an effort to treat his wife better; he'd have to pretend that he was interested in helping her put together a nursery for the little rug rat in the spare middle bedroom—the one she'd already painted a sickening bright yellow. Yeah, he was going to have to start some major sweet talking because aside from his personal financial problems, he liked his life and did not want it disrupted.

Not right now, anyway. Dayna sure had some fucked-up timing.

Their bedroom door was closed. Did his wife really have the audacity to lock him out? The lips that had been formed into a smile now twisted into a smirk. Damn, she was working his nerves. It was late, he was tired, and he didn't feel like smashing down a door, but that's exactly what he was prepared to do if he had to.

Making heavy steps toward the closed door, he wondered if she really thought the flimsy lock would keep him out of his own bedroom. Expecting resistance, he gave the doorknob a hard twist. To his surprise, it opened easily.

Reed's eyes wandered the room, his mouth gaped open in shock. The bedroom was in shambles. Clothes hangers, shoes, and piles of Dayna's clothing were scattered around the bedroom. Empty shoe boxes and lids were strewn about and carelessly tossed on the floor. Dayna's winter wardrobe had been dumped from giant plastic containers and was piled on top of the bed. Dresser drawers were left ajar with the contents spilling out and hanging over the sides.

He stamped over to his side of the closet, which he kept meticulously organized. He yanked open the door. His closet was in complete disarray, which made Reed livid. His neatly arranged shoes were haphazardly replaced on the shoe rack with mismatched shoes paired together. The mere sight of that atrocity made him want to hurt Dayna. His shirts and slacks, fresh from the dry cleaners, hung sloppily from hangers or had fallen off and lay in a crumpled mess on the closet floor.

Dayna's crazy ass must have gone on some kind of wild rampage, but she was really lucky she wasn't within reach because after slapping the shit out of her for desecrating his personal items, he would've shown her what a rampage was really all about.

Breathing hard, Reed stormed out of the room. Though

he still carried the flowers, he did not handle them gently. His hands tightly clutched the delicate paper that was wrapped around the stems, giving them the death grip he envisioned putting around Dayna's neck.

He opened the door of the middle bedroom, clicked on the light, and was damn near blinded by the brightly painted yellow walls. Dayna wasn't in there. Flicking off the light in disgust, he took long angry strides to the bedroom at the end of the hall. He tried the doorknob. The fucker was locked. Incensed, Reed clenched his teeth.

"Dayna!" he shouted. "If you don't open this damn door, I'm gonna rip it off the fuckin' hinges."

There was no response.

"Open this fucking door," he bellowed. Then, needing an outlet for his rage, he kicked the door, but the hinges remained intact and Dayna remained silent.

Reed took a few steps back and then slammed against the door with his shoulder the way they do on TV. Momentarily paralyzed by shooting pain that emanated from his shoulder down to his fingertips, Reed dropped the flowers, fell against the wall, and groaned in anguish. It felt like he had dislocated his shoulder.

When the pain finally subsided, he felt around his shoulder, squeezed it a couple of times and determined that it wasn't dislocated.

"Dayna!" he yelled. Not a sound came from the room. Infuriated by her stubborn and continued silence, Reed picked up the bouquet and began beating the flowers against the door. The floral arrangement was a weak and ineffective weapon. Multi-colored petals and leaves flew up in the air, swirled around, and then floated down, coating Reed's head and shoulders like giant-sized confetti. At the end of the tantrum, he shook off the petals and leaves and stomped back to his bedroom.

He glared at the bed, and then shoved the shoe boxes and some of the clothing off. But after assessing the total wreckage, Reed knew there was no way he could sleep in that trashed room.

He yanked the blanket off the bed, snatched a pillow, and trudged downstairs. Squirming restlessly for what seemed like hours, Reed tried his best to find a comfortable position on the sofa.

꒰ꕥ꒱ꕥ꒰ꕥ꒱

Groggy and disoriented from the sleeping pill she'd taken the night before, it took a few seconds for Dayna to figure out where she was. She sat up and looked around. *Ah, the guest room!* As comprehension washed over her, she was relieved to see that the dresser she'd used as a barricade to keep Reed out of the room was still in place at the door.

Knowing Reed as she did, she was certain he'd tried to break down the guest room door to get to her and start an argument that would last until the wee hours of the morning. Luckily, she'd been able to sleep through whatever hysterical reaction he'd had to their ransacked room and her departure from the marital bed.

Padding down the hall to take a shower, Dayna stopped and gave a reflexive jerk as she unexpectedly stumbled upon a ravaged flower bouquet. Reed, she surmised, had taken out his rage on innocent plant life. That knowledge gave her an uneasy feeling. With a slight shiver, she stepped over and around the slaughtered stems, petals, and leaves.

Shaking her head, she hurried to the bathroom to quickly shower before Reed woke up. The mere sight of him nauseated her now and if that weren't bad enough, to be harassed into listening to his warped sense of reasoning was a bit much for six o'clock in the morning.

Dayna shortened her typical fifteen-minute shower to five minutes, wrapped herself in a towel, and rushed back to the guest room to get dressed for work. She halted her steps at the doorway and shrieked in astonishment. Wearing boxers and a T-shirt, Reed lounged on the guest-room bed with his head propped up with pillows. He looked like a vile apparition and she was so startled, her first impulse was to turn around and run back to the bathroom and lock herself in. But she resisted the impulse and stepped inside the room.

"Did you sleep well?" he asked sarcastically. His bloodshot eyes held her in a smoldering gaze.

With just a towel covering her naked body and not knowing what retaliatory measures Reed had in mind, Dayna felt defenseless. "As well as can be expected," she said, trying to keep her voice steady.

"I didn't sleep a wink," he said bitterly.

Dayna covered herself with a robe and tied the sash. Feeling less vulnerable, she threw him a thin smile and said, "Maybe you'll find it easier to get some rest if you move into your own place."

"My own place?" he said with mirthless laughter. "I'm straight; I'm not moving anywhere. But if you're so unhappy with our situation, then you know what to do… *you* move the fuck out."

Dayna sat at the foot of the bed and applied lotion to her legs. She looked back at Reed. "I'd move in a heart-beat if I thought you could handle the mortgage and not ruin my credit. We both know who carries this house-hold, but if you've forgotten, let me remind you that I pay all the bills around here."

"You pay all the bills because you want to. Isn't that what fat, dumb bitches do?"

The blow from the sucker punch Reed had just landed hit Dayna hard. She flinched and then quickly regained her composure. "I have to get dressed. Would you please give me some privacy."

"I'm not giving you shit. You think you're running things now, so why don't you put me out?"

Dayna briefly considered provoking Reed into a physical altercation. A visible scar was a surefire way to have him ejected from their home. She winced, however, as she imagined being punched so hard that her face ended up discolored and bruised.

Then, she had a quick flash of herself with a blackened eye that was encrusted and swollen shut. No, that was definitely not the route she wanted to take. Imagining herself summoning the police to resolve the situation was a reverie too mortifying to even toy with.

Her best bet would be to consult her father and tell him the truth about her dreadful marriage; he'd give her sound advice. Despite Reed's intimidating presence, Dayna was somewhat calmed by the knowledge that her father would soon rectify the distasteful situation. She breathed deeply in hopes of achieving a state of complete tranquility.

After plugging in her lighted makeup mirror, Dayna slowly began her makeup ritual. She smoothed on moisturizer, patted on foundation, dabbed a touch of concealer under her eyes.

She tried to block Reed from her mind, though it was difficult with his sullen image reflected in the mirror. Searching for mascara, she emptied her makeup bag. Caught up in the process of applying mascara to her lashes, she managed to briefly forget Reed even existed.

He slid off the bed. *Oh good; he's leaving.* But instead of leaving, Reed sauntered across the room, drew back his hand, and in one fell swoop, he knocked every item of makeup off the dresser.

Dayna emitted a yelp of disbelief.

Reed smirked, looked down at the mess he'd made, nodded his head with hateful satisfaction, and then exited the guest room.

Chapter 19

His work day had been a bitch. He was dog-ass tired and his back hurt from sleeping on the couch. Reed would have loved to just go home, ignore Dayna, and climb into his unmade bed. But he couldn't. He'd committed himself to an eight o' clock meeting at the Hilton hotel with Chris Miller and a few other investors.

He was expected to arrive with a twenty-thousand-dollar cashier's check in hand. Now that was a joke, because all Reed was bringing was a new angle to stall his monetary contribution to the real estate investment deal.

He'd start things off by offering to pay for the first round of drinks. Then after everyone had mellowed a bit, he'd cap their heads up with some game so smooth, they'd be toasting him and paying for the rest of his drinks. Yeah, he had it like that— the smoothness. Some people called it charm, some called it charisma. Whatever it was, he had it and knew how to lay it on thick. As a child, he'd used the smoothness to get what he wanted from his mother, neighbors, teachers, and friends, and later in life; he found the smoothness to be particularly effective with women. He could talk a broad into damn near anything.

Realizing that he'd need some cash to buy that first round of drinks, Reed drove to an ATM machine on Stenton Avenue. He stepped up to the ATM, tapped in the PIN number and the amount of money he wanted.

Impatiently, Reed patted his foot waiting for the transaction to complete. Instead of hearing the sound the machine made when it kicked out cash, he heard an unfamiliar beep. He gazed up. A message in red popped up on the screen: *You have exceeded the daily limit.*

Huh? There had to be a mistake. Dayna had plenty of money in the savings account. He swiped the card again and tried to get money out of the checking account. Again, no cash. Just the same stupid message.

Reed's stomach clutched. He wouldn't have any money until payday and that was a week away. On the verge of storming inside the bank to demand an explanation, Reed's mind flashed to the scene he'd made in the guest room that morning.

Dayna was such an immature, vengeful bitch; she had withdrawn the money from both accounts. Moreover, since both accounts were in her name only, there wasn't much he could do.

After the wedding, she'd suggested joint accounts, but when she mentioned that she wanted him to fill out paperwork that would have his paycheck automatically deposited into the accounts, he vehemently refused. He wasn't about to turn his paycheck over to Dayna so she could dole out gas and lunch money. Fuck that! He controlled his own money.

And he liked having access to her money as well.

Dayna wasn't a very secretive person. She left her bank statements in her top dresser drawer. After opening them, she must have just given the statements a cursory glance because she had never asked him about his constant withdrawals from her savings account. The bank card he'd been using was sent as an extra and dumb-ass Dayna had never noticed it was missing. Once he had the card in his possession, figuring out her PIN number was easy. It was their wedding date. He laughed out loud at his wife's stupidity. But the laughter was cut off when his mind returned to the present predicament he faced. The bitch had found out what he'd been doing and had cut his cash stream off.

He had no money and no idea of how to get any. With increasing anxiety, he walked to his car and pondered the gravity of his circumstances. He sat in the driver's seat staring at nothing. As much as he hated to, he had to admit that he'd played himself with Dayna. He shouldn't have allowed her to provoke him like that. Now she'd trumped him by cutting off his access to cash.

He pulled out his CDs, but nothing looked appealing so he turned the radio on to WJJZ, the smooth jazz station. He needed something soothing to help him think. Larry Carlton's *Sleepwalk* was playing and like magic, an image of Buttercup appeared. He checked the time—

six-thirty. Good. If she'd followed his instructions, she should have been working for at least a couple of hours.

With his spirit bolstered, he cruised along Stenton Avenue and made a right on Mount Pleasant. Traffic ran smoothly and twenty minutes later Reed was opening the door to The Honey Club.

"Ten dollars, man," the big dude who collected the entrance fee said.

"Yo, bro, I'm not staying. I just want to speak to Buttercup." Reed wanted to step around the big man, but dude was blocking his path. While the doorman tried to figure out if Reed's request was permissible, a grinning Buttercup was already rushing toward Reed.

"Hey, baby," she said with an excited grin. "Whatchu doin' here so early?"

"I'm dealing with some issues," Reed whispered and pulled Buttercup to the side. Out of earshot of the doorman, Reed continued. "Yeah, as I was saying…the black stripe on the back of my debit card got scratched and I can't get a new card for three days. So I just swung by to see if you could let me hold a couple of dollars."

Buttercup had already started digging in her purse and pulled out two twenty-dollar bills. "It's still early and that's all I made so far. Is it enough?"

Reed was disappointed, but he didn't show it. He was hoping to get at least sixty dollars. "Yeah, baby. That's more than enough," he said with a strained smile. He took the money, gave her a quick kiss on the lips, and promised to come back and pick her up at ten o'clock.

The more he thought about it, the less sense it made to waste his time bullshitting Chris Miller. Until he was actually holding the cashier's check, he'd just duck the brother as well as all the other members of the club. The hell if he was going to waste his money buying drinks for a room full of dickheads.

Therefore, instead of going to the Hilton, Reed decided to spend his money at Lizzard's. Yeah, he hadn't seen Sensation in a while. He knew he didn't have enough to get with her after work, but he could afford a couple of beers while feasting his eyes on her.

Merely looking at Sensation's fine, phat ass would get his dick erect with a hardness that would last until Buttercup got off from work. Thinking about Sensation, he'd be able to bone Buttercup for a couple of hours. Then he'd go home feeling good enough to ignore Dayna and her stupid ploy to bully him into submission. Shit, moving out of their bedroom and threatening to get a divorce wasn't going to keep him locked up in the house with her boring ass.

Reed paid for a Corona. "What time is Sensation going onstage?"

The bartender turned his back to Reed and then turned around quickly, banging a chilled bottle on the counter. "She got canned," the man said smugly.

"She got what?" Reed felt panicked.

"Canned," the bartender repeated in a monotone.

"She doesn't work here anymore?" Reed glanced around anxiously as if expecting Sensation to appear from the shadows.

"I didn't stutter."

Reed immediately lost his taste for the weak beer and pushed it away from him. He wanted his money back. He also wanted to bitch slap the bartender for looking so damn pleased at his delivery of such bad news.

"Well, where's she working now?" Reed asked, distressed. He felt too desperate to try to conceal the urgency in his voice.

"How would I know?" the bartender said, and then turned his attention away from Reed and cracked a smile at a suit-wearing white patron who'd just taken a seat next to Reed. "Fuckin' faggot," Reed muttered and then chugged down the Corona. Without giving Reed and his quest to find Sensation another thought, the bartender turned around and became engrossed in mixing a martini for the suit.

Reed glared at the bartender's back, scooped up his change from the counter, and rose from the barstool. No tip for the obnoxious bartender. Plowing through a sea of smiling faces and humongous bogus tits, Reed stomped toward the exit sign.

He was feeling too cranky to drive all over the city looking for Sensation. Hell, he couldn't afford to look for Sensation. He shook his head at how fucked up his situation was. Gripping the steering wheel in anger, he drove to a deli and bought a six-pack of Old English. His private name for the malt liquor was "fire water" because it brought out the worst in him.

At the moment, with less than thirty dollars to his name, he had a right to bring out the beast in himself.

Dayna had put him in a hell of a quandary. The roof over his head was precarious at best; it was just a matter of time before her father figured out some legal loophole to have him evicted from his own home. And thanks to Dayna, his cash flow was cut off without warning, forcing him to have to rely on a drugged-out hooker for a little bit of chump change.

Yes, his wife was going to pay dearly for the unnecessary strain she was putting him through. If she thought she was going to strip him down to bare bones and suffer no repercussions, then she had sadly underestimated him. Sure, she had a master's degree while he had only a high school education, but by no means did those letters behind her name make her smarter than he was.

He snapped open a can of Old English, took a swig. He could feel the fire water coursing through his system, causing his mind to race with hateful thoughts. He didn't know how or when he would exact his revenge, but he knew with certainty that the penalty his wife would have to pay for her transgressions would be steep and life altering.

Three empty beer cans filled the waste bag in his Lexus to capacity. It gave his vehicle a cluttered appearance that was unacceptable. He drove around aimlessly for a few minutes until he happened upon an area that looked squalid enough that three crushed beer cans would fit perfectly with the setting.

After aiming and firing each can out of the window with the power and precision of a major league star pitcher, Reed pulled over to park on a small desolate street and snapped open the fourth can of beer.

Getting his bearings, he realized he was on Delancy Street, just a few blocks from Buttercup's crib. Images of freaky sex infiltrated his thoughts. He felt instant sexual tension that made his penis rise up and press against his slacks in a manner that screamed for immediate relief. But Buttercup was still at work. Damn! He rubbed his groin lightly, as if trying to pacify it into deflating.

Reed couldn't think straight with an engorged dick. His mind scrambled for alternative activities that would take his mind off his predicament until Buttercup got off, but nothing he thought of took away the dull ache.

He didn't want any more beer, he didn't want to chill with his PBP brothers, and the thought of going from one titty bar to the next to get a cheap lap dance gave him little consolation.

He wanted some pussy. Wet pussy was the only thing that would calm the beast inside.

The blood flow in the shaft of his penis caused Reed to feel disoriented. He wasn't even aware of starting the car. In fact, he had no conscious memory of pulling off and parking in front of Dottie's Hair Salon. He felt his fist pounding on the dusty door and later he had a faint recollection of the gnarled hand that admitted him. But in his current state, he was acting on pure animal instinct. There was nothing human about the urges he felt.

"How much do you charge, Dottie?" Reed asked, breathing hard.

"Did you bring me a bag of snuff?" The old woman was dressed in the same robe. It hadn't been washed and there were additional stains and congealed substances.

"I left your snuff in my car. I'll get it when we're finished," Reed heard himself say.

With the promise of a bag of snuff, the unwashed and senile old woman willingly lay down on the hard plastic couch and slowly opened her wrinkled thighs. The sight she offered was hideous and her parted legs emitted a foul scent. Remarkably, this revolting combination was giving Reed a brutal hard-on.

Like an animal in heat, Reed humped against her odiferous and hairless vagina. With fingers that trembled with depraved passion, he peeled open her paper-thin labia. There was not a drop of moisture inside the atrophied and extremely small vaginal opening.

Reed hawked up spit and smeared it inside the withered

vulva and plunged into the tightest and most vile pussy he'd ever penetrated. This sexual encounter was an act of sheer insanity; he knew it but couldn't stop himself.

Dottie cried out in pain, and then whimpered for a while, but that did not deter Reed from forcing himself as deeply as possible inside this bizarre batch of pussy. After a few moments, Dottie's whimpers changed to sounds of pleasure, and then escalated to orgasmic shrieks.

Dottie's shrieks along with her contracting vaginal muscles heightened Reed's arousal. He made guttural growling sounds and then an utterly inhuman roar as his sea of lust gushed inside the elderly woman. Afterward, drained and limp with satisfaction, he collapsed upon Dottie's frail chest. She grunted from the pressure of his weight.

"What the fuck?" he exclaimed as he inhaled the strong stench that filled the air. A frown of confusion covered his face. Then sanity slowly returned and he looked upon Dottie in horror. Jumping to his feet, Reed hurriedly stuffed his unclean member into his boxers and pulled up his pants.

Dottie lay on the plastic-covered couch with her legs gaped open. She shuddered. Moaned. Writhed. Reed wasn't sure what was wrong with the old bitch. Her spastic body movements strongly suggested she was having a seizure.

Dry heaving, Reed covered his mouth with his hand

and backed away. Feeling close to vomiting, he didn't dare risk going near her to check out her physical status. The best he could do was cast a curious last glance at the quivering figure on the couch before making a quick getaway.

Chapter 20

"You're gonna like your first client," Hershey said confidently. "Barry's real easy. No sex. He just wants a dinner date. You know…a companion. He loves my chocolate girls."

With a shoulder holding the phone to her ear, Chanelle gazed at her outgrown nails, which were badly in need of a fill-in. The appearance of her fingernails pretty much spoke to the state of her financial affairs.

"How much does this date pay?" she asked suspiciously. An easy date probably didn't pay very much. Chanelle appreciated Hershey for looking out and trying to ease her into the game, but her money was looking too funny to waste time getting her feet wet. She needed to dive right in and make some real money.

"It pays well."

"How much?"

"Five hundred for a few hours."

Chanelle almost choked. "He's paying that much money just to take me out to dinner?" She scowled at her nails. *I gotta make a quick trip to the nail salon; can't allow a five-hundred-dollar date to peep these trifling fingernails.*

"So how much do I have to give you?"

Hershey laughed. "Girl, don't be tryin' to count my money; I take mine off the top."

"I get the whole thing?"

"Uh-huh."

"Thanks, Hershey."

"You're welcome. So look, after his check clears, I'll drop the money off at your place."

"Suppose it bounces?"

"Barry's a regular; his checks are good. Anyway, don't start thinking every date is gonna be this sweet; just consider this as…you know…as a sign-on bonus. Starting you out with Barry is my way of saying, welcome to *Hershey's Smooches*."

At seven that evening, in a fancy downtown restaurant, Chanelle sat across from her client, a mature white man— oh hell, he was old, at least forty—but he was well-dressed and had a wealthy, distinguished look that worked for him.

Despite her beautiful French manicure, she felt awkward and unrefined. The double sets of silverware on each side of her plate intimidated her. She nervously wondered how she'd be able to handle the intricacies of social etiquette for two hours when she didn't even know which eating utensils to use.

Overtaken by a case of the jitters, she buried her face in the menu and scanned the appetizers: frisee salad with lardons, barigoule artichokes and leeks, black truffle dressing, caramelized onion and stout beer soup, warm potato blini…*what the fuck?* Nothing sounded appetizing or even remotely familiar. She sighed and prepared herself for a long, drawn-out evening.

"What are you having, Chanelle?" Barry asked.

It sounded weird for a client to use her real name, but somehow her alias did not fit with the modern art deco dining room. She looked up at Barry and was momentarily mesmerized by a painted glass mural on the wall behind him. If the richly decorated restaurant was indicative of the kind of things Barry had to offer, Chanelle figured it would be in her best interest to get over her nervousness.

"I'll have whatever you're having," she said, flicking her tongue across her lips flirtatiously and throwing him a sexy smile.

Barry blushed as if he'd been given a gift.

And a gift she was indeed, she reminded herself. After all, it was her beauty, her bangin' body, and her skin tone that Barry was most interested in, not her social skills. Still, she made a mental note to buy an etiquette book. Oh hell, who was she fooling—she hated reading. She'd be better off buying a DVD on the subject.

Barry ordered a bottle of wine as well as their appetizers. When the model-thin, Scandinavian-pale waitress whisked away, Barry leaned in and whispered, "*That* is not my idea of beauty; I think the western world has gone quite mad in encouraging young women to look like human toothpicks. You, on the other hand, are the epitome of everything desirable in a woman." He settled back in his chair, smiling and nodding approvingly.

Chanelle couldn't agree with him more, but decided it would be in poor taste to admit that she knew she was the bomb. "So, what do you do for a living, Barry?" she asked, changing the subject.

"Legal stuff," he said with a grimace. "I spend an inordinate amount of time kissing up to judges. But it pays off," he said with a modest shrug. "I earn a decent income." He frowned again as if his words were distasteful. "And I've made some good investments." He made another don't-blame-me-because-I'm-rich shrug.

Chanelle sized up Barry. Everything about him looked expensive: his suit, his watch, and his haircut, a stylishly tousled mass of layered locks, must have cost some bucks. Hell, she'd gotten a whiff when he stood up to greet her—Barry smelled expensive, too.

"Are you married?"

"Divorced." He shook his head and gave an uncomfortable chuckle. "Now, that was a very messy phase of my life. My wife ran out on me and then tried to take me for every cent. But she didn't win. I'm still trying to heal from that devastating experience, but overall...I can't complain."

Chanelle couldn't complain either. She felt like she'd hit the jackpot. This wealthy, yet unassuming and unmarried man was open game. Visions of a wonderfully idle suburban lifestyle danced across her mind.

The server returned with their appetizers: crab cakes surrounded by a spicy sautéed blend of vegetables. Hmmm. Chanelle hadn't seen any crab cakes on the menu. Now, if the menu items were called by their right names instead of describing everything in fancy terms, such as *pomme* this and *frisee* that, she could have ordered her own damn appetizer.

She watched Barry pick up a fork and a knife and imitated his choices. She sliced into the crab cake. "Mmm," she moaned, closing her eyes as she chewed.

"Oh, you like it?"

"Love it."

"Yes, the food here is of the gods," Barry said, picking up a piece of crab cake with his fork turned upside-down. Chanelle decided against mimicking that move. Surely, handling a fork in such an awkward manner would interfere with the enjoyment of her food.

When the server returned, Barry ordered the entrée, blackened sea bass. The side dishes had fancy-sounding names, but turned out to be sautéed celery, potato strips, and cucumber slices, all in their own tasty sauce. No bread was offered with the meal, so Chanelle didn't press the issue, but she sure could have used some bread and butter to sop up the various colorful sauces.

"There's nothing like a good bottle of wine," Barry said with a satisfied smile as the server popped the cork. "You're going to love this."

Chanelle took a sip and had to fight the impulse to spit

out the dry, bitter liquid. Quite frankly, *nasty* was the only word to describe the wine Barry had ordered. Swallowing was a serious struggle, but she felt obliged to indulge Barry. He seemed so proud of his choice. She took small sips to give the impression of savoring the taste. She even swirled it around in the wine glass as Barry did and she hoped all her swirling would give the nasty shit some badly needed flavor. It didn't. Damn, she wished she could add a shot of some peach schnapps to sweeten it up a bit.

Barry had kept up a continuous and often humorous stream of conversation throughout the delectable meal. Chanelle felt completely relaxed with him. She was so enamored of him—his intelligence, confidence, and his wealth—she'd already begun envisioning the indoor and outdoor Jacuzzis she'd insist upon after their wedding day.

"Do you have plans for later this evening?" Barry wanted to know.

"No, I'm free," she said without hesitation.

"Would you like to come back to my place? I promise I won't touch you; I'm really harmless," he said, holding up his hands in surrender. "I'm enjoying your company so much, I really hate for this evening to end."

Chanelle felt the same way, but she faced a moral dilemma. She couldn't in good conscience extend her time with Barry without further compensation.

As if reading her mind, he said, "Look, I'm willing to pay for your time. How does six hundred dollars for another few hours sound? You don't have to tell your employer about our little arrangement. I don't know what she paid you, but I paid her eight hundred dollars for your time tonight."

So...Hershey earned three hundred dollars. Hmmm. Not bad for just sitting on your ass. But man, I can't believe this dude paid for such an expensive meal plus eight hundred for two hours of conversation. Now, he's willing to kick in an additional six hundred for more conversation. Barry must be rollin' in dough and I plan on rollin' right along with him.

❧❧❧

Heart palpitations began the moment Barry pulled his Mercedes into his driveway. Chanelle gawked at the large modern home that sat on many acres of professionally landscaped grounds. Without even seeing the inside of the house, she knew she could get used to living like this.

Barry walked her through the huge living room, past a large den, and down a long hallway, then past a back stairway. Finally they walked into the media room. "I thought you might enjoy relaxing and watching a movie."

Speechless, Chanelle could only nod. The screen in the media room was almost as large as a screen in an actual movie theater.

"More wine?" he asked.

"Uh, do you have anything sweet?"

"Would you like a Kir?"

"What's that?"

"White wine with a shot of crème de cassis. I think you'll like it."

He left Chanelle ogling her surroundings, but was back in a flash with the drink in hand.

Chanelle took a sip. "Mmm. Now, this is good."

"Glad you approve. Look, check out the movie collection. I'll give you a tour of the place in a minute; I want to get out of this suit and put on something comfortable." He patted her on the shoulder and quickly made his way out of the room. Chanelle could hear his footsteps as he cheerfully trotted up the back staircase.

Uninterested in looking at movie titles, Chanelle decided to roam the downstairs unescorted. She wandered into the kitchen. It was a wondrous open area with granite kitchen counters. The island and counter bars seated up to eight guests. Fabulous! Chanelle couldn't cook, but she'd certainly start taping some of those cable cooking shows to prepare herself for her new wife/hostess role.

She climbed up on one of the leather-cushioned stools and swiveled around as she checked out her soon-to-be cooking area. Merrily, she took big sips of her drink. She'd already forgotten what Barry said the drink was called, but whatever it was, it was delicious and the way she was guzzling it down, she'd be ready for another drink soon.

A door in the kitchen opened to the terraced backyard. She had instant visions of elaborate, catered cookouts. She looked around as far as her eyes could see in search of a pool. With all this ground, there had to be a pool somewhere. She closed the door and returned to the media room to wait for Barry to start the tour.

While waiting, she snapped open her purse to admire the six hundred dollars he'd slipped her for coming to his home. Hershey would pay her the additional five hundred in three days, Chanelle assumed. Damn, she'd earned eleven hundred dollars for an evening of dining and chitchat with a rich, handsome man.

Good looking out, Hershey! she said to herself. *And good looking out to you, ex-wifey!* She raised her glass in a toast to Barry's ex-wife for paving such a smooth path for her. If things worked out as she planned, she'd never have to turn one damn trick. She'd be Mrs. Barry Whatever-the-hell-his-last-name-was as quickly as she could sweep him off his feet.

She just had to figure out what he was looking for. She'd be whatever he needed. She couldn't care less about the race thing, the class distinction, or the difference in their ages. Barry was husband material. That was all that mattered, she decided with a satisfied smile.

"Chanelle," a high-pitched voice called.

Startled, Chanelle jerked around. It sounded like a woman's voice; was she hearing things?

Chanelle gasped when Barry sauntered in. He was wearing makeup, an elaborate red wig, high heels, and a tight-fitting sequined dress. "Come, come." He beckoned with fluttering fingers. "I promised to give you a tour."

If this were a scene from a movie, Chanelle would have fainted, but somehow she held on to her composure. She mentally cancelled the wedding plans, but something instinctual made her go along with the charade. She'd made eleven hundred easy dollars off Barry. Treating him nice meant a constant flow of money; there was no point in insulting her transvestite cash cow.

"You look…um…fabulous, uh, Barry," she said as she trailed him from room to room of the home that just a few seconds ago held the promise of being her very own.

"Thank you, dear. But please, call me Rita," he said in a falsetto and grandly swung open a set of double doors that led into an elegant dining room that was dominated by a elaborate crystal chandelier.

Feeling numb from the disappointing fact that she'd never entertain in this grand room, Chanelle listened without interest while Barry/Rita droned on and on about every object in the room.

She thought of Barry's ex-wife whom a few minutes ago she'd considered crazy for leaving her rich and handsome husband. Now, seeing Barry dressed up like a woman…well, Chanelle couldn't blame the woman for fleeing her home. And Chanelle deserved to be well paid for the time put in with the woman's nutcase, female-impersonating husband.

Chapter 21

The school nurse had administered prescribed medication to the students right after lunch. It was now a little after one in the afternoon. A few children were hunched over their reading comprehension assignment wearing intense expressions. The majority of Dayna's students were slumped in their seats, motionless, and oblivious to their surroundings due to the recent scheduled doses of Ritalin, Adderall, and a plethora of other medications. The pharmaceutical industry had deemed these mood-altering substances the latest wonder drugs for children with ADHD.

Dayna hated seeing her high-spirited students subdued into a zombie state, moving in slow motion if at all. It was a heart-wrenching sight—a classroom filled with dull-eyed, sluggish children. She believed the medications were doled out to make the school day more manageable and less chaotic for the staff. As far as she could tell, there were no benefits to the students. If she could get away with it and not get fired, she'd tell every parent to refuse to allow their child to be drugged.

But that was just her opinion and her opinion didn't

matter, Dayna supposed. So while her students quietly and listlessly worked on the reading comprehension test, Dayna took advantage of the peaceful environment. She flipped open her cell phone to make a quick call to her father. She'd been leaving messages at his office for the past two days and hadn't heard a word from him yet. The hell with her own problems with Reed, she was starting to feel panicky about her father. What on earth would prevent him from returning her calls?

His secretary answered on the second ring with a cheery good afternoon.

"Good afternoon, Monica. Is my father in the office?" Dayna whispered.

"Uh…" The secretary paused. "No, Dayna, he isn't."

"Has he gotten the messages I've been leaving?"

"Yes, I've given him all your messages," she said in a clipped tone that suggested no other information would be forthcoming.

Dayna sighed in exasperation. Monica was typically very helpful, but not now. Her tone was almost defensive. Something was going on. "Is something wrong, Monica?" Dayna asked, concerned.

"No," she said quickly. "Why do you ask?"

"I don't know. I've been trying to track down my father for two days, and he hasn't returned my calls. I don't know what's going on, but I'm starting to get the feeling he's avoiding me…"

"Oh, Dayna, that's nonsense. Your father's been extremely busy. Look, the other line is ringing; I'll make sure I give your father your message." The secretary clicked off.

Dayna clutched the cell phone, not knowing what to make of her father's neglect. Monica was covering for him, but why? She could call him at home later tonight, but then she'd have to put up with his resentful new wife. It was sickening the way her father had allowed himself to become so henpecked.

She promptly pressed her mother's telephone number. Her mother was no doubt sitting around wallowing in her own misery and Dayna hated to involve her, however, she needed some answers.

"Hi, Mom," she said, keeping her tone low.

"Hi, darling." There was no enthusiasm in Pamela Hinton's greeting.

"Are you okay?"

"Actually, I'm not," her mother said gloomily. "Your father has been refusing my calls and Monica has been giving me the run-around. How many years has Monica worked for your father?"

"I don't know…she's been his secretary for as long as I can remember."

"Exactly. So how do you think I feel being treated like one of his pesky clients instead of his wife?"

"You're his ex-wife," Dayna reminded her mother.

"Mom, you should move on; Daddy sure has," Dayna said sternly, though she felt like crying. "Monica's only doing Daddy's bidding; don't blame her."

"Oh, I blame her plenty. She's been covering for him. You won't believe what I found out when I finally got him on the phone…" Pamela Hinton's voice cracked.

"What?"

"Your father got that bitch pregnant," she sobbed. "He's having a baby! Can you imagine that? At his age!"

Dayna's heart dropped. *Sh*e couldn't conceive a child and yet her father, who was well past his prime, was going to have a new baby.

"That's why he stood me up on Mother's Day. She told him the news and he took *her* to brunch instead of me. He replaced me with the mother of his unborn child."

The words *new baby* rang in Dayna's mind. She suspected that she'd been replaced as well. Her emotions were about to spin out of control, but she had to keep it together for her mother's sake.

"Mom, please don't cry. You really have to get on with your life. Join a support group or something."

"What can a support group do for me? Can a support group replace the years I wasted with your father? I was with him throughout law school; I helped him get his practice off the ground," her mother ranted.

Dayna had heard the spiel a million times. She wanted to console her mother, but her own pain was too severe to come up with one coherent word of comfort.

"I'm finished, Mrs. Reynolds," said Imani, one of Dayna's brightest students and one of the rare few who was not taking prescribed medication.

"Hold on, Mom," she continued whispering into the phone and then took it away from her ear. "Very good, Imani. Now, turn your paper over."

"Can I collect the papers?" Imani asked eagerly.

Dayna looked at her watch. "Not yet, Imani." Speaking to the other students, Dayna said, "Five more minutes, class. When I say stop, I want everyone to turn your papers over and put your pencils down."

She put the phone back to her ear. "Mom, I'm in class; I'll call you after school."

Dayna now had a clearer picture of what was going on. Her father was trying to cut his ties with her mother— probably at his wife's insistence—and in order to effectively disassociate himself from his ex-wife, he had put some distance between himself and his daughter.

My dad doesn't want a relationship with me. It was unnatural for her father to reject her—to break her heart like this. It's expected that a husband or a boyfriend might break a woman's heart, but not a father. A father's love was supposed to be unconditional, a love that could always be counted on. But another woman had stolen her father's heart and would soon give him a new child to dote upon—to distract his attention away from his first born. It felt like a betrayal and it cut like a knife.

Dayna bent over and briefly cupped her face in anguish,

then abruptly sat up. She'd be damned if she'd make one more call to her unresponsive father. She'd handle her problems on her own.

"Mrs. Reynolds." Ever vigilant, Imani brought Dayna out of her inner world. "Is it time to collect the papers?"

"Oh shut up, teacher's pet," a student said in a voice that was a slurred grumble. Amazingly, the student was being combative despite the drugs.

"Stop writing, class. Go ahead and collect the papers, Imani."

❧❧❧❧

Weary from a long day at school that included a Home and School Council meeting after regular school hours, Dayna arrived home and went straight upstairs to run bath water. A Calgon moment was truly in order. As she languished in the bathtub, she decided not to dwell on any of her numerous problems. Instead she cleared her mind and focused on the tranquility of the warm soapy water.

No sooner had she closed her eyes and slipped into a peaceful state when the locked bathroom door was suddenly kicked open. The door banged against the linen closet; it sounded like an explosion.

Dayna shrank back in fear, then bolted upright from her reclining position, splashing water as she scrambled out of the bathtub. Her naked body was covered with soap suds.

Reed stood in the doorway, leaning menacingly against the frame.

"What's wrong with you? Are you crazy?" she screamed at him as she grabbed a towel and wrapped it around her body.

Reed's lips stretched into such a hateful smile, Dayna hardly recognized him. "I had to show you that a locked door can't keep me out. When you stop locking doors around here, I'll stop kicking them down. This is *my* house and I don't want you to lock another damn door. Understand?"

"*Your* house! Now I know you're out of your mind." Dayna tried to push past him, but Reed blocked her path.

"Get out of my way!" She shoved him as hard as she could, but he didn't budge.

He gripped her jaw; hatred shone in his eyes as he dug his fingers in so deeply it felt like her teeth might crumble. "Don't put your hands on me again, Dayna," he warned. He kept a tight hold on her jaw and then released it with a spiteful shove.

She rubbed her face, wondering if it were bruised. "Let me out of this bathroom, Reed." There was a threatening tone in Dayna's voice.

His eyes ridiculed her. "What are you going to do? Knock me down?"

Dayna's eyes desperately swept the bathroom.

"Oh, I forgot about the window," he said mockingly and nodded his head toward the small single window.

"That's the only way you're getting out of here. So go ahead, be my guest. Jump out."

Standing there soaking wet, a naked captive covered with just a towel, she felt so degraded she wanted to cry. Acting on pure instinct, Dayna rushed toward the window, but instead of raising it, she grabbed a metal vase on the window ledge and hurled it at Reed's head.

Too stunned to duck, Reed was an unmoving target. "Damn!" he yelled and slumped against the wall. He covered his forehead with both hands. Blood gushed between his fingers, creating red speckles on the sink and tiled walls.

Dayna darted out of the bathroom and ran down the hall to the security of her bedroom. She locked the door and struggled to push the dresser against it. Panting, she pushed, pulled, and tugged until she had practically every piece of furniture in the room barricaded in front of the bedroom door.

Feeling safe enough to shift her gaze, she located the phone, which had fallen on the floor. She raced across the room to pick it up. She had to call her mother. Someone had to help her.

She picked up the receiver and to her utter amazement, she heard Reed's voice. "My wife is in here going crazy. She's trying to kill me. I need help *now!*"

"What's your location, sir?" asked the emergency dispatcher.

Reed gave their address. "Hurry up!" he hollered. "Get an ambulance over here before I bleed to death!"

Dayna quickly hung up. How badly had she hurt Reed? She ran an anxious hand through her hair as she pondered what she should do. *Get dressed!*

She raced to the dresser to get a pair of panties and a bra, but she couldn't open her lingerie drawer because it was pressed against the door. She made a beeline to the closet and snatched the first pair of jeans in sight.

Still damp from the tub, she struggled into jeans that were two sizes too small. *Why, oh why didn't I get rid of all my skinny clothes*, she wailed to herself. She got them over her hips but couldn't zip them up. There was no time to search through the clothing rack for something more comfortable. Dayna threw on an oversized T-shirt and a pair of sneakers without socks.

She picked up her cell phone to call her mother, but remembering her mother's fragile mental state, she called Cecily instead.

"I'm having a crisis over here," she blurted and was shocked that she sounded just like her mother.

"What's going on? Did Reed hit you?" Cecily shouted.

"No. I hit him. He called an ambulance. He's bleeding really badly."

"Dayna, listen to me. Grab as much stuff as you can and get over here. You don't want to be there when the ambulance arrives."

"Why not? It was self-defense."

"Do what I say. Hurry up!" Cecily hung up.

She thought Cecily was being overly dramatic but under the stressful circumstances and considering her own confused state of mind, Dayna was in no position to second-guess her girlfriend.

Badly shaken, Dayna walked in a perplexed circle for a moment. She didn't know where to begin. If she removed the blockade from the door, Reed could burst in and physically retaliate. But she knew she needed to try to escape while he was incapacitated.

Piece by piece, she pulled the furniture away from the door, yanked open the drawers, and began tossing lingerie and other clothing into a duffle bag. Then she rushed into the hallway.

A trail of blood from the bathroom to the stairs stopped her cold. Her hand covered her mouth to suppress a gasp. She could hear Reed moaning downstairs and was afraid to investigate the extent of his injury. *Oh God, is he dying?*

Finally, she mustered the courage to creep down the stairs. Reed was sitting in a chair holding a bloody towel to his forehead. Blood was everywhere—on his clothes, the chair, the carpet, the walls. But he was sitting up, so Dayna hoped the injury looked worse than it actually was. Ever so quietly, she inched past Reed and made her way to the front door. Just as her hand twisted the doorknob, she heard the blare of sirens.

Now she couldn't make her great escape. She'd have to stick around and endure the embarrassment of telling the emergency crew that she'd bashed her husband in the head with a vase. She'd explain of course that she'd only meant to subdue him, not cause him to bleed all over the house. Being his wife, she'd probably be expected to ride along in the ambulance with Reed. Damn! Damn! Damn! Dropping her duffle bag in defeat, Dayna opened the door to face the most humiliating experience of her entire life.

But it turned out worse than she could have ever imagined. The emergency rescue team arrived with the *police!*

Pointing a bloody finger at her, Reed shouted to the two police officers, "She tried to kill me; my own wife tried to kill me!"

"Can we get a statement, sir?" asked the male police officer.

"I'm bleeding to death. I need medical attention. She tried to kill me, what else do you need to know?"

The emergency team quickly rushed to Reed and began administering treatment to stop the bleeding.

"Sir, we'd appreciate a statement."

"Can I give a statement?" Dayna asked. "He started this whole thing. He wouldn't let me leave the bathroom—"

"She's lying. I'll give a statement," Reed said, wincing in pain as he lifted his head. "I came home a little late and she just went off on me, screaming and cursing, and before I knew what was happening she hit me with a vase."

"That's a lie—" Dayna began to protest.

"Did you use physical force against your husband?" the female officer interjected.

"Yes, but—"

"Did you feel threatened for your safety, ma'am?" the male officer asked.

"Yes," replied Dayna.

"I didn't lay a hand on her and I didn't threaten her," Reed countered as the female officer began snapping pictures of his head wound.

"Where is the weapon your wife used, sir?"

"It's upstairs in the bathroom…a vase," Reed groaned as if in agony.

The female police officer ran up the stairs and collected the incriminating bloody vase.

The male officer directed his next question to Dayna. "Did your husband use physical force against you tonight, ma'am?"

"Well…he grabbed my chin," Dayna said in a weak, embarrassed voice.

"I was rubbing her face, telling her I loved her," Reed said. "Do you see any marks on her face?"

"Did you use physical force against your husband?"

"Yes, because—" Before she could utter another word, she was read her rights, cuffed, and carted off to jail.

Chapter 22

"Baby, where've you been?" Malik asked over the phone. "I dropped by Lizzard's and they said you didn't work there anymore. What happened?"

Chanelle sucked her teeth. "You sure took your good ol' time to check on me, so don't even try to act like you give a damn. How you gonna let weeks pass by without a word and then call me like you haven't done anything wrong?"

"My bad; I know I'm wrong, but I've been upstate," Malik explained.

"You've been what?" She hoped he wasn't insinuating that he'd been in jail because that was a lame excuse that all brothers used whenever they went MIA.

"You haven't heard from me because I've been out of town."

"Oh, you've been on an extended vacation?" Chanelle felt the heat of anger scorching her face as she imagined Malik chillin' in Miami or some other glamorous location with his famous cousin while she ran around town looking for a job. "Well, that makes me feel better; thanks for sharing," she said sarcastically. "While you were living the good life, I got fired from Lizzard's."

"Baby, I didn't know. What happened? Why'd they fire you?"

"That jealous bitch, Lexi, lied on me and got me fired. But I shouldn't have to tell you that after all this time. Why the hell do you think I was blowing up your cell phone? You heard my messages, didn't you?"

"Naw, I never heard shit. I dropped my phone. Broke it. It took me a minute to get another one."

"That's no excuse. You knew I'd be trying to get in touch with you, so you should have called me. It's mighty suspicious that you got ghost the entire time I was doing bad, and now that I'm all right, you suddenly appear. What do you have, some kind of tracking system that tells you when it's safe to communicate with me?"

"Aw, baby. Don't be like that. You know I would have helped you out. But I was doing bad myself."

"Whatever. You call yourself my man, but obviously you're not. So I suggest you forget my number and continue to do whatever you've been doing all this time."

"Chanelle…baby…I wasn't having it all sweet like you think. I'm not trying to live off my cousin for the rest of my life. I've been out of town hustling, trying to get mine."

"Hustling what?"

"Rock."

Chanelle almost choked. "You're selling drugs?"

"Man, what else am I gonna do—work somewhere for minimum wage? There's too much heat in Philly, every corner is hot, so me and my dawgs been going upstate, where the honkies live. That's where the real money's at."

"I can't believe we're having this conversation. How can you go from working for your cousin to standing on a corner hustlin'?"

"It ain't like that. We work outta houses—nice houses. You'd be shocked at how many white people smoke crack—"

"I don't really care, Malik."

"Well, like I was trying to tell you, I'm my own man and I'm tired of taking orders from my—"

Chanelle cut Malik off.. "You know what? I don't care what you're doing or why you're doing it. All I know is you weren't there for me when I needed you, so please forget my name, my number, and everything about me." She slammed down the phone.

It rang a minute later. "Hello!" she hollered into the mouthpiece.

"Why'd you bang up on me? I wanted to ask you a question."

Chanelle took a deep breath and waited.

"You have a major credit card, right?"

The nerve of this fool. Chanelle was speechless. She made small indignant utterances, but was so deeply offended she could not find words to express her outrage.

"I need a rental car to handle my business. I've been taking the bus back and forth, but if you let me use your credit card, I won't have to sit out there in Williamsport for three or four days in a row. If I had a whip, I could can jet back and forth to Philly a couple times a week and spend some quality time with you."

Chanelle grimaced. Without his Stone Allen connection, Malik's value had plummeted. She had no use for him.

"So, whassup? You gonna let me use your credit card or what?"

"No."

"Aw, that's corny, Chanelle. Come on…hook me up with a wheel—a Magnum. They got a good deal at Avis. You can rent a Magnum for a week for just a buck-fifty."

Chanelle couldn't believe her ears. Throughout the entire affair, she'd been merely stringing Malik along; she'd always thought that he adored her to the point of worship. But now this…this nonchalant attitude regarding his disappearing act and his request that she risk her credit rating, not that she had one, but if she did, she wouldn't risk it on him. He'd already proven himself to be unreliable and that was evidence that he wasn't really feeling her either.

Malik had been using her, she realized. She'd been nothing more than a sex partner and eye candy, she presumed. It was a crushing blow to her ego and for a brief moment she felt off-kilter. Then she became angry. "Are you retarded?" she hissed. "I'm not letting your dumb ass use my credit card. And listen, if you call here again,

I'm gonna report it as a nuisance call." She quickly stabbed the button that would give Malik the dial tone.

Forget that fool, she told herself. She had other pressing business to attend to. Three days had passed and Hershey hadn't paid her for her date with Barry. It irked her that Hershey hadn't dropped off the money as she'd promised and it pissed her off even more that every time she called, she got Hershey's voice mail. If she'd known she was going to have to chase her down for her money, she wouldn't have agreed to work for her.

Feeling peeved, she picked up the phone and jabbed Hershey's number.

Surprisingly, Hershey picked up on the second ring. "Hey, whassup, Chanelle?" There was a lot of background noise. She could hear the happy high-pitched squeals and laughter of children. It sounded like Hershey was outside at a playground or somewhere with a million kids. How odd. She didn't get the impression that Hershey had children; she didn't seem like the motherly type.

"Um, I was calling to see if you had the money yet." Damn, she hated having to ask for her money; she felt like she was begging. If she continued to work for her, Hershey was going to have to come up with a better pay system.

"I can't believe you're sweatin' me over that little bit of cash," Hershey said with a chuckle. "Do you think I'm gonna skip town on you or somethin'?"

"That's not the point, I worked and I expect to get paid."

"And I told you it takes a couple of days for a check to clear. I just got your money today, Chanelle. I was planning to call you and let you know I'd drop it off sometime today, but I got tied up. I'm at the zoo."

"The zoo!" Chanelle repeated with raised brows. It was hard to imagine a diva trekking around at the zoo.

"Yes, the zoo. My godchild loves animals and I try to make sure she does all the fun stuff a little kid likes to do. Feel me?"

She wasn't feeling Hershey at all. She just wanted her money. What Chanelle could *feel* were the muscles in her face as they began to tighten. Hershey was really working her nerves. "So, how long are you gonna be at the zoo?"

Hershey sighed. "Another hour or so. I have your address somewhere, but give it to me again."

"It's 4814 Florence Avenue. It's a small street—between Baltimore and Warrington Avenue."

"Okay, see you soon," Hershey said and hung up.

Soon? How long was soon? To pass the time, Chanelle slid Beyonce's CD in her player and skipped forward to "Dangerously in Love" and put it on repeat. It was an old song, but it had been Chanelle's theme song at Lizzard's and was still one of her all-time favorites. As she listened to Beyonce pour her heart out to Jay-Z, she felt a pang of envy. Would she ever find that kind of love? Being that her primary goal was to find a rich husband, she doubted if she'd ever find someone to truly love.

Latching onto a rich husband and loving him as well was probably too much to ask for. It would be foolish to expect life to deliver such a delicious double treat. "But it sure would be nice," she whispered aloud and then gave a wistful sigh.

❧❧❧

Chanelle peered through her mini blinds when she heard the honk of a car horn. Hershey was sitting in her ride in front of Chanelle's front door. *It's about time*, Chanelle muttered to herself, then rushed outside to collect her cash.

She approached the car and was caught off-guard by the pretty little brown-skinned girl who was strapped in a car seat in the back. Chanelle gushed, "She's adorable."

"Thanks. That's my godchild, Markeeta." Hershey beamed with pride.

"Hi, Markeeta. How old are you?" Chanelle asked the pretty little girl.

Smiling bashfully, Markeeta held up three fingers.

"Don't do that, Keeta. Tell her how old you are," Hershey instructed, looking back at her godchild.

"I'm three and a half years old," the little girl said.

"Aw, aren't you the cutest," Chanelle exclaimed. "If I ever have a daughter, I hope she's as pretty as you, Markeeta."

"You better hope she's as smart as Markeeta. My girl is smart as a whip," said Hershey as she counted out five one-hundred-dollar bills. She handed the money to Chanelle, and then spoke in a whisper, "Fuck being pretty, I keep Markeeta focused on being smart. Feel me? Because between you and me…girl, we both know that the only thing pretty does is get you fucked."

Chanelle was taken aback by Hershey's comment. Stung by it. "That's your opinion; I'm not sure I agree with it."

"You don't have to. But that's the way I choose to raise Markeeta. I don't want her to end up having to rely on her looks to make a living."

Chanelle pondered Hershey's comment and decided it felt like a personal insult. "You're making it sound like being pretty is a curse or something."

"It is a curse if that's all you got." Hershey glanced into the rearview mirror. Markeeta had fallen asleep. "My baby is zonked out," Hershey commented. "Too much zoo activity, I guess. Oh Lord, I hope she don't think she's gonna sleep all day and stay up all night," she said, laughing.

"Does she live with you?"

"Uh-huh. I'm raising her. Me and her mom grew up together." Hershey lowered her voice. "Her mother's sick;

I'm taking care of Markeeta until she gets better." A look of pain crossed Hershey's face; she cast her eyes downward briefly and then, as if she'd shaken off a bad memory, she raised her face and said brightly, "Listen, I think I have a nice hook-up for you tonight." Then her tone became stern. "But let me get something straight, Chanelle…you can't be hounding me for your pay. I told you that I pay my girls anywhere from two to three days after the date. What kind of sense would it make for me to burn you? I'm a businesswoman, not a scam artist. Stealing from one of my employees would be bad business."

"I never accused you of stealing—"

"You didn't have to. Besides, why were you acting so pressed? I know Barry tipped you well."

"How do you know about that?"

"Oh, not much escapes me. Trust me. You'd have to get up pretty early in the morning to get one over on me. I know exactly how much cash you got from *my* client and I didn't say a word to you about my cut, did I?"

Looking contrite, Chanelle shook her head, but she was rather perplexed as to why Hershey felt entitled to *her* tip.

"All right, so give me the same respect."

Chanelle nodded.

"Barry's a trip with his cross-dressing self, ain't he?" Hershey said, lightening up the mood. "I want to warn you in advance…if you accept the date I've lined up tonight, you gotta be prepared to get your cherry popped. This client's not trying to wine and dine you. He's expecting to get laid. Still interested?"

Chanelle scrunched up her face as she contemplated the situation. *I pretended to be Malik's girl and had sex with him just to hang out with members of the NBA. So hell, why not do it for cash?*

"Yeah, I'm interested," she finally said.

"Good, I'll call you with the details later on tonight," Hershey said and started the engine. "By the way, the client you're seeing tonight is filthy rich; I like doing business with him, so don't fuck this up by having cold feet at the last minute."

Chanelle got a quick image of a big fat rich slob. She exhaled and managed a fluttery wave as Hershey pulled out of the parking spot. She walked back to her apartment with a vague sense that she'd not only waved goodbye to Hershey, but also to the life she'd known.

While other dancers tricked at the drop of a dime, she never stooped that low; she had too much self-respect for that. But that world of prostitution had been haunting her, pulling at her for a long time, and now she found herself mentally waving a white flag.

Stripper. Exotic dancer. Go-go dancer. Those labels would no longer apply to her. She let out a sigh of resignation. After tonight, she'd officially be a ho.

Chapter 23

Dayna spent an entire night and a half the next day in jail. The degradation was beyond anything she'd ever known. She didn't call her mother because her mother would need her father to handle things, and she was too embarrassed to call her father because she'd surely have to go through his secretary or his wife to get to him on the phone. Her shameful predicament was certainly not her father's wife or his secretary's business, so Dayna had no choice but to turn to Cecily to come to her rescue.

No bail was required. She was released on her own recognizance, but was ordered to vacate her home. Dayna was escorted home by two male police officers. Cecily came along for support. Dayna took a deep breath when the squad car parked in her driveway. Instead of ringing the bell, one of the officers pounded on the door. Dayna supposed that making unnecessary racket was standard procedure when the enforcers of the law came to call.

Reed opened the door. As she entered her home, her legs felt weak and she thought she'd collapse and wail in despair, but she'd shed so many tears while sitting in that awful cell, there were none left to cry.

"Mr. Reynolds, I'm Officer Porter," one of the officers said. "This is Officer Buckley." He indicated his partner by turning slightly toward the younger police officer. "We're going to escort your wife while she gathers her things."

Then the officer turned toward Dayna. "Mrs. Reynolds, do you understand that you're not allowed to come back to these premises until your hearing in thirty days?" Dayna bowed her head solemnly and nodded.

Reed wore a huge white gauze bandage on his forehead. He looked stricken. His lips twitched and his eyes blinked uncomfortably, then closed briefly as if everything—the wound inflicted by his crazy wife, her self-imposed exile from their home—was simply too much for him to bear.

But Dayna wasn't fooled for a second. As Reed struggled to look like an emotionally broken and physically abused husband, his lips twitched because he was probably fighting the urge to break out in a fit of uncontrollable and triumphant laughter.

"Do you want to start upstairs?" Officer Porter asked Dayna.

"Yes." Her voice was barely above a whisper. That she was being evicted from the home she'd bought and continued to pay for was an unspeakable travesty of justice.

She swooned ever so slightly. Cecily patted Dayna's arm soothingly and then squeezed it in support as she assisted her friend up the stairs.

"Stay down here, sir," ordered Officer Porter and then the two officers hurried up the stairs, following closely behind Dayna and Cecily.

She made her way to the top. The feet that had bravely climbed each stair step paused and seemed unwilling to cooperate further. An unexpected wave of lightheadedness made her stick out a hand to steady herself against the wall.

"It's going to be all right," Cecily murmured and gently nudged her along. Dayna detected a quaver in her friend's voice that could only mean Cecily didn't really think it would be all right. She was as befuddled as Dayna by this strange turn of events.

Sensing Dayna's weakening spirit, Cecily took the lead, steering Dayna and the two escorts to the guest room, where the majority of Dayna's personal possessions were stored.

"I'll pack the stuff on top of the dresser and in the drawers," said Cecily, snapping open a deep square beauty case. "You get your clothes out of the closet—your shoes, pocketbooks, and things."

The bathroom was next and then the master bedroom, where a few of Dayna's possessions remained.

Except for Reed's clothing and other odds and ends,

everything in the room—in the entire house for that matter—belonged to Dayna, yet the officers stood guard in the doorway with their arms folded, distrustful eyes glued to her as she sorted through the closet and rustled through the drawers. They stared at her suspiciously as if they expected she'd try to pull a fast one and slip something that didn't belong to her in one of the extra large trash bags that Cecily had the foresight to bring along.

Finally, it was over. All things she needed were packed in a set of Samsonite luggage, a cloth duffle, and plastic trash bags.

The police marched her and Cecily down the stairs. As they passed through the large and beautifully furnished living room, dragging baggage that contained only pieces of Dayna's life, a wayward suitcase bumped against an end table, knocking over a heavy silver frame.

Instinctively, Dayna stopped and readjusted the frame, momentarily forgetting she was repositioning a wedding photo of herself and Reed. She suddenly realized that Reed's eyes in the photo were those of someone far worse than a scoundrel. There was such evil in Reed's eyes, Dayna felt a chill. Why hadn't she noticed that before?

Reed was settled in a chair, his head tilted toward the arm of the chair, resting on a pillow. With a palm placed gingerly over his sutured and bandaged forehead, he clenched his teeth and grimaced dramatically as he used his other hand to shift himself upright. "I hope you realize you can't keep coming back and forth every time you think of something you forgot," he said scornfully.

Cecily jerked around. "Shut up, you no-good—"

But Dayna stopped Cecily's bitter words with a sharp tug to the hem of her blouse. She pressed her lips tightly together, refusing to dignify her husband's ignorant outburst.

The battle was far from over. She'd die before she'd allow her horrible husband to win. In thirty days she'd be back with a vengeance to reclaim her home and repair her shattered life.

Chapter 24

Hershey told her to always carry some kind of protection when out with a client, but Chanelle didn't feel threatened enough to actually pack a weapon inside her purse. Carrying a gun was out of the question, so she gave some thought to retrieving a steak knife from a kitchen drawer. Scowling, she shook her head. She'd pick up a can of pepper spray the first chance she had.

Swathed in a tasteful powder-blue sundress, Chanelle exited the cab in front of the Ritz-Carlton hotel. She carried a small overnight bag that was stuffed with exotic dance costumes.

In a matter of minutes she would be selling her body to the stranger who waited for her on the twenty-first floor. The thought of having anonymous sex filled her with self-pity, not fear. Adding insult to injury, the notion of walking unescorted into the lobby of the posh hotel gave her a serious case of the jitters.

Her imagination ran wild with horrific images. The worst-case scenario was the possibility of being apprehended by security for sex trafficking before she even stepped foot into the elevator.

Although she was in a state of panic, Chanelle entered the imposing hotel lobby with her head held high. She gave the impression of a confident young black woman, accustomed to the finest things in life. Putting on a show for nosey observers, she walked purposefully to the elevator, jabbed the button, and then impatiently threw up her wrist to check the time.

The elevator arrived and she stepped inside with a self-assured stride that conveyed ownership. Once alone in the elevator, she allowed herself the luxury of falling against the wall and hyperventilating before pressing the button that would deliver her to the twenty-first floor.

Chanelle stepped off the elevator and looked around for the arrow that would point her in the right direction. She located the room and knocked. She took a deep breath as she braced herself for an hour-long session with a horrible pervert.

The door opened. *Oh my God!* The words almost traveled from her mind to her mouth, but she quickly composed herself. The client nodded his head and gave her a devilish smile.

Ignoring her brain's command to stay calm, Chanelle's lips formed into a smile and then scrunched up and became a seductive pucker. The man standing in the doorway was fine as shit! Dark and swarthy, with straight black hair and angular features, he wore baggy shorts and a white sleeveless T-shirt. Obviously Italian, with a cocky air, this man was not the fat slob she'd imagined.

He invited Chanelle in with a sweeping gesture and moved to the side, allowing her a clear path, then he closed the door and leaned against it. His eyes, filled with lust, traveled her body. She flung him a provocative look and permitted her own eyes to journey from his hairy legs, past his broad shoulders and handsome angular face, up to the pitch-black hair on his head.

"Marc Tarsia," he said.

"Sensation," Chanelle said, offering her hand.

But instead of shaking it, Marc pressed her hand against his lips. Then he turned her hand over and kissed her open palm.

Her skin felt seared; she held back a gasp. Under normal circumstances, this act of boldness would have offended her, but not today—she was feeling sexually aroused. The moisture between her legs confirmed that. *This man is dangerous*, she thought, avoiding his eyes as she glanced approvingly around the luxurious suite.

"Can I get you something to drink?"

She brought her attention back to Marc. "Um... what do you have?" she asked casually as her eyes traveled to his left hand. His third finger was bare. No wedding ring. Deliriously happy, she wanted to shout *hallelujah*, but settled for tossing him a brilliant smile.

"I don't know. I haven't checked out the wet bar." He sauntered to the other side of the room and peered inside a glass cabinet.

She didn't really want anything more than a Pepsi, but

she needed Marc distracted for a moment while she gathered her wits.

"I see a couple bottles of Moët. Do you like champagne?"

She nodded her head.

"I can order of bottle of Dom if you don't like Moët."

Dom Perignon! Dayum, dude must be working with some stacks. "Moët's fine," she said sweetly, hoping the champagne would have a tranquilizing effect. She needed something to calm her frazzled nerves.

She thought about her personal motto: *The only thing a client can offer is a ticket out of the ghetto.* Allowing the significance of the words to settle into her mind, she sank into the well-cushioned sofa. But her body was telling her something entirely different. She cut her eyes at Marc and observed him on the sly. Without a doubt, he was the sexiest man she'd ever laid eyes on. He radiated power; it was palpable. *Dayum! He has it all…money, good looks, and power.* Power was an aphrodisiac for Chanelle. Her physical attraction to Marc rendered her stupid motto a moot point. Excitedly, she ran her fingers through her hair. *I'm in trouble*, she giddily admitted to herself.

"You're really pretty, ya know that?" Marc was standing next to her. Chanelle beamed a thank-you as she accepted the glass of champagne.

"You're much prettier than my boat."

"Your boat? What are you talking about?"

Marc laughed. "I chose you when the lady who owns the service ran down the list of names of the girls."

"Oh…" Chanelle said, still unenlightened

"And since I own a boat named *Sensation*; I thought me and you might really hit it off."

"Okay, I see," she said, really seeing things much clearer.

"You like sailin', baby? I'd love to take you out on my boat."

Did she like sailing? How the hell did she know? Unless you counted the ferry ride from Penn's Landing to the aquarium in Camden, New Jersey, she didn't have much sailing experience under her belt.

Chanelle took a quick sip from the glass, reminding herself to sip slowly. Marc drank straight from the bottle, looking extremely masculine and appealing as he tilted it to his lips. *Sexy muthafucker!*

Although Chanelle preferred her men taller, Marc's gorgeous face and ripped physique more than made up for what he was lacking in height. She turned inquisitive eyes to his groin and wondered if the chink in his armor lay there. *I hope not,* she thought and shook her head.

After taking a few sips of champagne, Chanelle said, "I'm gonna change into something more comfortable. Okay?" She gestured toward the bathroom.

"Make yourself at home."

She took another sip and set the glass down. Clutching her purse and overnight bag, Chanelle sashayed to the bathroom. Heat emanating from Marc's smoldering brown eyes scorched her back, then moved to her buttocks. Instinctively, she arched her back, causing her moneymaker to protrude even more. His eyes lingered on her butt cheeks until she was behind the closed door and out of his line of vision.

The bathroom was exquisite, she admitted as she gazed at the glass-enclosed marble shower. Damn, she deserved this kind of luxury twenty-four-seven. And Marc could give it to her. If she played her cards right, her lifestyle could change overnight. Excitement coursed through her body as she invoked a mental image of his left hand and recalled his bare ring finger. *Oh yeah, it's on!* Then she began to undress.

Wearing a one-piece red suspender thong, sheer red thigh-highs, and blood-red stiletto heels with ankle straps, she re-entered the room, throwing her hips from side to side as she made slow sensual strides toward Marc.

"You're looking hot, baby. Get over here."

She crossed the room, stood before him, and seductively placed a red stiletto on the sofa in the space between his thighs. "I might be too much for you. Are you sure you want to take this ride?" Her voice was low and sexy.

He planted a kiss on her well-toned thigh. He raised his head. "I can hang," he said with a confident glint in his eyes.

"Is that right?" Insisting upon a reversal in power, Chanelle turned around and pushed her rear end in the empty space, forcing him to open his legs wide to accommodate her butt cheeks as they brushed against his groin.

Skillful in the art of seduction, she gave him a lap dance that was perfectly timed to the music in her mind. She smiled triumphantly when she heard his lustful groan and felt his manhood spring to life. Yes, she was in control. She had to strip him of his power—make him weak.

He reached around her and cupped her breasts. Hot fingers deftly moved the fabric aside and encircled her nipples until they became as hard as pebbles. Chanelle gritted her teeth, gave up, and gasped. Damn, every part of her body felt sensitive to his touch. He had to stop touching her, she decided as she dropped to her knees. Marc quickly came out of his shorts. He wasn't wearing underwear. Interesting.

Usually, she would have saved the best for last. But this was an emergency. She and Marc were engaged in a power struggle. She was backed into a corner and had no choice but to pull out the heavy artillery.

She examined his package. It was a nice-sized dick— not too big and definitely not too small. Nice color, too. Light brown, smooth, even toned. Chanelle dampened her lips and flicked her tongue against the perfectly shaped mushroom cap, making moist circles until Marc thrust upward, silently begging her to take more.

She licked the shaft. Marc made a throaty gasp. She stopped, took a swig of champagne but did not swallow until she drew him back inside her mouth, coercing him to slosh through the cool sparkly liquid.

He desperately entwined his hands in her hair and cried out in exquisite pain.

Finally swallowing the champagne, Chanelle threw back her head and opened her throat, allowing him to drive deeper. She made her throat constrict, giving him the sensation of tightening vaginal muscles. Marc shuddered; Chanelle smirked. There was no doubt about it; she was a master at giving some good damn head.

"Stop," he pleaded in a choked whisper.

"Had enough?" she asked, dabbing at the corner of her mouth with the back of her hand.

"I surrender." Marc held up his hands.

"Completely?"

"I'm all yours."

"That's what I wanted to hear." She smirked again, took his hand, and boldly led him into the bedroom.

Chapter 25

J ust before they reached the bed, Marc stopped
unexpectedly and turned to Chanelle. Cupping her
face with both hands, he kissed her passionately. She
returned the kiss and embraced him in a python-tight
hold. Marc was everything she desired. He was the type
of man she could easily love.

Suddenly, Marc pulled his lips away from her mouth.
Chanelle uttered a small cry of protest but, unwilling to
appear weak in the midst of battle, she reluctantly dropped
her arms and summoned the strength to meet his gaze
with a self-assured smile.

"Sensation," Marc said softly, stroking the side of her
face. "I dig you, you're something special, ya know. But
I gotta tell you something…" He paused, allowing the
effect of unspoken words to sink in.

Chanelle swallowed hard. "Is something wrong?"

The hand that had caressed her face was now pointing
at her. "Do I look like a cunt?" he exploded. Anger sparked
in his eye so his furious expression wasn't a pretty sight.

"No!" she exclaimed, confused.

"So why ya treatin' me like I'm a fuckin' cunt?" he

demanded, gesturing wildly while his head moved furiously from side to side.

She felt the blood drain away from her face. Marc's sudden and terribly frightening rant was completely out of the blue. In a matter of minutes he'd gone from hot and horny to an out-of-control beast.

"What?" she finally squeaked out. Beads of perspiration dotted her forehead, betraying her fear.

"You callin' the shots around here?"

Chanelle was completely thrown. What had happened to the prince of a man who'd kissed her hand a few minutes ago? Too stunned to speak, Chanelle could only shake her head. Marc was starting to remind her of the crazy nephew on *The Sopranos*—the one who had his own fiancée gunned down like a dog. She'd been so attracted to Marc's good looks and wealth, it hadn't occurred to her that he might be a bloodthirsty member of the mob.

"I wear the fuckin' pants and—."

A rush of hysteria forced Chanelle to mentally cut off Marc's verbal rampage; she could not listen to another word. Frantically, she began to bargain with a higher power: *Dear Lord, if I get out of this alive, I'll never turn another trick; I'll go back to school and get my GED, I'll get a regular job, I'll—*

She halted her internal rambling when Marc draped an arm around her shoulders and concluded his tirade. "Understand?" It was more a command than a question.

Chanelle had no idea what she should understand, but was so relieved that his mood had shifted from murderous to mellow that she lowered her head in contrition and murmured, "Yes."

Satisfied, Marc put both arms around her and kissed her forehead.

All was forgiven. He wasn't in the Mafia after all! He was high strung and had a bad temper—that's all. Now back to the important matter at hand…his money and becoming his wife. If she wanted to reap the benefits of his long paper on a permanent basis, she'd have to pussy whip him into saying, "I do."

She was going to have to stay on top of her game and make sure she didn't push any more buttons that made him behave like Tony Montana in *Scarface* at the height of his rage.

He took her hand and pressed it against his erection. "See what you do to me?" he accused.

"Sorry," she replied.

"Well, get your ass over there." He shook his thumb like a hitchhiker and pointed her in the direction of the king-sized bed.

It was an insulting gesture. Disrespectful as hell. But, pleased to have another shot at the good life, Chanelle shrugged it off and pondered the best way to deliver the goods. Marc didn't like sexually aggressive women; he'd made that abundantly clear. And realizing that there was just a scarce few rich, handsome, albeit hot-tempered and possibly unstable single men left in her playing field, it was best to go along with his…hmmm…the only word that came to mind was *fetish*. Yeah, she'd have to start clicking off emotional switches in order to cope with his weird sex demands.

She stripped off the lingerie, tossing each piece into a fluffy red pile, and flitted over to the bed. With her entire financial future resting on her performance, she obediently stretched her shapely naked body on top of the shimmering 600-thread-count European duvet cover. Her body had never touched bed linen as luxurious as this. It was a pity her state of duress prevented her from fully enjoying its sumptuous pleasure.

Marc crossed the room and stood beside the bed. He gazed down at Chanelle, his face serious as he studied her position. With eyes filled with recrimination, he unexpectedly smacked the side of Chanelle's ass. "Spread your fuckin' legs," he ordered.

Chanelle winced, though not from pain. Marc was treating her like a common whore and she was deeply offended. The heat of indignation scorched her cheeks, but she was obligated—there was money on the line. So she indulged his crude request and ever so slightly parted her thighs.

Marc climbed on the bed to mount her. "Damn," he complained when he discovered her legs were not completely open. Using a knee, he forced her legs wide apart and muttered, "Open 'em, you fuckin' bitch."

Bitch! she shouted incredulously in her mind. Astounded by his audacity, she lay motionless wondering how she should respond to such extreme verbal abuse. And then she felt it—a warm stickiness accumulating between her legs.

With Marc's Gestapo-brand of foreplay, she should have been as dry as a desert, but instead, she was inexplicably turned on. Her pussy had betrayed her; it was sopping wet. *What the fuck was happening here?*

Squeezing her eyes closed tight while biting her lip, Chanelle tried to control the waves of pleasure that coursed though her when Marc used his thick undulating middle finger to probe her syrupy slit. "Mmm," she whimpered in defeat.

With his free hand, he grabbed a handful of her hair and forced her ear to his lips. "Are you ready for the smackdown?" He spoke in a rough whispery voice.

"No! I'm not into that freak shit. I'm not into pain," she shouted, horrified. She'd let this lunatic go too far and now she was about to get her ass whipped. Chanelle instantly raised up on her elbows; Marc's finger slipped out.

"Oh, you don't want the smackdown?" He asked slyly, as if she might miss out on a wonderful surprise.

"No, I don't!" She shrank back and wrapped her arms around herself protectively.

He examined his sticky finger. "Your wet cunt is telling me a different story." Then he looked her in the eye. "Your cunt is beggin' for the smackdown." His voice was low and sexy, diminishing some of her initial fear.

"I…uh, don't think I wanna be smacked around," she stammered, shaking her head emphatically.

Marc laughed hard, then suddenly grabbed her ankles and yanked her into a prone position, pulling her closer to him. Chanelle's eyes became huge circles of fear; she let out a small cry.

With the crook of his arms, he cradled the back of her kneecaps and forcibly spread her thighs. Sitting on his haunches, he positioned himself inside the open space between them.

"You're gonna love the smackdown," he boasted as he slowly slid the tip of his growing thickness into her secret place.

It felt so good, Chanelle ceased to breathe for a moment, and then, yearning for more, she arched her back and rotated her pelvis.

"Want some more?" His voice was hypnotic as he eased in another inch. Chanelle grimaced and writhed; her pussy screamed for more.

"You want the smackdown…don't cha, bitch?"

Both insulted and aroused by his offensive language, she heard herself shouting, "Yes!" She didn't know what to expect and no longer cared. Marc had awakened a different kind of passion and she had lost all semblance of self-respect.

At that moment, she was no longer Chanelle Lawson, a coherent, clear-thinking young woman with a personality, goals, and dreams. She had slipped into a state of consciousness where she was pure pussy—pulsating, throbbing, and ravenous.

As he drove deep inside her, Chanelle could hear her vagina making hungry slurping sounds, opening and closing at his command.

He pulled out slightly.

"Oh God, don't stop," she cried. "Feed my pussy… feed it!" she screamed and reached out to grab him—to pull him back. She wanted him buried deep inside her; she wanted the perspiration from their bodies to glue them together groin-to-groin.

Marc, however, had other plans. Changing her position, he pulled her to her hands and knees and then situated himself to mount her doggy-style. Chanelle felt like crying: her pussy had been abandoned and she wanted the dick to return.

On all fours, she thrust her butt upward, clenched her teeth and braced herself for the hard internal thrust her body craved. She felt his hands grip her shoulders; her pulse racing in anticipation. Then the head of his penis touched her slippery entrance, teasing it, and Chanelle pleaded in a hoarse voice, "Fuck me!"

In circular motions, he rubbed the head against her clit, taunting her, teasing her, making her beg. Unable to endure another second of this delicious pain, Chanelle pushed back hard and worked her vaginal muscles to capture and tightly hold the dick. A long sigh of satisfaction rushed past her lips as she clenched her muscles even tighter as if to squeeze out the very essence of his soul.

Greedy for deeper penetration, she released her hold for a nanosecond and Marc promptly wrenched himself free. Weakened from unrequited passion, Chanelle felt wobbly, but remained on her hands and knees, waiting determinedly to be pleasured from behind.

An unexpected stinging sensation took her completely off guard, causing her head to bang into the headboard. She gave him a stunned look and silently rubbed her tingling butt cheek.

"You like it rough?" Marc growled contemptuously.

Chanelle's response, a head nod and an orgasmic moan, was all she could manage as she pondered the possibility that she had absolutely lost her mind.

"Yeah, I thought so," he replied snidely. "Well, guess what? I'm gonna give it to you rough."

Burrowing her knees into the expensive bed cover, she steadied herself, preparing herself for the next blow. Marc smacked her ass hard. Chanelle jerked forward. He smacked her again. And again. She grabbed a pillow, buried her face in it to muffle her cries of passion.

Then the smacking suddenly stopped. Marc placed both hands upon her burning butt and lovingly caressed her cheeks. "Are you my good girl, Sensation?" he asked, changing his tone from gruff to sweet.

She wanted to assure him that she was indeed whatever he wanted her to be, but her voice caught; she couldn't speak.

Marc reached beneath her and cupped her firm breasts, squeezed them as he suddenly plunged into her pulsating pit of dripping hot lava. He drove hard and fast with wild abandon, knocking Chanelle off her knees.

He fucked her until she lay exhausted. Flat on her stomach, panting, arms and legs splayed, smacked down.

And through the haze of post-sexual rapture, she realized the slaps to her ass were merely love pats. His rock-hard dick had given her the real smackdown.

Chapter 26

Fate was on his side, and the occurrences of the past few days couldn't have turned out better if he'd written the script himself. Puffed up with pride after successfully overthrowing his tyrannical wife, a breakfast fit for a king was in order: pancakes, fried potatoes, eggs, bacon, grits, and buttered toast.

The sun shone brightly through the thin frilly curtains at the kitchen window as Reed rubbed his growling stomach and took inventory of the food on hand. There was so much diet shit in the refrigerator and in the cabinets; he hoped he didn't have to make a quick run to the grocery store. Delightfully surprised, he found every single item required for his feast.

Whistling as he whipped pancake batter, Reed couldn't recall ever feeling as light and free as he did today. Dayna's presence, he now realized, had been a persistent dark cloud hanging over him—suffocating him.

Stupid bitch, he thought bitterly. Dayna, with all that education, didn't have a bit of common sense. *"Reed, I want a divorce; I'll buy out your share of the property. If we handle this like mature adults, we can have this whole thing resolved in ninety days and with your share of the money from the house, I'm sure you can find a really nice place,"* she'd announced, calm and self-assured as if it were perfectly reasonable to suggest a man just up and move from his own home. But her little stunt backfired—she was out and he was in!

He shook his head, amused by the uncharacteristic violent nature his wife had displayed the other night. It wouldn't take much to get her rattled again. If he jumped out of a corner and yelled *boo*, that jittery bitch was liable to start slinging knives at him. He hoped she didn't miss because the next time she spilled a drop of his blood, her prissy ass had better be prepared to do some hard time.

But he'd cross that bridge when she returned from her thirty-day exile.

He picked up the last forkful of scrambled eggs, chewed quickly, and gulped them down. His stomach was full, but he felt a sudden gnawing irritation brought on by another kind of hunger—a hunger so ravenous it refused to be denied. However, undigested food made him feel sluggish; he didn't feel like leaving his new bachelor pad to hunt down some pussy. Not yet; maybe later.

Scooting his chair away from the table, Reed sprang up to go get a stack of pornographic DVDs that were tucked away secretly in his car—an emergency stash he relied upon when times were hard. Like now.

He came back inside the house and shuffled through

the freakish images on the DVD covers, but nothing suited his mood. Then he came across a DVD case that featured a fresh-faced young jogger, abducted and mistreated by a group of crazed sex-freaks. The sweet-faced young woman was kept on all fours and locked up in a chicken coop. Though he'd seen the film countless times, he vividly imagined the rough sex and torture scenes, which shocked and aroused him anew.

Disregarding his head injury, Reed sprinted up the stairs to grab a tube of lubricant. Smiling when he returned to the living room, he popped in the DVD, unzipped his pants, and curved his fingers into position to pacify the stiffening that had already begun.

With the remote in his other hand, Reed settled in for a few hours of undisturbed pleasure.

❧❧❧❧

By two that afternoon, Reed needed a quick fix. No more self-administered manual relief. Blasting music in his Lexus while cool air pumped from the vents, he cruised around the city, getting out of his car only occasionally to check out a strip club here and there.

But as expected, the pickings were slim on this sweltering June afternoon. Only burned-out druggies and skeezers of the worst type were traipsing about in strip joints at this hour of the day.

There was no sense in trying to seduce a regular woman. The kind who earned a regular paycheck was still at work trying to get away with doing as little as possible until she could grab her purse and jet at five o'clock on the dot.

It didn't matter because with the exception of Dayna, Reed didn't have any use for regular working women. His casual affiliations with the women on his job didn't amount to much, being that he didn't have the patience to try to persuade them to do the kinky things he liked.

Having sex with his wife had been bad enough. In fact, it became an unbearable chore. *Prissy Dayna*, he thought grimly as he shook his head. His wife couldn't fuck worth shit. He'd only married her because she seemed so eager to give him a ticket to the good life. Hell if he was going to turn down a free ride.

After their marriage, however, she'd started trying to change him, turning up her nose at everything. She no longer liked his car—an old but reliable '94 Honda. She didn't seem to mind it when they'd first met, but she didn't think the Honda looked like the type of vehicle that should be parked in the driveway of their impressive new home. So, he just sat back and let her think she was handling things. She seemed so self-satisfied and smug when she co-signed for his Lexus, like she expected him to kiss her ass for the next couple of decades. Fuck that! He didn't owe her anything. All she wanted was to use him as a sperm donor.

Fuck that stuck-up bitch, he thought with a sneer as he

turned onto Delancy Street. He figured Buttercup was probably still asleep. *Too bad; she's just gonna have to wake the fuck up.* He pushed his firm penis in a more comfortable position and got out of the car.

There was a deadly look in Reed's eyes as he approached the front door. He gave the old wooden door several hard, defiant raps. He hadn't forgotten nor did he appreciate what Buttercup's great-grandmother had made him do the last time he was there. If she knew what was good for her and if the nasty old crone liked living, she'd better stay the hell out of his face today.

He knocked and knocked but no one answered, so he kicked the old wooden door. Still, no one responded. This baffled him because he could hear the TV blaring in the living room, a clear indication that someone was home.

Confused and frustrated, Reed stepped back onto the pavement, cupped his mouth, and shouted toward an open upstairs window, "Buttercup, I mean, um...Darlene!" He alternated calling both names loud enough to awaken Buttercup, but careful to keep his voice at a volume that wouldn't alarm neighbors nearby.

Then it came to him—the idea to try the side basement door. Break the lock and sneak in. Maybe he'd creep upstairs and reenact one of the rape scenes from one of the movies he'd viewed earlier that day. It would serve her lazy ass right for sleeping the day away.

With a pocketknife, he worked on the rusty old padlock swinging from the basement door. Perspiration poured from his scalp and soaked into the bandage. The salty sweat irritated his wound and plastered his curly hair to the exposed part of his forehead. Using the fabric of his T-shirt, he wiped the sweat from his face and persisted in twisting the knife this way and that until at last the lock popped open.

He looked up and down the quiet street and decided the entire block was taking a siesta. As he entered the dank, dark basement, knocking cobwebs out of his way, he formulated a devious plan.

He'd pounce upon Buttercup's sleeping form and with his knife pressed against her throat, he'd silently warn her not to make a sound. Then, when she settled into complacency, he'd take her forcibly from behind. Ah, the thought of giving life to a mere fantasy was as intoxicating as quickly guzzling down a forty-ounce bottle of Old English.

Since Buttercup considered herself his girl, he knew she'd laugh with him afterward and playfully punch him for scaring her out of her wits.

Squinting in the dark as he stealthily made his way through the smelly basement, Reed startled himself when he bumped into the hot water heater. It rumbled in response. No sooner had he recovered from that little fright when he heard a rustling in a corner and a dreadful whiny sound.

Deathly afraid of rats, he groped around for a light switch, gave up, and frantically began waving his hands in the air searching for a chain or a string, anything that would shed some light on this awful situation. Finding nothing, he decided to leave. *Fuck it…I'm out!*

He heard more rustling sounds and then a frightened, shrill voice called out, "Who's that?" Suddenly realizing the voice belonged to Dottie, Reed let out a breath of relief.

Crazy old bitch, he muttered, and then angrily moved in her direction. *I can't believe I fucked that old bitch; it's a wonder my dick didn't fall off.* Perhaps he'd give her a sharp kick for scaring the shit out of him or grab a handful of wooly hair and give her head a good shaking.

"Dottie," Reed whispered with annoyance in his tone. He could have easily ignored her and continued with the plan he had for Buttercup, but he wanted to extract some measure of revenge. Hurting Dottie, just a little, would make him feel better about what had happened between them. After messing with her, his dick felt so dirty, he cleaned it with soap and water and then showered his jawn with an entire bottle of Listerine.

Reed kicked his foot out as he inched his way toward the area where he thought she was hiding. Then he heard a wheezing cough. He drew his leg back as far as he could and then kicked out—hard. But instead of landing a blow to a bony leg or a soft stomach, he felt something hard and metallic, then heard something fall to the floor.

Whatever he kicked drew Dottie from her hiding place. It was pitch black, but his eyes had adjusted slightly to the dark and he could see the light-colored fabric of her housedress.

Muttering and cussing, she scooted across the floor in pursuit of the rolling metallic object. Unable to catch up with it, she switched to an awkward crawl and then pounced upon it. From Dottie's unintelligible murmurs, Reed made out the words *thief* and *money*. He instantly remembered Buttercup's claim that her great-grandmother had money hidden in a coffee can.

Dottie sat on the floor hunched over, her arms wrapped tightly around her prize. Reed crept up on the old woman and crouched down. Did he dare to hope that Dottie was actually holding on to a can filled with money?

"What do you have there, Dottie?" he asked, using a gentle tone. Then he roughly tugged at her wrist and peeled away one gnarled finger at a time.

Dottie let out a yelp and twisted away.

"Make another sound and I'm going to crush your skull. Now, give me whatever you're trying to hide." Reed didn't care if he had to snap both her arms like brittle twigs— that can filled with money was his!

Overpowering the helpless old woman, Reed pried her arms apart. A short stout can tumbled out; it made a loud clatter as it again rolled across the floor. Reed stuck out a foot and stopped the rolling can. He picked it up and used it to knock Dottie upside the head hard enough to silence her annoying whimpers.

Chapter 27

Cecily invited her to share her small apartment, but not wanting to overburden her friend, Dayna turned down her offer.

Lugging suitcases and trash bags, she'd shown up unannounced on her mother's doorstep. One look at Dayna's tear-swollen eyes and her mother was forced to come out of her own depression to comfort her daughter. With her head nestled in her mother's bosom, Dayna divulged every tawdry detail of her marriage to Reed, ending with the humiliating thirty-day eviction.

Furious, Pamela Hinton eased Dayna from her chest and stood up abruptly. "I could kill him!" She spoke through clenched teeth. "I'm your mother and even if you couldn't see past his good looks and smooth demeanor, I should have immediately sensed that he was nothing more than an opportunist." Dayna's mother began pacing and wringing her hands helplessly. "Instead of protecting you, I encouraged you to marry that...that monster."

"Mom!" Dayna said sharply. Wiping tears with the back of her hand, she stood up. "Mom, it's not your fault. I was in love with Reed when I married him." Dayna paused in thought. "Or maybe I was in love with the idea of getting married. Whatever the case, there was nothing you could have done to stop me."

"But I was so wrapped up and embarrassed by my own predicament, I allowed you to marry someone you hardly knew just to keep up appearances."

Uncomprehending, Dayna tilted her head to the side.

"Being recently divorced, I felt like such a failure. But your marriage redeemed me. If my daughter was marrying such a handsome, upstanding man, then I could believe that at least I hadn't failed you." Her mother covered her face with her hands and sobbed.

Dayna bent slightly to hug her mother. "The way I've allowed your father to treat me..." Her mother's muffled voice broke off in a low whine of anguish. "I know I've been a terrible role model, sweetheart," she sobbed, shaking her head regretfully. "I'm so sorry. I'm going to do better; I promise."

"You couldn't help it, Mommy." Dayna's voice came out in the tiny voice of a six-year-old. "You miss Daddy and I miss him, too. But he left us; he moved on and we have to try to move on, too." Locked in a tight embrace, the two women silently mourned their shared loss.

Drained from the encounter with Reed and feeling too emotionally weakened to attempt polite small talk with her mother, Dayna retreated to her former bedroom in her parents' home.

❧❧❧

Two days later, Dayna lay on her back and stared at the ceiling. She sat up when she heard her mother's soft, hesitant knock on her bedroom door. "Come in."

Her mother peeked her head in. "Cecily's on the phone. Do you feel like talking?" Dayna pondered the question and decided two days of wallowing in self-pity was long enough. She nodded. Out of the corner of her eye, she saw her mother's look of relief as she entered the bedroom, handed Dayna the phone, and then quietly left the room.

"Hi, Cecily." Dayna tried to inject some sunshine into her tone.

"You stood me up the last time I invited you out, so I'm not taking no for an answer," Cecily said, sternly. "My friend Kendrick is having another art exhibit."

"When?" Dayna asked, wearily.

"Tonight at seven."

"Tonight!"

"Yes. We're going; I told you I'm not taking no for an answer."

"Okay," Dayna agreed, surprising herself. "What's the address?"

"You're kidding. Are you really gonna go?" Cecily asked, sounding surprised. Her no-nonsense tone had softened considerably.

"You said you weren't taking no for an answer. Do I

have a choice?" Dayna groused playfully. She wrote down the address and promised to meet Cecily there.

To hope that she'd actually have a good time was a big stretch for a woman with limited expectations, but getting out and mingling with people was better than lying in a single bed staring at the ceiling. It was time to practice what she preached; it was time to move on.

❧❧❧

The sun still shone brightly at seven o'clock. Black folks in all their glory filled the three-story stone house and many people were chilling in the backyard, eating barbecue and fried catfish. These people who came out to view art were as vibrant and beautiful as the oil and acrylic paintings that graced the walls on every floor.

Mesmerized by the lively and colorful setting, Dayna wasn't quite sure where to place her focus. She'd find herself enthralled by a particular painting and then quickly shift her gaze to one of the spectators whose fashionable attire demanded attention.

Garbed in a colorful array of African fabric, men and women floated through the house with the proud carriage of kings and queens. Others, dressed to impress in a range of fashions from trendy jeans to business suits, also provided interesting and pleasant visuals as they gazed at the displayed artwork.

"I don't see Kendrick," Cecily said, peering through

the crowd in the main room. "Come on; let's go get something to eat. They're grilling ribs and frying catfish in the backyard. Kendrick is probably somewhere near the food," Cecily said, laughing.

"Go ahead; I'm not hungry yet," Dayna said, easing closer to a colorful eye-catching painting of palm trees and blue-green water.

Cecily looked Dayna up and down like she couldn't believe her ears. "You're not hungry?"

"Nope."

"Okay, I'll be right back." Cecily turned to leave and then turned back abruptly. "Are you sure you don't want a plate?"

Dayna shook her head and smiled wanly. "I haven't had an appetite lately."

"I can tell. I didn't want to say anything, but honey, your slacks are sagging something terrible."

Looking down, Dayna examined the slacks. Both women burst into laughter. "I was shocked at how loose these pants had gotten," Dayna admitted. She tugged at the loose waistband of the peach linen slacks. "Do I look sloppy?" she asked, worried.

"No, you don't look sloppy; I was just playing. Look, you're swimming in those pants, but that's a good thing. There's nothing wrong with dropping a few pounds." Cecily craned her neck and squinted. "Oh, there's Kendrick; I'll be right back."

Dayna watched Cecily approach the young man she'd

met at the club in Manayunk. Dayna nodded in approval; Cecily and Kendrick looked good together.

Turning her attention back to the painting, Dayna approached the canvas slowly, reverently. It was a whimsical yet powerful piece, showing a man and a woman in a rowboat, the woman's head resting upon the man's chest. Palm trees swayed in the background. If only her life could be that peaceful. She scanned the painting as she searched for the name of the artist. AMMON 2005 was penned in the bottom right-hand corner. No last name; just Ammon. How intriguing. She wondered if Ammon were male or female. Beneath the painting was a card tacked to the wall with the painting's title: "Serenity." There was also an eight hundred dollar price tag attached. Whew!

The painting was calling her, seductively whispering her name, but she refused to respond. Homeless people such as herself did not purchase expensive art. Especially homeless people with limited funds in their savings account. She was about to get nauseous just thinking about her recent discovery of all the money Reed had been siphoning from her savings account.

Dayna forced herself to step away from the painting and move on to the next piece. Browsing, she admired more of Ammon's paintings as well as the work of several other artists, but nothing struck her quite like "Serenity."

"Oh, there you are," Cecily called. In one hand, she balanced a plastic plate that was piled high with mounds of food; she held a glass of wine in the other. She also had Kendrick in tow.

"Dayna, you remember Kendrick, don't you?" Cecily said, looking around for a place to sit and enjoy her food. She spotted a metal folding chair and pulled it over, plopped down, and started eating.

"I sure do. How are you, Kendrick? These paintings are really impressive. Are the artists here?" Dayna inquired.

"Yes…" Kendrick paused and looked around. "I just saw Ammon a few minutes ago. He's around here some-where." *Ah, so Ammon is a man*, Dayna thought and found herself even more intrigued. "The other artist, Aaron Joseph, is over there." Kendrick pointed to a light-skinned brother who was holding court near a group of his paintings. "Looks like he's mingling with prospective buyers."

"How's it going?" Cecily asked.

"Good. Real good. Ammon's work is selling like crazy."

"Has 'Serenity' been sold?" Dayna asked, sounding panicked.

Cecily gave Dayna a curious look.

"I don't think so. I'll have to check. Are you interested?"

Dayna didn't answer right away. "I'm not sure," she said, feeling foolish. She didn't want to commit to buy-ing the painting; she just wanted to know whether or not it was available.

"You haven't been upstairs yet, have you?" Cecily cut in. Dayna shook her head. "Well, you need to look at everything before you make a decision," Cecily said.

Dayna nodded, grateful to be off the hook. What was wrong with her? She needed an eight-hundred-dollar painting like she needed a hole in her head.

"Well, feel free to look around. There's plenty of food outside and drinks in the backyard and in the kitchen," Kendrick said to Dayna.

A newly arrived couple waved to Kendrick. "I'll be back soon." He bent and gave Cecily a kiss before he went to greet the couple.

"I'm cool. Handle your business," she said, blissfully content as she shoveled food into her mouth.

"Cecily! He's wonderful," Dayna said quietly. "I didn't realize you two were so…close."

"We're getting there, but you know the game. He's holding all the cards; it's his world and I'm happy to be in it. If it were up to me, our relationship would be sealed tight. We'd be married right now or at least living together, but you know how it goes. A sistah's gotta act indifferent if she expects to stay in the game."

"You're doing a damn good job; you sure had me fooled. Girl, you've got skills."

Cecily laughed, then turned serious. "Dayna, please go get something to eat. I don't think it's healthy for you to just stop eating. Don't you feel weak?"

"No, I'm fine."

"You're not fine. You haven't eaten in days and I'm afraid you're gonna collapse if you don't eat something. I'm sure they're serving food that's low calorie, low carb, or whatever it is you eat. Come to think of it, I saw a fruit and raw vegetable spread in the kitchen."

"All right, I'll go make a salad. Be right back." Dayna cast a fleeting glance at "Serenity" and then drifted toward the kitchen.

Numerous large wooden bowls containing fresh fruit and raw vegetables were lined up in a long row on the kitchen counter. There was a short line of people waiting, holding plastic plates. Dayna found a plate and stood at the end of the line. Suddenly ravenous, she hoped the wait wouldn't be too long.

When someone got in line behind her, she caught a pleasant whiff of cologne. She twisted around slightly to compliment the person wearing the scent, but she abruptly closed her parted lips when she looked up and gazed into the hazel eyes of a man with golden brown skin.

It was him! The gorgeous bartender from Carmella's. What was he doing there? She looked down at her slacks. Not only were they much too baggy, but they were wrinkled as well. Why'd she wear linen? Damn! Looking unkempt made her feel insecure. Dayna wanted to run for cover, but instead forced her lips into a polite smile.

He returned the smile. Her pulse went crazy and the room seemed to spin. She ran an uncomfortable hand down one thigh and then the other as she self-consciously tried to smooth out the wrinkled fabric. "Have we met?" he asked with a slight lift of a silky brow.

"I saw you at Carmella's but we weren't introduced."

She was amazed that her words came out in a smooth melodic flow as if talking to this man of unearthly good looks was an everyday occurrence.

"Okay, I knew you looked familiar," he said. He leaned back a little and gave her an intense look as he tried to envision her at Carmella's. Then his face lit up with recognition. "Oh yeah, I remember you!" He nodded and gave her another smile. A big smile. Was it her imagination or did he emphasize the word *you?*

"I work at Carmella's part-time. Hopefully I won't have to stay at that gig much longer," he said, shaking his head. His locks seemed to dance. "Yeah, I'm getting tired of waking up feeling like I just smoked a pack of Newports." His laughter was infectious and put Dayna somewhat at ease, but she wasn't following him. She really didn't have a clue as to why his job made him feel like he'd smoked a pack of cigarettes.

When he noticed her puzzled expression, he quickly explained, "You know… inhaling all that secondhand smoke. It gets into your lungs, your hair, your clothes."

"Oh!" she blurted a bit too loudly. "Oh," she repeated in a much softer tone. Damn, she hated the way she acted around attractive men—so nervous and ill at ease.

"What's your name?" he asked as they finally approached the salad bar.

"Dayna," she said as she picked up a pair of tongs and dug into a bowl of mixed salad greens.

"Ammon," he said softly. But the effect of those two syllables had the power of an electrical jolt.

Dayna almost dropped her plate. "You're the artist?" she said with awe.

"Yes, but not The Artist Formerly Known as Prince," Ammon said, with a burst of laughter. "I'm just a regular Joe."

Dayna smiled. "A regular Joe you're not. I saw your paintings; a regular person doesn't express his inner feelings the way you do. I fell in love with "Serenity," but I'm…uh, I couldn't purchase it because I'm between places right now and…" Her rambling trailed off and she gave an apologetic sigh.

"Hey, I'm glad you like my work," he said in a sincere voice that assured her there was no need for her to feel uneasy. "Kendrick promised a big crowd and the brother delivered. He's already setting up my next exhibit."

"That's awesome. Congratulations," Dayna gushed.

"Thank you," Ammon said, and lowered his eyes humbly. He scooped up a mound of couscous. "Want some?" When Dayna nodded, he carefully shook the grain over her salad.

His gallant behavior took her off guard, and she struggled to get the surprised look off her face. Being married to Reed for so long, Dayna had no frame of reference for this simple act of kindness from a man. Reed had been charming, but never kind. A taker, never a giver.

She gave Ammon a long look. He was about six feet tall, with the chiseled features of a Greek god. Beautiful light-brown locks touched his shoulders. He was dressed in a cotton tunic and matching loose-fitting slacks, shell jewelry adorned both wrists, and a pair of leather sandals completed his majestic look. This sensual brother was the truth. A shiver ran down Dayna's spine as she acknowledged her serious physical attraction to Ammon.

"I'm sitting outside. Care to join me?" Ammon asked after they finished filling their plates.

Dayna didn't know what to say. She couldn't just leave Cecily waiting in the other room. But on second thought, maybe she could. Cecily would certainly leave her at the drop of a hat to get her mack on. In fact, she'd done just that the night she met Kendrick. "Sure, why not?" Dayna said, nonchalantly.

Ammon held the door open for Dayna. She took a deep breath as she stepped out into the open air. Outside, Ammon pointed to two unoccupied lawn chairs. After sinking into the seats, Dayna and Ammon balanced the plastic plates on their laps. A part of her was aware of the festive atmosphere in the backyard as she picked up bits of conversations and heard the tinkling sound of laughter, but everything and everyone seemed distant, far away like props and background music. Ammon had her undivided attention. Ammon held center stage.

She was frightened by her sudden and powerful attraction to him. She was so distracted by worry; she could hardly keep up with his conversation. What would he do next? Would he ask to take her out, ask for her phone number? Or would he finish his plate, stand up, and thank her kindly for her time and be about his business?

Imagining the awkward silence that would hang between them if Ammon stood up abruptly after he finished his meal, Dayna began to chew quickly, racing to finish first. She wanted to be the one who said, "It was nice meeting you." She desperately needed to adjourn this curious encounter to protect herself from the shame of being left outside alone.

Hadn't she experienced enough shame in the last week to last a lifetime? She nodded her head in response to her silent question, picked up the half-eaten plate of salad greens from her lap, and abruptly leaned forward with the heel of her palm pressed determinedly on the wooden arm of the chair.

"You leaving?" Ammon inquired, his brow furrowed in confusion.

"Yeah, I, uh…have to check on my girlfriend; she's probably wondering what happened to me."

"Oh, excuse me. I was so concerned about losing you again; I didn't even think to ask if you were alone."

Concerned about losing me again! So, it wasn't her imagination, they truly had shared a moment at Carmella's. A moment so intense, she'd fled from his gaze and sought refuge in her car. Dayna eased against the back of the chair, relaxed her hand from escape mode, and fastened her eyes on his.

Ammon tilted his head and asked with a chuckle, "Can I get a phone number or something?" Then his voice turned serious. "I'd like to see you again."

"You'll have to give me your number; I'm staying with my mother right now and I don't…" She could have easily given him her cell phone number, but she wanted to see how he'd handle the situation. Would he offer just his cell phone number or would he give up his home number? She'd heard somewhere that a man who only gives his cell phone number is usually unavailable—a cheater. Like her no-good husband. She recalled how secretive Reed was about his cell phone; always keeping it turned off whenever she was in close range.

"No problem," Ammon said, placing his plate on the ground while he fished around in his pocket. Clipping a business card between two fingers, he said, "Here you go. You've got both my numbers…home and cell."

She felt like jumping up and down and squealing in glee, but Dayna calmly accepted the card and promised to call soon. As she quickly whisked away, she mouthed the word *yes!*

She walked as fast as she could as she wrestled with an overpowering urge to dance or skip…or hell, she might even start turning somersaults all the way from the back-yard to the main room of the big house.

Chapter 28

The old woman had squirreled away fifty-two thousand dollars! Reed had never seen so much cash in his life.

Rolls upon rolls of twenty- and fifty-dollar bills had been tightly packed and stacked in an old rusty coffee can. The top was homemade—aluminum foil folded over the rim and secured with a rubber band.

"Look at all this paper," he muttered in amazement. Tightly curled bills covered the kitchen table, and no matter how much pressure he used to smooth the money out, it stubbornly refused to unfurl.

Perspiring from excitement, he counted out the bills for the third and final time. Astounded by his good fortune, he shook his head and mopped his brow. Then, filled with a sense of smug self-satisfaction, he gave a loud whoop and raised both fists high in the air.

He wondered if there was still time to get in on that real estate action in Chester. But then again, did he really want to part with twenty thousand dollars of such hard-to-come-by cash? He scratched his head in thought and decided he'd deal with that situation when he had more time. Right now, the go-go bars were screaming his name and he could not ignore the alluring call.

Reed pulled the ironing board out of the kitchen closet, set it up and plugged in the iron. He grabbed a couple rolls and began pressing the money, attempting to give the crinkly old bills a more presentable appearance.

After showering and dressing, he decided to remove the unsightly bandage that was plastered against his forehead. He couldn't go out in public looking like he'd been victimized. In his car, he took a closer look at his injury. He pulled down the visor, looked in the mirror, and frowned at the ugly black sutures that zigzagged across his forehead. He looked like a fucking monster—like Frankenstein! Fuming, Reed closed the mirror with a heavy thud, which he emphasized with a twisted grimace that aggravated his injury and caused him tremendous pain.

At that moment, had Dayna been sitting in the passenger seat, he would have grabbed the back of her neck and banged her head into the dashboard repeatedly until he heard her brains rattle. Consumed by rage, Reed pushed hard on the gas pedal. He started to feel better and could feel his anger dissipate as he watched the odometer needle zip past one hundred.

Fifteen minutes later, he strolled into Lizzard's like he owned the place.

"Corona, with a slice of lime." He spoke to the bartender without bothering to look at his face. Reed's eyes were fastened on the stage. An Asian chick he'd never seen before who had a blanket of black hair that touched the crack of her ass was swiveling her slender hips, slicing the air with sharp, hard thrusts.

Reed was intrigued; he'd never had any Asian nookie. He made a silent declaration that tonight he would.

Reed saw the grubby hand of the bartender set down the bottle of Corona. Refusing to look at the man, Reed tossed him a slightly coiled twenty-dollar bill.

"Still looking for Sensation?" the bartender asked with a snort, demanding Reed's attention as he pushed Reed's change forward.

Reed felt wealthy and magnanimous and had planned to give the man a tip but, irked by the bartender's ignorant-ass comment, he sucked his teeth and snatched up his change like it was the last money in the world.

When the slant-eyed beauty came off stage, Reed beckoned her by waving a twenty. She floated toward him wearing a phony smile.

"Hello," she said, standing before him, wiggling her waistline. She rubbed her tiny breasts, her fingers carefully avoiding the star-shaped rhinestone pasties that covered her nipples.

"Hey whassup, little lady?" Reed inquired, still clipping the twenty-dollar bill.

"My name's Amy," she said, her lips still smiling mechanically while annoyance flickered in her narrowed eyes.

"Can I get a couch dance, Amy?" He smiled wide, proud that he could finally afford to blow money on an expensive dry fuck at Lizzard's.

She glanced over at the designated couch dancing area. "No, the room is full right now; maybe later." Her words were tinged with irritation but, anticipating Reed's money, she maintained a twitchy smile.

Though the rules of the game were not rigidly set in stone, Reed knew full well that he should pay Amy for her time. But suspecting Amy didn't want to get it on with a black man, Reed put the twenty back in his pocket and exchanged it with a one.

"What the hell is this?" Amy exploded when Reed tried to hand her a crisp dollar bill. "We don't accept dollars here!" Her eyes shot daggers at him as she recoiled in disgust. She twirled toward the bartender. "Bernie, call the manager."

"Call the manager, Miss Ching Chong!" Reed hurled the slur with a sneer "What's the manager gonna do— kick me out?" he scoffed.

"Hey, Bernie," he said, now addressing the bartender. "Save yourself some trouble, man," Reed rose from his seat. "I'm outta here!"

He took a healthy swig from the chilled bottle of Corona and slammed it down on the counter. Intent on provoking Amy further, he summoned his alter ego as he walked away, assuming the slow, impudent movements of a street hoodlum. With one shoulder hunched up while the other was dipped way down, Reed dragged his feet across the floor, exiting the premises with an arrogant thuggish glide.

It didn't matter that Amy was a bitch; she was still a sexy little chink. He didn't know if she was Chinese, Korean, or Vietnamese, but whatever her heritage, her spit-fire temperament had put him in the mood for some tight-eyed twat.

He swung his Lexus to the curb on Thirty-Eighth Street and parked illegally, trotted half a block to Spruce Street, and ran into the WaWa convenience store.

He picked up a copy of *The City Paper*, which was in a bin in the front of the store. Reed flipped to the back and perused the small block ads until he located the heading Massage Parlors. He ran a finger down the page until he spotted a photo of a young Asian woman holding an umbrella and smiling invitingly—at him!

The massage parlor was called The Song of the East, an establishment located on Bustleton Avenue, way up in the northeast section of the city.

He cut in front of a long line of WaWa customers. "Yo, buddy…you got a pen?" Reed asked the harried young cashier.

Sighing before he handed Reed the pen, the grungy-looking youth cautioned, "You gotta give it right back, man."

Reed picked up a brown paper bag from the counter, ripped off a piece, and jotted down the address. Having no further use for the newspaper, he flung it across the counter along with the pen.

Driving to the far northeast was a hell of a hike, but the opportunity to sample some Chinese snatch made the trip well worth his while.

¿¿¿¿

The Song of the East was in a strip mall. Reed pulled into a parking space in the lot. Before getting out of the car, he checked his reflection in the mirror and noticed that his stitches looked hard and dry and were jutting out every which way like jagged threads from a broken seam.

From his glove compartment, he retrieved a small container of medicated Vaseline and dabbed on a bit to soften and smooth down the stiff sutures. After snapping on the cap, satisfied that he looked more like his usual handsome self, Reed walked briskly to the place where he expected to receive some freaky sex…Chinese-style.

"You want massage?" inquired a plump Asian woman the moment Reed walked through the door.

"Yeah, how much?" He looked around, surveying the surroundings. The place was sterile, no character or personality, and no Asian ambiance.

"Fifty dolla," the woman said, holding out her hand.

"What do I get for my fifty?"

"Very nice massage," she said, smiling and nodding.

"What else do I get?" Reed asked, suspiciously.

"That up to girl. You tip her; not me."

He briefly thought about what the woman had just said and concluded that if he gave a tip, there was no doubt that he would get more than a lousy massage. Reed felt a little better, but not much. He had hoped for an erotic Asian experience, had fantasized a scene with a hot little Chinese girl walking on his back, washing his feet, and then skillfully using a set of chopsticks to feed him something exotic before the main event. To get all that, he now realized, he'd have to go somewhere like Las Vegas…or, hell, with all his dough, he could go straight to Beijing!

"So where are the girls?" He looked around, wondering where they kept their sexy little China dolls.

"Pay fifty, I show you."

It seemed like a scam; Reed was annoyed at being hustled. His first impulse was to tell the woman to fuck off, but he had driven too far for a piece of Chinese pussy to turn around and slam indignantly out the door. So he reluctantly dug in his pocket and pulled out the cash.

After he paid the woman, she led him down a narrow hallway past five or six closed doors and ushered him into an undistinguished waiting room equipped with a vending machine, a microwave, a table, and chairs. "Have seat;

I come right back," the chubby lady assured him and vanished.

The woman returned with three fairly average-looking young Asian women. "They all very nice," she said, her eyes all atwinkle.

Reed felt his disappointment wrestling with frustration. None of the women had the looks of the smiling beauty that posed in the newspaper ad, or were even as pretty as Amy for that matter. But what the hell? He'd come this far, he might as well pick one of them so he could hurry up and get his fuck on.

The young women met Reed's scrutiny with nervous smiles. They chattered anxiously amongst themselves in Chinese, Vietnamese, or whatever—gesturing and acting ill at ease. He got the distinct impression that none of the three homely broads wanted to service him.

"What's the problem?" Ticked off, Reed arched an eyebrow.

"They wanna know why scar?" The woman pointed to Reed's stitched forehead, which glistened with medicated petroleum jelly.

"Why scar?" He touched his forehead, chuckled, and said, "Oh, I had a little accident." *Why don't you mind your business, bitch!*

The older woman spoke to the Asian hookers in their language. Reed didn't know what she was saying, but she was being long-winded and basically working his nerves.

With all the cash he was carrying he could purchase some poontang anywhere. He didn't have to deal with this shit.

Reed breathed out heavily and shifted his feet. He was about to demand his money back when the woman practically shoved one of the girls in his path. The girl was a scrawny little thing, possibly the youngest of the three and definitely the worst-looking in the bunch.

"Come with me," the girl said sorrowfully and with a thick Asian accent. As she led Reed out of the waiting room, she cast a regretful last glance at her friends, and then bravely lifted her chin.

Chapter 29

The room was small and barren. No frills. There was just a massage table and a wicker shelf nailed to the wall, which was filled with numerous bottles of lotions and oils that emitted a pleasant citrus scent.

"Take off," the girl said, then looked down.

"What?" *Speak English*, he wanted to implore.

With an unhappy upturned face, she repeated the two-word request.

Reed patted his shirt and then his pants. The girl nodded. "Right back," she said sulkily, and promptly left the room.

In a flash, Reed was naked and lying on his back. He thought about the masseuse. The girl seemed so sad and unpleasant, he wondered if she was working there against her will. He'd read about the Asian mobsters who supplied a steady stream of women from China. They forced them to work for free in the network of Chinese brothels here in the States until they paid off the price of their airline ticket and the money spent for their room and board.

Yes, the girl was probably a sex slave, Reed thought, liking the idea. He reached down and stroked himself to hardness, wondering how much it cost to get his own personal Asian sex slave.

A few minutes later, the young woman returned with a towel folded across her arm. She took a look at Reed's erect member and her face scrunched up into a frown. "Wrong way," she said in a harsh voice, then gestured for him to turn over.

Reed reluctantly complied. "You got me lying on my kickstand," he said with a chuckle. "I'm not comfortable lying on my stomach." He sat up.

The masseuse didn't understand a word he said. "Half-hour massage," she replied. "Five dolla extra for hot oil," she continued as if reading from a script.

"Massage this." Reed pointed to his hardness. "No hot oil!"

The girl fled the room and returned with the matronly woman, who'd lost her twinkling smile. "What wrong?" she asked Reed, pretending not to notice his now semi-hard-on.

"How much extra for sex?"

"No sex!" the woman said sternly, and waved a finger for emphasis.

"What do you mean, no sex?" Reed asked in a calm but menacing voice. "You said if I tip the girl I could get something extra."

"Hot oil massage…you tip girl. Warm towel rubdown… you tip girl, but no sex with girl," she insisted, standing her ground.

"You said whatever happened in here was between me and the girl," Reed said, beginning a slow seethe.

"Yes." She nodded her head. "With experience girl. This new girl," she pointed to the little waif. "We break her in." The woman was now smiling but the young girl maintained a solemn expression with her head slightly bowed.

I'd like to break her in, he thought maliciously. "Well, I don't want her if she doesn't know what she's doing. Send in another girl—and make sure she can speak English."

The woman began fussing at the girl in Chinese and pinched her arm for good measure before they exited the room. The girl yelped and Reed was satisfied that she'd been sufficiently punished for causing him such aggravation.

He was also aroused, wishing the woman had allowed him the pleasure of inflicting a fair amount of pain upon the girl. He had to admit he had developed some sadistic tendencies and was finding it increasingly difficult to limit himself to ordinary sex.

A few minutes later, the door opened and the tallest of the three young women entered. "I'm Nancy," she said, smiling.

It was a strange name for a Chinese woman, probably fake like Amy, but Reed really didn't give a damn.

"No massage?" Nancy wanted to know.

"No massage," he confirmed. Then added, "No hot oil, just sex."

"Awww!" She covered her mouth and fell out laughing

like Reed had cracked a big joke. "No sex! Topless massage for extra."

A topless damn massage! "That's all you're offering?" he asked, still unconvinced that he couldn't pay for sexual intercourse.

"Hot oil massage, five dolla. Topless massage, twenty dolla. You pay extra." Nancy gave a weary smile.

Reed was tired, too. Tired of hearing the heavy accents, tired of arguing with women about sex. He jumped off the table. "I want a refund; go tell that woman to give me my money back."

"No refund," Nancy said sadly, shaking her head.

"Yes refund," Reed said, clenching his fists menacingly.

"Okay, handjob fifty more dolla. How 'bout that?"

"Blowjob," Reed suggested. "Now, how about that?"

"Too big!" She pointed at his penis and shook her head.

"You Chinese people with your broken English try to pretend like you're so innocent. But I'm not stupid." Reed paused, waiting for Nancy to protest. She didn't, her expression was blank, and so he continued. "I realized something tonight. You people are nothing but bunch of scam artists, always trying to beat a brother out of his hard-earned cash," Reed fumed as he went to his pants to extract an additional fifty dollars.

Nancy tucked the money away fast and quietly reached for one of the bottles on the wicker shelf. "Relax," she told Reed as she shook a generous amount of oil into her cupped palm.

Lightly squeezing his member, she slowly moved her hand up and down his shaft. "Ah. This is very big; very nice," she murmured. Her voice, no longer annoying, was now soothing. She increased the speed and the pressure, murmuring softly.

It was a real turn on—the foreign language and the squishy sounds made by the friction and oil. Reed's sexual tension mounted as Nancy whispered to him in Chinese. Breathing hard, Reed pumped hard into her oil-lubricated fist.

Past the point of rational restraint, he clamped his hand around the back of her neck and held it in a powerful grip.

"Suck it!" Reed insisted, applying more pressure and tightening the stranglehold on her thin neck. Under his fingers, he could feel her pulse quicken; her fear and vulnerability inciting him to cross the line that separates man from beast.

He was motivated now by the single-minded quest to find a warm moist place to deposit his sperm. He dug his nails into the Asian woman's neck and growled through clenched teeth, "Open your fuckin' mouth!"

With her throat constricted, the poor woman was unable to scream. Her fear-filled eyes bulged and wept. Unwilling to completely submit, she fought silently, twisting and thrashing, arms flailing as she tried to claw her assailant.

But when Reed's raging knuckles crashed against the side of her face, Nancy could no longer oppose the unrelenting force of the dark rigid flesh. She gagged and choked to no avail; the rock-hard shaft determinedly pushed past her lips and invaded her mouth, unstoppable until it pressed against a soft barricade of tonsils.

"Ahhh!" Reed groaned as he made his deposit—a gush of thick milky fluid that streamed down the Asian woman's throat.

＊＊＊＊

When he came to his senses, he expected the masseuse to run screaming from the room, accusing him of being a vile pillager, a rapist, scum! Reed's frantic eyes searched the barren room for something he could use as a weapon to defend himself against the three women he expected to burst through the door at any moment. He had a horrible vision of the female battalion of three, hoodied up like ninja warriors—shrieking war cries, wielding nunchakus, and hurling poisonous ninja stars.

Astonishingly, an atmosphere of calm permeated the small room. Nancy wiped her mouth with a towel and then dabbed her teary eyes. "Hundred dolla extra," she said, completely composed.

Reed gave her two hundred dollars. Hush money, just in case.

Back in his car, safe from harm, Reed started up the engine and thought about the massage parlor episode.

He couldn't control his savage behavior; he was a sex-fiend—no doubt about it. But he was perplexed by Nancy's willingness to keep it on the low. Shrugging, he supposed she was abiding by some Chinese code of honor, some antiquated need to save face. After all, how could she remain in her kinfolks' good graces after swallowing a black man's cum?

The session with Nancy was like an appetizer. His dick was still hard and he felt hornier than ever. He needed a depraved sex experience and the yearning scorched his loins. What he now required was a sex slave.

Reed wondered if he could find one on the Internet. *No, fuck that!* That kind of search could take days or even weeks. For the time being, he'd have to find a hooker from Philly. He needed someone he could connect with tonight.

Reed let out a loud guffaw. Finding a playmate should be easy enough; it was his world. His money could buy anything.

He pushed a button and music blared from the speakers. He turned a dial to put his music on blast. Feeling good, feeling powerful, Reed accelerated out of the lot.

Chapter 30

"Spirit!" The beautiful forty-something yoga instructor dramatically spoke the word while moving with the grace of a dancer. "The word *spirit* means breath." She paused, seeming to look Dayna in the eyes. "And together, spirit and breath create life." The woman was convincing. She looked strong, lean, and healthy, as if she'd never ingested anything inorganic in her entire life.

"You cannot imagine the power of proper breathing," she concluded. "Now, remember…breathe through your nose. Take a long, slow, deep breath, hold it, for ten seconds, then exhale."

A collective intake of breath sounded in the large gymnasium. Sitting on her mat, her spine erect, Dayna took a deep breath, but couldn't hold it longer than a few seconds. She wondered why a simple thing like breathing was suddenly so hard. She cut a curious eye at her mother, who sat next to her. With her eyes closed, wearing an expression of inner peace, her mom seemed to be doing just fine. Good. At least one of them was feeling peaceful.

"Maybe we should take a yoga class. We could both

benefit from the relaxation," Pamela Hinton had said the day before. Wanting to support her mother in anything that would distract her from pining for Dayna's dad (who had recently confirmed that he and his wife were expecting a baby), Dayna had agreed to take the class in the gymnasium of a local high school.

Surprisingly, Dayna's mother did not fall apart. The news that her ex-husband was starting a family seemed to give her closure and the strength to rebuild her life.

Dayna closed her eyes again. She tried to concentrate on breathing, but rapid eye-blinking became a problem. She gave up, opened her eyes, and peeked around. She noticed that everyone else in the class seemed to have the hang of it. The instructor smiled at Dayna, her eyes radiating patience and understanding.

Suddenly her cell phone squawked. Dayna was mortified; she'd thought the phone was on vibrate. Startled eyes popped open and stared at her—the peace-breaking culprit. Embarrassed, she fumbled through her bag to shut off the blasted thing, but unable to find it, she grabbed her bag and rushed out into the corridor.

"Hello," she said in a breathy whisper after she retrieved and flipped open the phone.

"Gurrrl…" It was Cecily, sounding typically exuberant as if she had the most exciting news in the world to share.

"What's up? I'm in a yoga class," Dayna whispered with a tinge of annoyance that she hoped would encourage Cecily to quickly get to the point.

"A yoga class! Stretching into those painful positions?"

"Yes, I'm with my mom. We're working on breathing right now. I'm out in the hallway, but I think I'm disturbing the class."

"Can you go outside for a second?"

"Why?"

"Gotta run something by you."

Dayna sighed, but started walking toward the exit sign. Actually, talking to Cecily was a better deal than the impossible task of deep breathing. "Okay, but make it fast. If I don't hurry back; my mom is gonna have a conniption fit."

"Okay, listen. Kendrick asked me to call you because your new friend…" Cecily paused and made the sound of a drum roll with her tongue, "Ammon Abdullah," she said with a lilt in her voice, "has been anxiously awaiting your call."

Dayna's heart did a pleasant flip at the sound of Ammon's name. His full name, Ammon Abdullah, which she was hearing for the first time, had a very nice ring to it.

"Ammon painted a mural on a wall somewhere in West Philly…"

"Uh-huh," Dayna said, indicating Cecily should continue.

"On Haverford Avenue, or was it Parkside Avenue? I forget, but anyway, his mural won an award. He's being honored by the mayor at a really glitzy affair downtown at the Bellevue Stratford. He wants to take you as his date."

Suddenly incapable of breathing, Dayna inhaled deeply

and held her breath until she felt her chest expanding. "Are you serious? He wants me to be his date?" She felt lightheaded and giddy.

"Yes! We're all going together. Me, you, Kendrick, and Ammon! Isn't that exciting?" Cecily began to scream like a teenager. Had her mother not been within earshot, trying to achieve a state of nirvana, Dayna would have broken into a happy dance and harmonized with Cecily's joyful scream.

"Now hurry up and call him so we can go shopping to pick out something fabulous to wear."

"I'm scared," Dayna whispered. "I can't remember the last time I called a man. Anyway, I gotta get back to the class."

"Gurrrl..." This time there was the hint of a threat in the word. "If you don't call that man right now." Cecily paused and chuckled. "I'm gonna drive over to that class and twist your body up like a pretzel! And I guarantee you that yoga teacher you're so eager to get back to won't be able to undo the damage."

"All right, Cecily. Tell Kendrick I'm gonna give Ammon a call in an hour."

"An hour! Come on Dayna, call the man now!"

"The class doesn't let out for another half-hour," Dayna explained. "Cecily, I have to go. I'm gonna call him at two o' clock. I promise."

After the class, parched from all that inhaling and

exhaling, Dayna and her mother bought tall Styrofoam cups of fresh carrot juice from a man who had set up a stand in the back of the gym. Sipping the juice, which was surprisingly tasty, Dayna stood in the background while her mother mingled with the other lingering participants.

Pretty and petite, Pamela Hinton had long, gray-streaked black hair. Dayna observed her mother as she interacted with people she'd just met. She felt satisfied in the knowledge that with or without the status of being the wife of prominent attorney Joshua Hinton, her mother would always be the quintessential social butterfly.

Dayna gave her mother a proud smile. She glanced down at her watch and was shocked that it was already one-forty-five. With only fifteen minutes to make the scheduled phone call, Dayna's heart did a double flip. *Should I call at two o'clock sharp or wait until about two-fifteen?* Although she didn't know the appropriateness of calling a man at the exact appointed time, she knew one thing with certainty…she wasn't going to call Ammon until she was in a private place, preferably in her own bedroom or somewhere where she could close a door.

Dayna shot an impatient look at her mother, who was now chatting with the yoga instructor and appeared oblivious to her daughter's anxious frame of mind.

Dayna finished the juice and then traipsed across the room to toss the empty Styrofoam cup. She caught her mother's eye, gave her a long anguished look, and began to wring her hands in anxiety.

Mercifully, her mother bid her new yoga friends farewell and hurried to her daughter's side. "What's wrong, honey?"

Hmmm. She hadn't prepared an excuse. "I have to go to the bathroom," she blurted, sounding like a two-year-old.

"There's a bathroom at the top of the stairs, Dayna." Her mother sounded slightly annoyed.

"I know, Mom. But I *really* have to go," she said, telling a little white lie.

"Oh!" her mother said, finally getting it. Dayna would *never* move her bowels in a public place. "Come on, Sweetie, let's get you home. I don't want you to get constipated."

Sliding in her mother's car; Dayna maintained a facial expression of extreme discomfort. To get her mother to really press down on the gas pedal, Dayna winced and rubbed her stomach. Admittedly, there were certain benefits to being the child instead of the parent.

❧❧❧

She looked at Ammon's business card. *Home phone, cell phone—which one should I call?* It was ten minutes after two and Dayna still hadn't made the call. She decided to call Cecily instead.

"Help me out."

"Out of what? Have you talked to Ammon?"

"No. I need you to call him for me."

"Why?" Cecily balked. "You're a grown woman, stop acting like a child."

"Cecily, I can't. Please do this for me. Just call him and make up some reason why I can't call him. Give him my number and tell him to call me."

"This is so pathetic. I'll do it, but I'm only doing it because I want to get dressed up and go to the ball."

"The ball! I thought we were going—"

"That's just an expression. Calm down. I don't even think there's such a thing as a ball anymore. We're invited to an event held in a hotel ballroom. Relax, Dayna. Jeez!"

Dayna exhaled and gave Cecily Ammon's number.

Then the gnawing thought that she hadn't disclosed her marital status began to bother her terribly. *He didn't ask!* she reminded herself.

The deep breathing technique she'd practiced in yoga class came in handy while she was waiting for Ammon to call. The sudden ring of her cell phone jolted her, but she said, "Hello," in a voice that was calm and clear.

"How are you, Dayna; this is Ammon."

"Hi!" she said, sounding surprised and happy.

"This is kind of embarrassing, being that it's so last minute and everything…" Ammon lapsed into silence and Dayna didn't know what to say to fill the gap. "Your friend Cecily said she told you about the award ceremony…"

"Oh yes," Dayna piped in.

"Uh, I don't usually attend those types of events, but Kendrick thinks I could use the publicity to sell more of my paintings. You know what I mean?"

Dayna nodded as if Ammon could see her. "It can't hurt," she said, unable to come up with anything clever or profound.

"So, do you think you can make it? It's next weekend, Saturday night at seven."

"Sure, I'd love to," she said sincerely. "Oh, by the way, where exactly is your mural?"

"Ah, the mural's on the corner of Forty-Sixth and Haverford." Ammon laughed self-consciously; Dayna found his modesty endearing. "It's painted on the exposed side of a multi-story apartment building. You can't miss it," he said with a chuckle.

"I can't wait to check it out."

"Thanks. So…I guess I'll see you next week."

"All right, thanks again for inviting me."

"Uh, thanks for accepting," he stammered.

Aww. Ammon seems almost as shy as I am, Dayna thought wistfully. She was surprised; he'd seemed so self-assured when they met.

"I guess I'll talk to you soon."

"Okay, bye."

The day couldn't have been more perfect. She and her mother were working through their pain together, supporting each other, becoming friends, and talking to Ammon was the icing on the cake. Dreamily, she recalled the sound of his voice, hearing him say. *I guess I'll talk to you soon.*

Maybe this thing called life wasn't so bad after all. Did she dare to hope for a happy ending? Dayna cast a glance in the mirror and smiled. For the first time in years she was truly satisfied with her reflected image.

❦❦❦

Born and raised in Mount Airy, Dayna wasn't too familiar with West Philly. Following directions she'd downloaded from Mapquest . She exited the Expressway at Thirtieth Street, then drove along Market until she reached Forty-Sixth Street, the heart of the inner city. She made a right, which would take her to Haverford Avenue.

Her breath caught the moment she made the turn. She experienced a small thrill at the sight of Ammon's work—a larger-than-life-sized mural painted on a three-story building of a black man with strong arms embracing a woman and child. It was a beautiful but heart-wrenching reminder of Dayna's most cherished dream.

Repressed emotions instantly began to bubble to the

surface. Dayna wanted to make a quick U-turn, afraid a closer look would bring on the pain and the awful yearning. But she swallowed her apprehension, bit her lip in determination and bravely continued on—though at a very slow crawl.

When she finally reached the building and parked the car, the beauty of the mural was so astounding that she quickly got out. Standing before the exposed wall with her mouth agape, Dayna was awestruck by the intricate details in the painting that were now revealed.

Cars whisked past with music blaring from open windows, horns honked, brakes squealed, screeching tires made sharp turns, laughing children passed by, the wheels of a shopping cart piled high with freshly folded laundry rattled by. These sounds of urban America sounded muted and distant as Dayna stood transfixed, interpreting the mural.

The eyes of the man in the portrait were closed as if in ecstasy; his face buried in the woman's braided hair as if intoxicated by the scent. The woman's face, the picture of pure bliss, smiled down at the child, which she held close to her breast.

The man's closed eyes spoke of a love supreme; his bulging muscles declared him the protector of this woman and child. The woman appeared to be in a state of rapture…peaceful and secure in the knowledge that she and her child were loved beyond measure. In the background was a magnificent landscape—the sun beaming brilliantly through tall leafy trees; pebbles and rocks washed by a running stream.

Nothing this extraordinary could be accomplished by man alone. Surely, God and his angels had inspired this painting.

Dayna approached the wall, taking tiny, awe-inspired steps. Kneeling on one knee, she read the caption: "Family" by AMMON 2005.

Tears streamed down Dayna's face. Her heart ached for what she'd thought she'd found in Reed. She mourned the loss of the child she would never have.

Chapter 31

"Sensation!" Hershey said with a smile in her voice. "I got another date for you."

Chanelle wasn't so sure this was good news. If Hershey was calling to tell her about a date with someone other than Marc, she might as well just hang up the phone.

Why didn't Marc ask for my number? she wondered, brooding. She couldn't understand why he insisted upon using Hershey as the middle man. Didn't he know she'd see him in a heartbeat; it didn't matter whether or not he paid the required fee?

That's right! she boasted to herself, feeling the cockiness of a dick-whipped woman who didn't give a damn what other people thought. Fuck Hershey and fuck her commission; if she could get her hands on Marc right now and if he permitted, she'd climb on him and ride him like he was a horse named Trigger, all day and all night long, absolutely for free.

Chanelle shook her head incredulously. What the hell was happening to her? As much as she loved and needed money, how could she even entertain such a crazy thought?

Maybe she was in love? If so, love was nothing like

she'd imagined. Over the course of the past three days, she'd been lying in bed with the covers pulled over her head, feeling hollow and lost and keenly aware of each hour that ticked past without a word from Marc.

"Hellooo, are you there?" Hershey asked, snapping Chanelle from her musing.

"Oh, yeah…I was just thinking about something. So tell me—whassup?" she asked, hoping to sound indifferent.

"I've got a client lined up for this evening. He's so sweet; the hour session is so easy; girl, dealing with him is a piece of cake."

Chanelle was instantly deflated, anyone who was described as being easy couldn't possibly be Marc. However, holding on to the thread of hope that the client might still be Marc, Chanelle muttered, "Uh-huh…" in a tone that came out sounding as if she were only vaguely interested at best.

"His name is Wes. If you're smart, you'll grip him up and keep him as a regular."

Overtaken by disappointment, Chanelle wanted to bang on Hershey, but reality had begun to set in.

After paying her rent, cable, and cell phone bill, she was practically broke. And embarrassingly, she'd run out like a nut and bought a pair of three-hundred-dollar sunglasses to accessorize the ensemble she was planning to put together when she went sailing with Marc on his boat. Her eyes rested on the sunglasses, gleaming on top of the fancy case. She sucked her teeth at the ever-present reminder of her stupidity.

"Your version of easy isn't necessarily the case," Chanelle said saucily. "That guy, Barry, turned out to be a real jerk. Dressing up like a damn woman…umph, umph, umph. What an asshole!"

"If I remember correctly, you liked that asshole's cheddar and his generous tip," Hershey hissed. Chanelle had forgotten about Hershey's short fuse and her sharp tongue. "Shit," Hershey continued her harangue, "I let that shit slide when I could have easily taken my money off the top before I paid you for the date you had with Marc Tarsia."

Her money! This was the second time Hershey had mentioned Barry's tip. Chanelle made a mental note to address the issue at another time. At the moment, however, she was in the throes of severe lovesickness. Just hearing Hershey speak Marc's name made Chanelle weak in the knees, while at the same time giving her an inexplicable glimmer of hope that the mention of his name would compel Hershey to start spillin'—to give up the tapes and reveal that Marc had admitted he had fallen hard for Chanelle.

But no such luck. Hershey went on jabbering about Wes. "He claims he's a doctor, but who knows, who cares. As long as he's spreading money, he can tell me anything.

He can claim to be a fuckin' brain surgeon," Hershey said, giggling.

Chanelle failed to see the humor. "Where am I supposed to meet this guy?"

"At his house; he lives in Bensalem."

"His house!"

"Yeah, it's cool. I've sent dozens of girls there. Girl, trust me…I wouldn't send you anywhere if I didn't think it was safe. But safe or not, you should still pack some heat. I mean, in the world we live in, you never know."

"What are you talking about—a gun?" Chanelle asked, clearly alarmed.

"Yeah, I'm talking about a gun. I used to carry a little .22, but not anymore. With all the money I'm handling, I stay strapped with a baby nine."

Chanelle was disgusted and decided to ignore any further mention of guns. "Where the hell is Bensalem?"

"Girl, it's way up there—way past the northeast. You gotta hop on the Roosevelt Boulevard and stay on that bitch forever. Eventually you'll end up in Bensalem."

"I don't drive and you know it," Chanelle said sullenly.

"My bad; I forgot. By the way, what's up with that?"

"I can't drive."

"Well, pay for some driving lessons; I need you to be able to get around. I already told you that ninety percent of my clients are white and in case you haven't noticed, there ain't hardly no white people left in Philly. Yeah, girl, the ones handling the real paper done hauled their asses the hell outta Philly and moved to the peaceful suburbs."

After listening to Hershey's commentary, Chanelle's thoughts ricocheted back to Marc. She wondered where he lived, but fought the compulsion to ask Hershey to give her the 411. There was no way she would play herself like that.

"Do you want to get someone else for this guy, Wes?" Broke or not, Chanelle was feeling so depressed, she doubted if she had the energy to put up with a paid date.

There was silence while Hershey thought about it. "No. Take a cab; I'll tell Wes he has to pay for your transportation."

Chanelle's shoulders sagged; she really wasn't feeling this Bensalem trick. But she'd be a fool to turn down money outright while she was so badly in need.

"Oh, be sure to pack some exercise wear—a tank top and a pair of sweats."

"Why?" Chanelle asked wearily.

"Wes is into physical fitness."

"And…"

"I guess he wants you to exercise," Hershey said sheepishly.

Chanelle sighed. "I thought you said this dude was gonna be easy."

"He is easy," Hershey said defensively. "You won't have to even work up a sweat. He'll probably want you to strike a pose while you're holding a two- or three-pound dumb-bell."

Already regretting her decision to date this pervert, and unable to think of a coherent word to express her disdain, Chanelle simply uttered, "Umph!"

"Oh yeah, Wes likes his girls to arrive on time, so why don't you order a cab now to be on the safe side," Hershey suggested.

Fuck what Wes wants. Chanelle was really starting to hate Wes. Not because of his penchant for fitness, but because he wasn't Marc.

❧❧❧

The cab ride came to sixty dollars plus a tip. *I could have rented a damn limo for this kind of money.* As Chanelle paid the cab driver, she reminded herself she'd get her money right back from Wes.

"Can you pick me up in an hour?" she asked the cab driver. Thankfully, he agreed.

The crib was cracked; Wes was really living large. He even had an indoor pool, which was where their little rendezvous would take place.

Unfortunately, Wes was a creepy little thing and none of his material possessions could change that fact. Standing at about five foot three, he looked like he weighed about a buck twenty. *A fitness fanatic, my ass!* Chanelle thought snidely. The puny little wimp didn't have an athletic bone in his body.

"There's a bathroom right down the hall if you want to change," Wes said, raising both brows double-time in a creepy, suggestive manner.

Eew! He repelled her; this had to be the worst night of her life. How could she do anything with this awful little man after being with someone like Marc?

Though she was fuming inside, she picked up her duffle bag indulgently. Careful not to swing her hips sexily, Chanelle left the pool area, striding as stiff as a soldier as she marched to the bathroom. Wes, as far as she was concerned, did not deserve a tantalizing rear-end view.

She emerged from the bathroom wearing a skintight white tank top that bared her navel and tight abs. Hip-hugging white nylon capri sweatpants and a pair of white Nikes completed her titillating athletic look. Although her appearance was wasted on the likes of Wes, Chanelle's spirits lifted when she saw her reflection. All that white fabric against her dark brown skin provided a very attractive contrast.

Her mood instantly darkened again when her eyes rested on Wes, who was swimming in the pool naked as the day he was born.

"Do ya like skinny dipping?" he called out with a twinkle in his eye, and then he did the creepy double brow lift again.

"Not really; I can't swim," Chanelle replied. She could barely disguise her revulsion.

"I'll tell you what."

Chanelle cocked her head inquiringly.

"I'll do the swimming and you do the flexing. What do you think about that?" He dove underwater and swam a while, as if to give her time to mull over his request. His tiny feet kicked and splashed water as Chanelle jumped out of the way.

Flexing? She didn't know what he was talking about and she refused to try to figure it out. The hell with the money; she didn't deserve this shit. She was a second away from picking up her cell phone to call the cab and get the hell out of this nut house.

Wes popped out of the water, causing another great splash. Chanelle rolled her eyes at him.

"Ready to do some flexing?"

"What are you talking about?"

"You know, make a muscle. Wait a second, I'll show you." Holding on to the ledge of the pool, Wes pulled himself up and hopped out. Chanelle averted her gaze from the unattractive sight, but he called out, "Look... flex like this."

The naked little man bent over and flexed a bicep like he was posing for the cover of *Muscle Magazine*. "See...I want you to flex like this," he said trying to pump up his puny bicep.

It was clearly time to leave, but she'd have to wait for the cab. She sighed. Hershey was right; she really needed her own car. Learning how to drive was now a top priority.

"Hershey said you wanted me to do some arm curls or something with a dumbbell."

"I don't know why she told you that; I don't have any dumbbells. I just want you to flex like this." He did the pose again and Chanelle wanted to throw up. On second thought, maybe she should throw Wes's dwarfed ass in the pool and drown him.

She thought about how much Hershey was paying her for this supposedly easy gig and suddenly four hundred dollars didn't seem like enough. "I can't do that, I don't know how," she protested.

"It's easy! Do just like this." He bent over to give another demonstration.

"Okay, okay. I got it. You don't have to show me again," she shouted. She could not bear to see him do it again. Feeling more than ridiculous, she balled her fist and flexed her bicep. She didn't, however, perform the pose bent at the waist like Mr. Fucking Universe.

"Not like that! You're doing it all wrong. I said.do it like this."

Sighing and flustered, Chanelle endured another demonstration from the bossy little dwarf of a man. Satisfied that he'd given a thorough demonstration, Wes stood straight up and beamed with pride.

"All right; I see what you mean, but that's gonna cost you extra."

"How much?" he asked with a forlorn expression. "None of the other girls ever asked me to pay them more."

"Look, I don't know what your deal is and I don't care, but you're gonna have to give me another bean if you want me to act like a damn bodybuilder.

"Another bean?"

"Another hundred bucks," she said with frustration. Having to decipher street jargon was annoying.

"Okay, I'll give it to you before you leave."

She folded her arms across her chest. "Sorry, I need it now."

Sloshing over the wet tiled floor, Wes, still naked, stomped out of the pool area to go get Chanelle's cash.

Looking perturbed, he returned with the money. "Here," he said in a gruff voice and handed her two fifty-dollar bills.

Chanelle folded the money and put it in her duffle bag, gave a sigh, and struck the ridiculous pose. She thought she'd sunk to an all-time low until she noticed that Wes, reclining on a lounge chair, was jerking on his dick, which had grown shockingly large.

"That's right, baby, pump it up for me," he said as his hand worked at top speed. With her hands on her hips, Chanelle stood up straight. "What the hell…"

"Don't stop…I paid you…Come on, baby. Pump it up, pump it up!" he pleaded.

Figuring there were people who'd done far worse for money, and desperately wanting to get this insanity over with, she gave in and resumed the position.

Wes ejaculated; the long stream that shot high up in the air truly resembled a geyser. It splashed down near Chanelle's feet. "Aw, man. I don't know what happened. I can usually do amazing cum shots that hit the ceiling." He pointed to several suspicious stains on the ceiling. "See? Do you see what I mean?"

༺༒༺

She opened her eyes when the cab made a left on Florence Avenue. Grateful that the driver didn't try to talk her ears off, Chanelle gave him a twenty-dollar tip.

Inside her quiet apartment, she broke down in tears. Her life was shit and she didn't know how to change it. She was so tired of being utterly alone.

Chapter 32

Too squeamish to look at the instruments of torture the doctor used to remove the sutures, Reed kept his eyes closed throughout the procedure. He didn't know which hurt worse, getting his head stitched or having the stitches removed.

"Last one," the doctor said cheerfully, his hand holding a shiny metal object of torture, coming toward Reed's head.

Reed winced. "What's the big rush, Dr. Oliver? Can I have a second to catch my breath before you start working on me again?"

"It's better to get it over with," the doctor explained patiently.

"Better for whom? Me or you?"

"You, of course," said Dr. Oliver with a chuckle.

"You just finished yanking out a stitch. Now, give me a break...my head is killing me. Shouldn't you have given me something for the pain?"

"I'll give you something after the procedure, okay?"

"I hope it's a lot stronger than those baby aspirins I got at the emergency room."

"What were you prescribed?"

"Motrin," Reed said in a huff.

"I'll write a prescription for Percoset, but be careful. No driving or operating heavy equipment."

Whatever! Reed thought and rolled his eyes. The doctor had moved behind him, seeing only the back of Reed's head as it bobbed up and down in understanding. Dr. Oliver had no way of knowing that Reed held him in contempt.

"Okay, here we go. Think of something pleasant. You're only going to feel a little pinch."

"Look, I'm not in any shape to go back to work..."

"All right; I'll write a note for you to go back to work... let's see...how about in two weeks?"

That sounded good to Reed.

"Okay...ready?"

Reed closed his eyes and scrunched up his face, bracing himself for what felt to him like unendurable pain. "Ow," he yelled. His hand flew up to his forehead, covering it protectively, and remained in that position throughout the drive to the pharmacy and during the entire ride home.

At home he took a Motrin. He'd take a Percoset late at night when he was ready for bed. Right now, he had important business to attend to and needed to be fully alert.

He uncurled the *City Paper* that was left behind in the physician's waiting room. He quickly turned the pages, eager to get to the back, and quickly found what he was looking for. There were more than a dozen ads placed by women who were looking for a dominant man. He perused the selections and finally made a choice: "Submissive young woman desires to be enslaved." There was an immediate hardening inside Reed's pants. He caressed it—stroked it. He tried to console it, but it became harder and lengthened considerably. The hardness demanded special attention and would not calm down until Reed unzipped his pants and set it free.

His dick was in his left hand; with his right hand he pressed the numbers and excitedly listened to the phone ring.

"Greetings, Master," said a sweet-sounding female.

"Uh. I'm calling about the ad…uh…the one in *The City Paper*."

"Yes, Master. How can I serve you?"

Damn, this was the shit! And it was turning him on. He felt like he was gonna bust a nut while merely talking on the phone.

"Well, I wanted to get together. Is that possible today?"

The woman giggled. "Forgive me laughing. It's just that I'm so honored that you'll be spending time with me today. I can hardly wait to sit at your feet."

"What's your name?" Reed asked.

"My name is Patience," the woman said. "But you can call me whatever you like. Personally, I like to be called slut…bitch or slave. But it's not my place to choose."

"Stop it," he said in a gruff whisper as he unconsciously

stroked his dick. "You're going to have to stop talking like this…you've got my man down here all upset…" He paused and looked down, fondled his penis, and wiped away the pre-cum with his thumb. "I wish you could see what you're doing to me; my man is about to explode." His tone was husky and so lustful, he hardly recognized the voice as his own.

"You're making me blush, Master," Patience said with a giggle. "Would you mind getting a pen to jot down my address?"

After carefully writing down the woman's address, Reed asked, "How much do you charge for this?"

"Oh, I don't charge; I enjoy being submissive. I do, however, accept contributions… you know…to pay the rent."

"Cool, I can contribute something."

"Is ten o'clock tonight okay?" she asked sweetly.

He wanted to see her as soon as possible, but thought it best not to impose his will just yet. "Sure, ten o'clock is cool."

Reed couldn't get over how sweet she sounded; her tone was filled with such a willingness to comply. He felt he'd finally found the kind of woman he really needed. Had he not been experiencing residual pain in his forehead, he would have excitedly leaped into a back flip.

Most pressing at the moment, however, was the need to relieve himself. Reed pounded up the stairs, eager to get his private party started. He grabbed his special bottle of baby oil from the dresser in the bedroom. This lubricant was used for one purpose only—to assist in self-administered manual release.

This time he didn't require an X-rated video to help him along. He needed only to think about his new playmate, his sex slave. The movement of his oil-slick fist became slower as he looked up in thought. *What should I call her?* The name Patience didn't suit him; it sounded too prim—too old-fashioned. Settling for one of the choices she provided, Reed decided to call her Slut.

His hand moved fast and furiously; a hot sensation rushed through his loins.

"Ahhh," he roared as he climaxed, then collapsed across the bed.

Depleted of strength, he curled up to take a nap. He'd need rest to rejuvenate his semen supply; he had big plans for later in the evening. He planned to fuck Slut until she cried.

❧❧❧

Patience came to the door wearing a short frilly two-piece white set. She had almond-shaped brown eyes and cascading auburn hair.

"Greetings, Master. Welcome to my home," she said breathlessly, and politely bowed her head.

Patience had the face of an angel; she looked soft and tender—vulnerable. She gave off virginal vibes, and was the perfect example of the kind of woman Reed yearned to defile.

This is the shit! he thought excitedly as he appraised her through eyes that had narrowed into lustful slits.

Patience beckoned Reed to come inside. The living room was also frilly and feminine, with oodles of fluffy and fringed throw pillows. There was also an unsettling collection of what seemed like dozens of life-like dolls. The dolls representing various nationalities, were all dressed to the nines. They sat atop miniature wicker chairs, straddled tiny bicycles, carried picnic baskets, lay in cradles…Reed thought it was entirely too, too much.

"Mind if we do this in the bedroom?" His tone annoyed him; it was a tad too sweet. He should have barked out an order and walked her to the bedroom on a leash.

A leash! Agitated, he rubbed the scar on his forehead. He didn't have any kind of equipment; nothing to intimidate a sex slave into cowering obedience, nothing that would instill fear. He'd have to brush up on the subject and start collecting the objects he needed to dispense both pleasure and pain.

"Certainly, Master. The bedroom is upstairs, first door on the right. Make yourself comfortable, I'll join you right away. But first…" Patience blushed and lowered her eyes. "Forgive me if I seem impudent, but I would be remiss if I didn't inform you that the contributions start at two-fifty." Her fingers brushed her lips in a demur manner; her lashes fluttered bashfully.

"That's not a problem," Reed said and really meant it. He dug deep and gave her an extra fifty. Her soft voice and the way she spoke—so proper, so respectful—were enough to drive him mad. The three hundred dollars he gave her was just a drop in the bucket. He would have paid any price to demean and violate such a pretty little fragile thing. Just the thought of debasing her made the blood rush to his head.

Pulling open a pair of sliding double doors, she excused herself and motioned to the stairs. "I'll be with you in just a second, Master."

This shit is serious, Reed thought as he climbed the stairs. Every sexual act he'd ever engaged in was nothing more than foreplay. Being lord and master without apology was the lifestyle he deserved; it was the life he was destined to live.

Filled with a sense of self-importance, Reed opened the door to the bedroom. More beady-eyed dolls stared at him.

Reed frowned and sighed and determined he was going to have to put his foot down for sure. *Slut is gonna have to get a grip! She's gonna have to get rid of all these dumb-ass dolls and all this childish bullshit!*

Patience appeared in the doorway, a vision of virginal

purity. She smiled at Reed and inquired in her breathy whisper, "Master, should I crawl to you?"

Her words made his pulse race. He felt his manhood stiffen and throb and to his horror, he exploded in his pants.

He never dreamed it would happen this way, but there was something in the way she looked at him—so eager and willing to please. She offered everything he'd ever hoped for, but her gift was more than he could handle. He was just a novice, he realized now, and all this was too much, way too soon.

Embarrassed, he apologized profusely and rushed to the bathroom to clean up the mess. With a damp washcloth he rubbed the front of his semen-smeared boxers, and then wiped the thick gooey substance that trailed down his thigh.

Startled by two soft knocks on the bathroom door, Reed splashed water on the front of his pants. "May I assist you, Master?" Patience asked. There was pity in her tone.

Her pity angered Reed. "No!" he bellowed. "I don't need your help." In his mind, the accident was all her fault for talking so much shit and deliberately making him cum.

He yanked open the door and nudged her out of his way. She was lucky he didn't break her neck or throw her down the stairs. He ran down the stairs with the fretful love slave close on his heels.

"Do you want to try it again—in a day or so, perhaps?" she inquired anxiously.

Unwilling to commit, unable to trust he could perform as a true master, Reed shook his head. "I don't know; I'll have to get back with you. I'll give you a call."

Before he left, the telephone jangled. Patience picked it up. "Speak," she commanded. Her voice was suddenly rough and strong. "This is Mistress Veronique. State your name, slave!"

Reacting to her harsh tone, Reed stared at Patience with his mouth hanging open. Amazingly, she had transformed from a docile sex slave into a dominatrix before his very eyes.

She covered the mouthpiece and turned to Reed. Reverting back to a sugar-coated whisper, she said, "Farewell, Master; I'll be anticipating your call."

Then Patience removed her hand from the mouthpiece, gave Reed a faint, fleeting smile. She fluttered a farewell with her fingers and turned back around and resumed the persona of Mistress Veronique as she began barking into the phone.

Reed trudged solemnly to his car. His listless hand searched his pocket for his keys. He looked down at the dark wet circle on the front of his pants. It was a soggy reminder that he had been played.

Chapter 33

"Cecily," Dayna called from inside the dressing room. "Can you zip me up?"

Cecily squeezed into the tiny room and tugged on the zipper. The two friends scrutinized Dayna's image in the magnified mirror. Cecily frowned. "I don't like the fit; it's too big."

Dayna pressed her lips together, attempting to suppress a big smile. "Look," she said, reaching over her shoulder to display the tag that dangled at the back of the dress.

Cecily stepped behind Dayna, pulled out the tag, and gave it a suspicious look. "Oh, my God," she squealed. "It's a size twelve!"

"I know...I think I need a smaller size. I may need a ten," Dayna said, sounding shocked. She and Cecily shared a look.

"A ten!" Cecily echoed, astonished. "You've slimmed down to a size ten?"

"We'll soon find out," Dayna replied.

Cecily dashed out of the dressing room and was back a few moments later. "This was the only size ten left on the rack," she announced, happily waving the dress, a whimsical dusty-rose-colored sequined sheath.

Dayna pulled the dress over her head and when it fell over her hips without requiring even a light tug, she flashed Cecily a sly grin. "Zip me up," she demanded gaily.

Cecily zipped the dressed and stood back, cradling her chin thoughtfully. "It's perfect. And you are truly wearing that dress," Cecily complimented her, and gave Dayna a quick hug.

Dayna spun around, gazing approvingly at herself in the mirror. "I can't take any credit for this weight loss. I guess Reed is good for something." She gave a wry chuckle.

"Have you talked to him?" Cecily's expression turned serious. "Have you made a decision...you know...about the house?"

Dayna took off the dress and carefully placed it on the satiny hanger. "I don't know," she said with a sigh. "I've been doing some thinking and this may sound strange, but I might let him have it. I don't have the energy to fight over that house."

"What are you saying? Reed can't even afford to pay the mortgage."

"It doesn't matter. You don't know him like I do. He'll never allow me to live there peacefully, so I'm just going to walk away. He can have it."

"Are you sure you want to start all over? You love your house; Reed doesn't deserve to have it. You've paid the mortgage all these years and *your* father paid the down payment on the house."

"Girl, you're preaching to the choir." Dayna shook her head and then her expression brightened. "Hey, it's okay," she said with a consoling pat to Cecily's back. "Look, I spent three years in a loveless marriage and managed to maintain my sanity; I survived. My goal is to find inner peace, to be at peace with myself. Right now, I'm focused on getting out of this marriage. I want a quick and pain-free divorce. No squabbling over property. A no-fault, uncontested divorce only takes ninety days."

"Hmm. You're probably right. What do I know; I've never been married. Still, I just can't imagine giving up everything so easily."

"*Things* come and go, Cecily. Living with Reed was killing my spirit. I'm finding more joy living in my former bedroom than I ever had while living with him in that big, unhappy house," Dayna said defensively.

"You have a point," Cecily conceded. "And looking on the bright side, all your trouble with Reed led you straight to Ammon."

Dayna grinned, then giggled. Cecily was relieved that the somber mood had lifted.

The two friends fell in line and then paid for their purchases. "I meant to tell you that I saw Ammon's mural."

"Really?"

"Uh-huh, I drove to West Philly to see it a few days ago. It's on the corner of Forty-Sixth and Haverford."

"You're so sneaky," Cecily teased. "You saw the mural and didn't say a word?"

"I got so emotional after seeing it, I needed a little time to recover."

Cecily's eyes shot up heavenward.

"Seriously, Cecily. The brother is really deep. I was moved to tears. His mural is the most beautiful painting I've ever seen. He painted a portrait of the life I've been dreaming of…a man, a woman, and their *baby*." Dayna's voice cracked; her eyes glistened with emotion.

Cecily nodded, feeling her pain. "Kendrick constantly sings Ammon's praises. He says he's a genius and he's certain that Ammon is going to take the art world by storm."

"I don't doubt it." Dayna's mind drifted off in thoughts of Reed. She hoped he would allow her to move on gracefully, peacefully.

Respecting Dayna's mood, which seemed close to morose but was actually pensive, Cecily didn't attempt to be chatty or funny. She simply walked in silence beside her friend. Outside in the parking lot, they gave each other air kisses, got in their cars, honked their horns, and drove their separate ways.

⋅⋅⋅

Several hours later as Dayna prepared for bed, her cell

phone rang. Ammon's name flashed, sending a flood of emotions through her ranging from joyful panic to fearful dread. Suppose he was calling to break their date! Since she was already perplexed by his interest in her, she wouldn't have been a bit surprised.

Bravely, she flipped open the phone and prepared herself for the blow.

"I was thinking about you," he said. "I hope I'm not calling too late."

The comfort of his voice was palpable; her hand pressed against her thumping heart. "Not at all; it's nice to hear from you." There was a lull and, remembering that Ammon acted bashful when talking on the phone, Dayna filled the gap with light banter. "It's getting close to your big day. Nervous?"

"Not at all. But I'm sure I'll be nervous around you."

Whoa! What was she supposed to say in response to that? At a loss for words, she cleared her throat.

"I get embarrassed when I think about how I talked you to death over at Kendrick's place—at the exhibit."

"No, you didn't," she assured him.

"Well, when you consider the way you jumped up all of a sudden and ran back inside…what's a brother supposed to think?" Ammon gave a good-natured chuckle.

"No, I found you fascinating. You have to forgive me." She paused, and then said teasingly, "I was in the presence of a talented and handsome man. I momentarily lost my head and became socially inept. Do you accept my apology?" she asked playfully. When was the last time she'd been playful with a man? She couldn't recall; it had to have been eons ago!

She sat curled in her bed with her head propped with three fluffed pillows. Hit by a sudden realization that all was well in her world, Dayna beamed with self-satisfaction.

"I saw your mural, "Family." There was reverence in her tone. "Ammon, I stood in front of your painting, transfixed. It took my breath away."

"Thank you." He did that bashful chuckle that he seemed to do when the spotlight shined on him too brightly.

"You're so talented," she gushed. "It's no wonder you're being honored by the mayor."

"That's enough. You should see me. I've got this big cheesy grin on my face; my cheeks are actually starting to hurt."

Dayna laughed. "Okay, I'll stop, but I want you to know…I'm really proud of you."

"I'm not the only artist being honored, you know. Several others are receiving awards," Ammon said, trying to temper her enthusiasm. "Do you know how many murals there are in Philadelphia?"

She didn't.

"Twenty-four hundred. Philadelphia is called the City of Murals," Ammon said with pride.

"Wow. Now, that's something I can talk about in class."

"Oh, yeah. Right. Your students could learn a lot by taking the tour."

"What tour?"

"The mural tour. You've seen those historic trolleys?"

"Uh-huh."

"The Mural Arts Program provides a tour of the city's murals and they use those old historic trolleys."

"Interesting. I'd love to take my students, but school's going to be closing soon for summer vacation. I won't be able to take them on the tour until the next school year."

"If you'd like to check it out personally, you know, to see what's in store for your students, I'd love to take you. Would you like to go?"

Dayna didn't hesitate. "Of course."

"How about next week. How's Wednesday around five?"

"Wednesday works fine for me."

"I'd love to say I'll pick you up, but I don't think you'd enjoy riding on the back of a bike."

"A motorcycle?" Dayna was scared to death of those things.

"No, a regular bike."

"You're full of surprises, aren't you?"

"No, that's just me—a nonconformist, I guess you could say. Well, I'm gonna let you go. Sweet dreams."

"Goodnight, Ammon." Dayna smiled as she clicked off. She closed her eyes dreamily. It was hard to believe that she'd been invited on not one, but *two* dates with a handsome, talented, wonderful, extraordinary man.

Chapter 34

Chanelle had a taste for her favorite food—mushroom cheese steak. In her opinion, Larry's on Fifty-Fourth Street and City Avenue had the best cheese steaks in the city. She didn't live in the vicinity of the deli, but she hoped to sweet-talk whoever picked up the phone into making a delivery to her neighborhood.

A man with a foreign accent, Greek perhaps, told her they didn't make deliveries anywhere. "Pick-up only," he said. Damn; she'd have to take a cab.

In the backseat of the cab she fretted over bumping into Malik. Larry's Deli was a favorite spot of members of the Seventy-Sixers. Knowing Malik, he had probably given up on hustlin'. Yeah, he was probably right back with his cousin—kissing up and enjoying the good life.

Chanelle jumped out of the cab and darted in the restaurant. No sign of Malik or any members of the basketball team. Good. She was out of Malik's good graces and she supposed the team members would have felt obligated to ignore her, which would have stung. Her feelings were too close to the surface right now to endure being snubbed.

Her food, hot and steamy and packed nicely, was waiting for her at the counter. Not having to wait pleased her; however, she was slightly miffed at having to shell out twenty-five dollars for the cost of a cab ride to the restaurant and back. She definitely had to start the process of getting her driver's license very soon.

At home, she spread out her feast, which consisted of a large mushroom cheese steak, a double order of cheese fries, a Mountain Dew soda, and a pack of Tasty Kake Krimpets. At eighteen years old with a youthful, revved-up metabolism, greasy foods had no effect on her twenty-two-inch waistline.

The food was supposed to make her happy, but it didn't. Throughout the meal, which she merely picked at, Chanelle couldn't shake her gloomy mood. She gave up, wrapped up the cheese steak and fries, put them in the microwave to eat later, and turned hopefully to the Krimpets. After just a single bite, she tossed the pack in the trash.

Nothing was working. Food wasn't the remedy. She wanted Marc; she wanted to get the "smackdown."

Brashly, she picked up the phone and called Hershey. She didn't beat around the bush. "Hershey," she said in a serious voice, "do you have a number for Marc Tarsia?"

Hershey snorted. "Why do you want *my* client's number? You know I don't roll like that."

"It's sort of an emergency. I left something important

in his room." Chanelle frowned; she should have prepared a better lie. She held her breath, waiting to see if Hershey would buy it.

"Is that so," Hershey replied in a distrustful tone.

Chanelle really disliked Hershey sometimes. Hell, she couldn't stand her most of the time.

"Are you gonna give me his number or not?" Chanelle asked snippily.

"Let me give you some advice. Don't get your heart involved with a trick, because—"

"Who said my heart was involved?" Chanelle protested a bit too loudly. "I just want the number so I can—"

"I didn't just get in this game. I've been around for a minute and like I told you before, you'd have to get up pretty early in the morning to chump my ass, so girl, don't even try it. Now, I know Marc looks good, he's loaded, and he's slinging some good-ass dick…"

How does she know about the dick? Chanelle wondered, alarmed.

"But girl, take it from me. You don't wanna get emotionally attached to a trick. Your role is to get their money and get them hooked on *you* so they'll wanna keep on spending. You're not supposed to start huntin' their asses down. Dayum, girl, what's your problem? What are you trying to do? Give away a shot of pussy for free?"

Hershey was throwing slurs right and left, but Chanelle

did not feel a bit of shame because Hershey had it all wrong. Chanelle didn't view Marc as a trick; a trick was someone disgusting like Wes.

Chanelle was mute. So Hershey continued to lay it on her thick. "I knew you were green but since you'd been strippin' for a minute, well, I figured I didn't have to give you any life lessons. Now, I'm gonna tell you something that might help you get your head back on straight." She paused and Chanelle's ears perked with interest.

"I was going to hook you up with a bachelor party Friday night. It pays a thousand dollars for the night."

Chanelle felt instantly deflated. She thought Hershey was going to provide some pertinent information regarding Marc.

"The party's being hosted by one of Marc's friends." Hershey paused for emphasis.

Marc! With renewed interest, Chanelle murmured, "Okay…"

"The party's being held on Marc's boat and Marc's the guest of honor. He's getting married Saturday."

Chanelle gasped.

"I take it you're not interested in working the bachelor party?" Hershey didn't have any of her usual sarcasm in her tone. Frankly, she sounded like she felt sorry for Chanelle. And rightly so, because Chanelle was trembling so badly, she dropped the phone and slumped into a kitchen chair.

She could hear Hershey's concerned voice. "Are you

all right?" She definitely was not all right. Dazed, she hung up the phone and began to drift aimlessly from room to room.

Chanelle suddenly reached the sad conclusion that she and Marc had shared sexual chemistry and nothing more. During her adolescence, she'd escaped the normal love affairs experienced by most girls as early as middle school. Those great love affairs that inevitably turned to heartbreak had put calluses around their hearts as protection against future heartbreak. Chanelle's inexperience had caused her to mistake great sex for true love.

Wracking sobs hurt her chest, but the tears she cried were cleansing. She realized she'd had enough. No more tricking and no more stripping.

She wiped her eyes and vowed to get a real job, start a new life and find herself a regular man. No more dealing with men who couldn't see past her body.

Since losing her mother, Chanelle had been utterly alone. There was nothing to tie her to Philly? Perhaps she should move somewhere far away; somewhere where she didn't run the risk of bumping into any of her former customers from the strip clubs or the men who could certainly point a finger at her, identifying her as a whore.

That sordid secret would go with her to her grave. Yeah, she was going to get the hell out of Philly. Hopefully she'd meet someone nice—a regular working guy— get married, and start a family of her own.

Chapter 35

The man approached while Reed was in his driveway washing his car.

"Hey man, how ya doin'?" The pleasant-looking man, who mopped his perspiring bald head with a white towel that had been draped around his neck as if part of his summer wardrobe, looked to be around Reed's age. There was friendly laughter in his voice.

Taken off-guard, Reed spun around. He didn't recognize the man, who beamed as if he expected Reed to drop the hose he held and embrace him.

"Aw, don't tell me you forgot me, man." He had a twinkle of knowing in his eyes.

Squinting, Reed tried to place him.

"I'm Bo!" The man extended his hand.

"Bo?" Reed questioned as he gave the stranger a limp handshake.

"I'm Bo Miller…Chris Miller's cousin. You're Reed Reynolds, right?"

"Yeah, I'm Reed Reynolds, but I don't remember meeting any of Chris's—"

"Chris wanted me to bring you these papers," Bo

interrupted, and snapped open his briefcase. "He wants you to look this paperwork over. You know, concerning the real estate deal he's working on in Chester."

"Yeah, right, right," Reed said dully. His interest in the deal had diminished to nonexistent.

"You mind?" Bo asked, setting his metal briefcase on the back of Reed's car.

Reed minded a great deal, but didn't say a word. He didn't want to slight Chris's cousin because Chris was wealthy and had connections. There was the possibility that Reed might need a favor one day. Still he chastised himself for not letting Chris know he wasn't going to participate in the real estate venture.

Giving Chris money that he had charmed out of Dayna's pop was one thing, but things had changed and there wasn't a chance in hell he was going to give the dude *his* money. What kind of fool would invest his own money in something that wouldn't start turning a profit for years to come?

He glanced at Chris's cousin and was seriously annoyed. The man was flipping through papers as if he was searching for something really important like the deed to a mansion in Palm Springs or Beverly Hills. Reed fought the urge to spray the interloper with the hose he held in his hand. Why didn't this asshole hurry up and be on his way?

"Here you go, Reed." Bo said, smiling even more

broadly. He stuck out his hand as if to solidify an important deal.

Reed shook his head. If the fool only knew how fast those papers were going to be thrown in the trash, he could conserve some energy and forgo the handshake.

Reed accepted the thick envelope but didn't give it even a cursory glance. Just to get rid of him, Reed forced a smile and shook the man's hand. "Good looking out, brother. Thanks for taking the time to bring these papers by."

"Damn, I almost forgot," said Bo, patting his pants pocket. Reed couldn't contain a huge sigh.

"Smile, man," Bo said suddenly, snapping a picture with a camera that seemed to have materialized out of thin air. He quickly secured the camera in the briefcase, gave it a snap, and turned the lock. "You've been served; that's a divorce petition. Your wife wanted me to tell you she'd see you in court." Bo turned away, doubling over in laughter. Damn, he loved the work he did! Being the sort of man he was, fun loving and a real practical joker, Bo got a big kick out of witnessing the shocked and stricken expressions of those whom he duped into thinking he came as a friend.

Too bad Reed didn't have a camera handy when he turned up the water pressure and sprayed Bo with the hose. Getting a picture of Bo haul-assing it to his car would have given Reed a small measure of satisfaction. However, a photograph of Dayna with a bullet hole in her head would make him giddy with excitement. In fact, he'd be overjoyed.

Leaving his car half-clean, he jabbed the numbers to his wife's cell phone. When she answered, he launched into a thundering, incoherent tirade, which ended with "This is my house, too; you can't put me the fuck out!"

"Did you look over the papers?" she asked with a calm voice usually reserved for use when one finds oneself in the unfortunate position of having to talk some sense into a raving lunatic.

"I don't have to read them; I know what you're trying to do. You're a violent person. The court ordered you to vacate the house and you can't deal with it. Being homeless is humiliating and you want to take your revenge out on me."

"That's not true."

"Sure it is. But let me tell you something, Dayna," Reed said ominously. "I'm not going anywhere. The last time I looked, my name was on the deed, too. I don't want to hear a long conversation about how you pay the lion's share of everything around here. Because all that's changed now. Baby, I don't need you; I can hold my own." He laughed maliciously.

"Good for you, Reed. I'm glad to hear that because I won't be making any more mortgage payments."

"Yeah, I knew that was coming and I'm one step ahead of you."

"Oh, really?"

"Yeah, really."

"That's good news."

"For whom?"

"For you."

Suspicious that Dayna had a trick up her sleeve, Reed became quiet.

"If you look over the papers, you'll see that I don't want anything. I just want to move on," she explained. "Being that property is involved, my attorney advised me of several options. We can simply sell the house and split the proceeds or we can determine the equity value, subtract any outstanding mortgage from the market value of the home, and split the remaining value."

"Your lawyer's talking shit. We have a thirty-year mortgage. What kind of equity do you think we have?"

"Not much, that's why I suggested a no-fault divorce. We won't have to worry about a property settlement. Sign the papers and we'll be free of each other in three months."

"I'm not signing shit. You fucked up this marriage."

"Fine. Whatever!" Dayna said, exasperated. "If you don't sign the papers, this divorce could drag on for two years or more."

"Let it drag. And now that I know where you stand, don't expect me to act like a married man when that court order's lifted and they let you come back home. You want a divorce? You want to be single again? Yeah, all right, I'm going to show you how a single man behaves."

"You've shown me how a single man acts for three years. And I'm not coming back. I don't plan to ever come anywhere near you or that house again." Dayna hung up.

Absence had definitely not made his heart grow fonder. Reed hated Dayna as much as always, and with all this divorce talk, it was possible he hated her even more. He ripped open the envelope, but nothing made sense; it was all legal gibberish. Oh well, she said she wasn't coming back, that he could have the house. So be it.

He looked around the spacious home, delighted that it was now his and his alone. He thrilled at the thought of never having to see Dayna again or hear her complaining, whining, nagging voice.

Aside from that slip-up with that phony submissive, Reed was on a winning streak. Life was throwing him fastballs and he was hitting nothing but home runs.

There was one thing, however, that disturbed him... the mortgage payment. Paying that crazy-high monthly note would put a big dent in his new windfall. He hadn't intended to use that money for bills; it was his personal stash to be used strictly for self-indulgent pleasure.

Muttering obscenities, directed at Dayna, Reed stamped to the kitchen. With his arm held high in the air, he leaned back, aimed, and then dunk shot the divorce papers straight into the waste can.

A pile of unpaid bills lay on the countertop. Bills that he assumed would soon be paid by his wife. Some, he noticed, were enclosed in attention-demanding pink envelopes. Reed supposed it couldn't hurt to take a look at what he was up against, so reluctantly he picked the bills up. There was a bill for everything: mortgage, gas, electric, cable, water, alarm system, home phone, cell phone, credit cards, car insurance, and a bill for his student loan. It was mind-boggling; he'd never paid for anything except his car insurance and monthly car note. Anxiously, he bit his lip, wondering what he was going to do, now that it appeared Dayna would no longer be paying the household bills.

Then he had a thought. Perhaps it was just wishful thinking but if memory served him correctly, didn't Buttercup say her grandmother had money stashed away in *two* coffee cans?

It was early in the day, Buttercup was probably still sleeping and old Dottie…well, he hoped for her sake she was having a lucid day. If she didn't point him in the direction of that other coffee can, he was going to snap her scrawny neck!

ﻪ

Reed's eyes nearly popped out of his head. The house was boarded up and appeared abandoned. "What the hell?" he mumbled as he got out of his car. Hurriedly, he approached the house, scratching his head.

Unlike the last time he was there, when he was quiet

and his movements around the property had been stealthy, he banged loudly on the boarded door, demanding that someone let him in. They had to be in there, where else would they go? The hell with Buttercup; hopefully, Dottie was inside refusing to come out.

"Who ya lookin' for?" A woman called from an open window next door.

"I'm looking for Darlene," he said, using a professional tone.

"Gimme a minute; I'll be right down." In a matter of seconds, the woman came barreling down the stairs and was outside on her stoop. "You're Darlene's friend, ain't you? I know I saw that car before." There was suspicion in her voice, or at least it sounded that way to Reed.

"I wouldn't refer to myself as a friend. Darlene has an addiction and I'm one of her counselors." The lie rolled off his tongue with such ease, he amazed himself.

"Her drug counselor, huh. Well, you shoulda kept up with her more better. That girl done got locked up for prostitutin'. You know she was only doing all that nasty stuff so she could go out and buy herself some drugs."

Reed lowered his head and shook it regretfully. He raised his head suddenly and asked in a voice that sounded eager to hear good news, "What happened to her great-grandmother?"

The neighbor closed her eyes and shook her head in sorrow.

Reed furrowed his brow, his voice oozed with concern. "Is she dead?"

The woman shook her head. "No, she ain't dead, but poor Dottie was in there all by herself for two or three days or more. Ain't nobody knew nothing about it, though. If we did, we sure would have helped her. I guess she just went crazy from hunger because she came outside and started digging around in all the trash cans. Right here on Delancy Street! Eating garbage out of the cans!" The woman scrunched up her lips and shook her head vigorously, as if telling the tale of old Dottie's downfall was taking a terrible toll.

To keep the woman talking, Reed shook his head and uttered, "Umph, umph, umph. Is Dottie in the hospital? Are they going to let her come back home?"

"Oh, she's too far gone for that; they done put her in that Philadelphia Nursing Home. You know that place that was on CNN news last year?"

Reed didn't know what she was talking about and he damn sure didn't care.

"Yeah, some nurse went wild up in there and cut up about four or five feeding tubes," the neighbor continued.

"Umph," Reed grunted. "So what's going to happen to Miss Dottie's house? Where's Darlene going to live when she eventually comes home?" Reed inquired, worried sick over the possibility that a money-filled coffee can might be somewhere inside the abandoned house.

"Ain't nobody paid no taxes on that house for years." The neighbor reared back and stretched her neck and looked over in the direction of Dottie's house. "There was a sign tacked up on one of them boards; I guess one of those bad kids tore it down. I sure hope the city does something about that place before the drug addicts and the rats take it over."

Nausea gripped the pit of Reed's stomach at the thought of a wretched crackhead, exercising his squatter's rights and lucking up and finding the money.

"Well, it was nice talking to you," Reed said, giving up but still treating the neighbor with respect. There was a strong possibility that on a desperate night, he might come back with a crowbar and a flashlight. And if the neighbor caught him sneaking around, he wanted to be sure she thought of him as a friend.

Chapter 36

Chanelle felt conspicuous wearing the waitress uniform. The little cap she was forced to wear was enough to make her puke, but what could she do? The uniform came with the gig. Finally earning an honest dollar, she was determined to make the best of it.

She'd honed her people skills when she'd worked as a stripper, so at least her tips at the restaurant were pretty good.

The only thing she hated about working in a public restaurant was that she never knew who would walk through the door. She'd die from embarrassment if one of her former co-workers from Lizzard's caught her wearing the corny waitress uniform while she hustled tables for tips.

"May I help you?" she asked the gentleman who sat in an empty booth in her section. He was nice looking, and older than she was. She guessed him to be about twenty-five or so. Then it hit her. He'd sat in the same booth a few days ago and had left her a nice tip. "Hi," she said in recognition. "How are you?"

"I'm good." He nodded, pleased that she remembered him. "And how are you?"

"Pretty good," Chanelle said, smiling as she rattled off the daily special and waited for him to make up his mind. Not only was he handsome, he also dressed nice. She checked out his watch. It looked expensive.

"I'll have the catch of the day."

"Something to drink?

Contemplating, the man gazed upward, rubbing his chin. "How about a glass of lemonade."

"Okay, be right back." She gave him a sincere smile. As she traipsed back to the kitchen with his order, she hummed her favorite song, which was a sure sign that her depression was finally lifting.

"What's your name, pretty lady?" the man asked when she returned with the beverage and garden salad appetizer.

"Chanelle."

"My name's Greg." He studied her with a curious arched brow. "Is this a part-time job? Are you in college?"

She laughed. "No, I'm not in school. Hopefully, I'll go back one day. Right now, I'm just trying to pay the bills."

"You young people don't understand the value of higher learning—"

"Oh, check you out," she interrupted, amused. "You're not that much older than me."

"I'm probably old enough to be your father."

"No way," she said in a burst of laughter.

"How old are you?" he asked.

"Eighteen."

"I'm thirty-five."

Chanelle gawked. "Really? Dag, I didn't think you were that old." Wanting to know if he were truly old enough to be her father, she tried to work the math in her head but gave up and started scribbling figures on her pad.

"There's a seventeen-year age difference," Greg informed her. "I could have had a kid at seventeen."

"That's wild."

"What's wild?"

"That someone who looks as young as you is actually old enough to be my father."

Shaking her head in wonder, Chanelle excused herself to go to the kitchen to get Greg's entrée. She rushed right back, wanting their conversation to continue.. Surprisingly, she enjoyed talking with the mature and intelligent older man and thankfully, she wasn't real busy. She'd be getting off in another hour, so why not have some fun on the job? She could probably learn a few life lessons from the distinguished gentleman.

She waited on her remaining customers but kept checking on Greg. There was something about him that was kind and patient. He didn't seem interested in her body, only in her mind."

When he asked her to tell him about herself, she was careful not to talk about her work in the sex industry. She did, however, tell him about her mother's passing and that she had no family that she was aware of.

"I'm in awe," he said.

"Why?" she asked, blushing.

"To have overcome so many obstacles and not succumbed to drugs or a teenage pregnancy…well, I'm amazed, truly amazed."

Chanelle enjoyed the compliment though she didn't feel she deserved it. *If you only knew*, she wanted to say.

<hr />

Standing on her feet for eight hours took an enormous toll, so when Greg offered to give her a ride home, she gladly accepted. Cab rides were no longer an affordable mode of transportation. Chanelle got around the city traveling on public transportation, which sucked big time.

"Would you like to stop and have a drink or a cup of coffee?"

Chanelle was tired to the bone, but Greg was so nice, she decided one drink wouldn't hurt. It might do her some good to relax and unwind.

They went to a bar in a hotel near the airport. He ordered a bottle of Perrier water with a twist of lemon; Chanelle, relieved that she didn't get carded, ordered a Long Island Iced Tea.

"Excuse me, I have to go tinkle," she said with a girlish giggle that she recognized as sounding a bit too loud and giddy. She'd forgotten how strong the drink was, and reminded herself to sip slowly and monitor her tone.

"Are you feeling okay?" Greg asked when she returned from the restroom.

"I'm a little tipsy, but in a good way. Don't worry, I'm not drunk."

"I have to confess, I feel guilty for hogging your time. You've had a long day and I know you must be tired."

"A little," she admitted.

He smiled kindly. "Okay, Princess, drink up and I'll take you home."

Princess! She liked being called Princess, she thought, as a hazy feeling came over her. *I had too much to drink.* She hiccupped, giggled, and covered her mouth. *I sure hope I don't puke in front of this nice man.*

Next she had a vague impression of being outside; she felt herself being half-dragged, half-carried to the car. *He's so sweet!* she thought as she felt the seatbelt being strapped across her chest. The metallic sound of the seatbelt being snapped into place was the last thing Chanelle heard before she drifted into a blissful sleep.

Chapter 37

"You look just like a princess! Stand over there near the light." Dayna's mother pointed to a well-lit area near the bay windows and excitedly snapped a picture of her daughter.

"Okay, Mom," Dayna said, concluding the photo session when she spotted Cecily turning into the driveway. "Cecily's here."

Pamela Hinton frowned. "Why would a man invite you to an important function and not escort you properly?"

"Ammon had to be there early," Dayna explained. Under her mother's disapproving glare, Dayna fidgeted self-consciously. "It's more convenient for me to ride with Cecily. Besides, Ammon doesn't have a car. He rides a bicycle."

Her mother gasped. "That's so dangerous. Listen to me, Dayna…If you ever decide to ride on that thing with him, I hope you have enough sense to wear a helmet."

Dayna groaned; she hated it when her mom started acting over-protective. "He doesn't ride a motorcycle. His mode of transportation is a regular bicycle," she explained.

"A bicycle!" Her mother just shook her head. Her eyes beseeched her daughter to be cautious, to keep a level head. Artists were known to be eccentric and this Ammon sounded like a real character.

"He's an artist, Mom, not a CEO or a *lawyer*," she threw in, making a soft jab. "Besides, I'm not concerned about appearances. That's your department, remember?"

Cecily honked twice. "Smooches!" Dayna blew her mother a kiss and rushed out the door.

When Dayna and Cecily entered the Bellevue's main ballroom, Dayna's nervous eyes scanned the throng of elegantly attired attendees as she searched for a glimpse of Ammon. The discomforting feeling that she was perhaps dateless was mercifully brief. Within seconds Ammon and Kendrick, looking dapper in dark-colored suits, appeared seemingly out of nowhere.

"You look beautiful," Ammon said to Dayna. His lips sought her cheek, but she turned her head slightly, causing his lips to brush her neck.

"Thanks," she uttered with eyes downcast, trembling from the feel of his soft lips. She returned the compliment when she was finally able to meet his gaze.

Ammon smiled in appreciation. "I've got something to show you." He reached for her hand. "We'll meet you two at the table," he said to Kendrick and Cecily as he guided Dayna in the direction of the prominent display.

He held her hand tenderly. It was a token of affection

she should have enjoyed, but the fear that her palm would soon become drenched with sweat kept her from deriving any pleasure from the moment.

Sitting atop an ornate pedestal was a framed replica of Ammon's mural. Dayna was momentarily startled; a rush of air escaped her lips. In bewildered fascination, her head turned from the framed print to Ammon. "Are there prints available for sale?" She asked anxiously.

"Not yet. My piece is being featured in a book called *The City of Murals*. After the book release, 'Family' will be available in print."

"When is the book release?" she asked, sounding somewhat frantic. She *had* to have that painting.

"Um, I think October or sometime next fall." There was a clatter of platters that were set up on carts and wheeled into the ballroom. Ammon slipped an arm across Dayna's shoulder. "Hungry?" he asked. "Ready to eat?"

She wasn't; she could have stood gazing at the painting all night. But she nodded consent and allowed herself the luxury of enjoying the arm draped around her. The feeling was utter bliss.

After the meal and after several artists accepted their plaques and words of congratulations, the mayor of Philadelphia finally called Ammon to the stage. The print of his mural was brought from the back of the room and now stood front and center on the stage.

Dayna was breathless, bursting with pride as Ammon

rose and strode proudly to the front of the room. On the edge of her seat, she listened intently to every word the mayor spoke in regard to Ammon's numerous accomplishments.

"For his work at The State Correctional Facility at Graterford, where he teaches the inmates the art of creating murals…" The mayor paused, his voice rose ceremoniously. "On behalf of the City of Philadelphia and the Perry Foundation, we are proud to present Ammon Abdullah with a fifty-thousand-dollar grant."

There was a thunderous applause. A series of lights flashed from cameras as Ammon and the mayor shook hands.

Shortly after the award ceremony, Cecily and Dayna excused themselves and went to the restroom. "If you don't solidify your relationship with Ammon, I'm gonna dump Kendrick and make a move on that gorgeous hunk of masculinity! Do you hear me, girl? That fifty-thousand-dollar check he just got is looking pretty good to a sistah, but the hell with that. Ammon can have any woman in this ballroom, with or without that check. I'm not playing, that brother looks good!" Cecily and Dayna broke into titters of soft laughter. "I'm serious, gurrrl. He's as talented as he is gorgeous." Cecily became suddenly serious. "Dayna! Honestly, you should see the way he's been looking at you all night."

"For real?" Dayna asked timidly.

"For real! Now stop playing and jump on that!"

Cecily was right. It was time to stop deluding herself. Her attraction to Ammon was not something casual; her feelings could not be described as merely fondness. She was no longer inclined to stifle her emotions nor would she sit back and reveal her feelings slowly over time.

She'd been struck by love—there were no other words to describe her condition. She'd felt it the first time her eyes locked on Ammon. When he looked at her while he worked behind the bar at Carmella's, the electric jolt sent her running to her car. And she'd been involved in a marriage at the time, a marriage she had hoped to save.

Her thoughts flitted to her wedding day. *What a charade*, she thought, saddened by the memory. Though their names were printed on a piece of paper that was embossed with a legal seal, her marriage to Reed was never a real union or a blending of two loving hearts. There were no words to adequately describe the misery of three years of marriage to Reed, but to say it was a *living hell* came close to summing it up.

Then, shaking away those painful memories, she went to the mirror and glossed her lips.

Waiting for Dayna, Cecily stood near the door. "Ready?" Cecily asked.

"Yes, I'm ready!" Dayna said, enthusiastically emphasizing each word.

The double meaning behind Dayna's words was not

lost on Cecily. She laughed and Dayna joined in. Their laughter left a joyous echo in the restroom as the two friends edged their way through the festive crowd and joined their men at the table.

❧❧❧

"Can you make sure Dayna gets home safely?" Cecily asked Ammon.

"Sure, if she doesn't mind riding on the back of a bicycle that's not meant for two," he replied humorously.

Dayna shot Cecily a look. Cecily inched over and pulled Dayna to the side. "I don't know about you, but I'm feeling extra horny," she whispered. "I'm following Kendrick home. If you know like I know, you'll go home with Ammon and get your freak on."

"Cecily! I didn't mean I was ready for *that!*" Dayna said, looking stricken.

"What did you mean?"

"I meant I was ready to be honest and express my true feelings and…you know… tell him about Reed and how I'm adapting…"

"Oh, you're so corny," Cecily interjected. "All right, whatever. I did my part. It's Ammon's responsibility to get you home."

Ammon approached. "I hope you're not seriously worrying about a ride. I'm a rich man now." He chuckled. "I can afford a cab."

Kendrick and Cecily waved good-bye and walked to the parking garage hand-in-hand.

Ammon hailed a cab. "She's going to Mount Airy and then you can drop me off at Twenty-fourth and Fairmount," Ammon told the cab driver.

Dayna gave the driver her mother's address. "Take the scenic route," Ammon demanded with laughter.

As the cab rolled along, the driver seemed compelled to point out areas of interest as if he were giving Dayna and Ammon a guided tour.

The driver's voice sounded far away as Ammon whispered in her ear. "Have a good time?"

"The best. Thank you for inviting me."

He silenced her with an affectionate peck on the lips, and then a soft but tentative kiss. Dayna pulled him closer, showing him that she wanted, no, needed to feel his lips pressed against hers. She wrapped both arms around his neck. Her fingers became entangled in his locks, which felt like ropes made of velvet.

Their breathing increased; Dayna bent back her head and slowly parted her lips. Her tongue touched his. His mouth tasted like tangerines. Ammon's hand worked its way under Dayna's dress and up her thigh. She quivered at his touch. It had been so long since she'd felt a kiss or even a gentle touch.

Dayna broke the kiss, released a long, pent-up sigh, and asked breathily, "Would you like some company tonight?"

Ammon scrunched up his face to express the depth of

his yearning as he nodded his head and replied, "Mm-hmm."

With Dayna bundled in his arms, Ammon informed the driver: "Change of plans, driver. Make a left turn at the light. We're both going to my place."

Chapter 38

S he was having a terrible dream. A nightmare. The kind her mother used to refer to as "the witch's ride." She couldn't move and was unable to open her eyes. Chanelle tried to scream, but could only make a tormented, muffled sound. She twisted and struggled, then, suddenly aware that her strongest efforts were ineffective, she stopped struggling against the invisible dark force.

Then she recalled something her mother had told her. "When that witch is riding your back, don't try to fight it. Just be calm and start reciting the Twenty-third Psalm. That'll get it off you," her mother had advised.

Halfway through the Bible verse, she heard a man's voice and became keenly and horribly aware that she was not in the midst of a bad dream.

"Are you awake, Sleeping Beauty?" The voice sounded kind; perhaps he would explain what was going on. She felt extremely groggy, like she'd been drugged, but she managed to turn her head in the direction of the voice.

Chanelle forced her eyelids open. She blinked frantically as her long lashes fluttered against a blindfold. She grunted through the electrical tape that covered her mouth, wanting desperately to rip it away. She made an attempt to move her hands, but couldn't; her wrists were bound. In a panic, she groaned and tried to kick out her feet, which were tightly tied to the bed posts.

Twisting at the waist, she realized she was lying in a bed—naked. The horror of being naked and tied up in a stranger's bed compelled her to thrash and buck wildly. She screamed loud and hard until her throat felt raw, but the only sound she was able to emit was a thin muted wail.

"You're a real wildcat, aren't you?" the voice said. There was no longer even a trace of kindness in the tone.

Poked with a sharp pointed object that traveled from her throat to her navel, Chanelle became paralyzed with fear and whimpered the unintelligible words *"Help me, somebody. Please!"*

As if in answer to her prayer, she felt fingers untying the blindfold. Her eyelids blinked rapidly as her eyes adjusted to the light. Nothing she saw made any sense. If only she could rub her blurry eyes, perhaps her vision would become clear and reveal that she was at home in her own bedroom.

But as her vision improved, she realized there was nothing familiar in this room. She saw an unfamiliar closet with a set of double doors, an end table, a Tiffany lamp, a bureau, a vanity table and stool, and floral prints hanging on the walls—evidence that she was not in her own bedroom, where posters of rap and hip hop artists adorned the walls.

Her eyes shot up toward the ceiling. Through sheer fabric that cloaked the bed posts and cascaded down the sides, she glimpsed a covered light bulb. She was imprisoned in a beautiful canopy bed.

The man who'd untied the blindfold crept from behind her. To her amazement, she saw it was Greg! The nice man who was supposed to take her home. And for a few fleeting moments, she dared to hope he had come to rescue her from this terrible harm.

His expression, however, quickly dashed all hope. The once smiling mouth was now twisted contemptuously. Chanelle's eyes bulged with fear when she glimpsed the shiny knife Greg shook tauntingly in her face. "Oh God, please help me. What's going on?" she pleaded, but her words came out in a garbled murmur.

"We just keep bumping into each other. We really have to stop meeting like this!" He laughed spitefully.

Too frightened to speak and unable to verbalize even if she tried, Chanelle made terrified humming sounds.

"That's right. I drugged you and dragged you here to my lair," he said with a snort and then circled the bed menacingly. "Oh, that's right…I was supposed to give you a ride home. My bad!" he shouted in a mocking tone. "You didn't think I knew the jargon of those street thugs—those young hooligans you like to fuck…"

Her eyes squinted in incomprehension. She had no idea what this madman was talking about.

"Don't play dumb," he said in response to her confused expression. "You know what I'm talking about, don't you, Sensation?"

Sensation! How did he know her former alias? Her mind did a frantic search but came up blank. She couldn't recall having ever seen him when she worked as a dancer and she certainly didn't know him through Hershey's escort service.

"You forgot me!" He looked sincerely hurt. But the expression of hurt swiftly changed to rage. "You bitch!" he bellowed. "You really forgot me. I thought you were just pretending not to recognize me; trying to keep your waitress friends from learning that you're nothing but a pole-swiveling ho."

An eruption of tears streamed down her cheeks. Her shoulders shook from the pressure of her agonized muffled sobs.

"Stop crying!" he demanded.

Chanelle sniffled and trembled like a frightened child.

"You're nothing but a dick teaser, Sensation." He smiled and spoke in a voice that was low and pleasant-sounding, as if he were giving her a compliment. "It seemed like you knew me pretty well when I was stuffing money in your crotch. And I didn't see you crying back then," he said and shook his head.

"Set after set, I gave you my money—every single dollar.

Most of the time I didn't stop spending until my pockets were empty." He looked off as if remembering those days. "I'd run out of money and then rush out to the ATM machine, withdraw some cash, and make it back before your next set."

Okay, this guy was a regular at Lizzard's. Chanelle tried to remember him, but for the life of her, she couldn't place him. Over the course of the two years she danced there, there were so many men, so many faces, they all became a blur.

But if this guy was as devoted as he claimed to have been, maybe he still had some feelings for her. Perhaps she could reason with him. If he would just remove the gag, she would instantly start spilling her guts. First, she'd try to talk some sense into his head. If that didn't work she'd start rappin' about anything he wanted to hear. She'd pretend she suddenly remembered him...*Oh, yeah! Come to think of it, I do remember you!* If given a chance, she'd tell him how much she'd always loved him; she'd tell him anything he wanted to hear. And she'd *do* just about anything to get away from this crazy man.

"I was just trying to get to know you better," he continued. "I noticed you didn't shed a single tear on the nights I went home broke. You gave me your ass to kiss and kept on shaking it. Dancing and flirting with other men—right in my face. Now *that* was disrespectful and disrespectful bitches like you have to be dealt with."

With her head tilted to one side in confusion, Chanelle

stared at him with wide eyes that proclaimed her inno-cence—frightened eyes that swore he had to be mistaken. She'd never told him to kiss her ass; she'd never treated him disrespectfully. *Dear God, if you get me out of this*—

Without warning, he slapped her hard across the face, ending her silent plea to the Lord.

It took a few seconds for her to understand what had happened. Reflexively, she wanted to rub her face, but couldn't. Her hands were bound. And until that moment, she hadn't realized how badly her wrists hurt.

The man named Greg balled a fist and shook it in her face. "Don't look at me like that again!" He advanced closer, drawing his fist back threateningly as if about to strike.

Chanelle squeezed her eyes shut, whimpering as she waited for the crushing blow. When several excruciating seconds passed, she opened her eyes.

"I changed my mind; I don't want to mess your face up…not yet. I'm going to have a lot of fun with you before I kill you."

His promise of murder was more than she could bear. Fear of this magnitude should have been the catalyst for an instant nervous breakdown. Chanelle screamed, but the black tape on her lips kept the scream trapped inside her mouth. Her eyes, wide and terrified, pleaded with the insane man to spare her life.

He sat down on the bed beside her. "I've been waiting

for this moment a long time. But before we continue this conversation, I want to tell you my real name. I don't mind telling you because my identity is going to be our little secret. A secret you'll take to your grave."

She squirmed uncomfortably. She didn't want to know his name. If he kept his identity to himself, she might see the glorious light of another day.

But before she could utter a grunt of protest, he leaned close to her ear and whispered, "My name is Reed. *Master* Reed to you."

She hadn't stepped foot inside a church since her mother's funeral and she felt like a shameless hypocrite when she started praying to God, promising all sorts of things, reminding Him that she'd stopped tricking and had gotten a real job.

"You played me, Sensation," Reed said, interrupting her internal prayer. "Remember that night you left me sitting in my car outside Lizzard's?"

She shook her head no. He smacked her face. "Stop lying!"

With her system in a state of shock, her body shuddered and jerked.

"Yeah, you had me waiting outside the club for you and then you came out and waltzed right past me... waved at me like I was some kind of insignificant chump and then you jumped in that Bentley with that basketball star. I guess my Lexus wasn't good enough for you."

Malik! This maniac saw me get in Stone Allen's whip with Malik!

He reached toward her mouth. Chanelle edged away, but he popped her on the side of her head as a warning to be still. At first, he peeled gently and then with sudden savagery, he impatiently ripped the tape away.

She yelped from shock and then gave a cry of pain.

"Now, what's my name?" he demanded.

"Reed," she blurted through lips that hurt from being sealed together. With hunched shoulders, she shrank away in case he was prepared to deliver another blow.

"Master Reed," he corrected. "Fuck it…just call me Master."

With her mind and vocal chords badly out of sync, Chanelle was silent for a few seconds—a few seconds too long. A sharp smack to her cheek prompted her to blurt, "Master! Your name is Master!"

The urge to pee was overwhelming and with her legs spread-eagle, her feet tied to separate bed posts, she was unable to squeeze her thighs together to suppress the urge.

"I have to go to the bathroom, Master."

"Hmm," Reed said, stroking his chin. "I hadn't thought about that. Let's see now…can't have you pissing up the place, so I'm gonna untie you, but don't try any tricks." He walked over to the bureau, pulled open a drawer, and rummaged around until he retrieved something that made an awful clicking sound.

Standing over Chanelle with his hand snaking up her naked thigh and inching toward her pubis, he flicked a lighter and pointed the flame near her neatly trimmed mound.

An intake of breath was her single expression of fear. She was afraid that making harsh sounds or sudden movements might incite the maniac to set her aflame.

"Not much down there to start a forest fire." Reed chuckled, referring to her trimmed pubic hair. "If you try something slick while you're in the bathroom…" He paused and grabbed a handful of the hair on her head. "I'm gonna set this shit on fire."

He untied her hands and feet, yanked her off the bed, and dragged her down the hall to the bathroom. Reed sat on the side of the tub while Chanelle released a long stream of urine.

After finishing she stood, waiting for him to tell her what to do next. Reed kicked her on her hipbone and growled, "Wash your hands, you nasty bitch." Shaking, she soaped up and quickly washed her hands and just before she turned to ask for a towel, he sent a thundering blast to her ass.

It wasn't the sensual smackdown she'd experienced at Marc Tarsia's hands. This was excruciating pain produced by a doubled-up leather belt.

"On your knees, slut. Did I say you could walk?"

She dropped to all fours. "Crawl!" he snarled and then gave her a swift kick in the behind as a reminder to obey quickly. Being on her hands and knees and feeling the bottom of his dirty shoe on her bare ass was beyond any humiliation she'd ever experienced in her life.

Assuming he wanted her to go back into the bedroom, Chanelle began crawling in that direction. She hesitated for a split second as she approached a winding, elegant flight of stairs, but the sole of Reed's shoe and the threat of a vicious kick dashed any hope of escape and encouraged her to continue crawling.

Back in the bedroom, Reed pointed a finger at her. "Kneel!" he commanded, and then placed his foot in the center of her back forcing her to lie on her belly. Her face was buried in the thick carpet. "Kneel like a dog!" he roared.

Chanelle quickly assumed a sphinx-like position.

"Now, this is the deal. You're my slave; I'm your master." Reed kicked her in the side. She cried out in pain. "Look at me when I'm talking to you."

With wounded eyes, she looked up at him. Her injured side throbbed but she dared not rub it.

"Your life can be extended as long as you do as I say. I'm going to get fuming mad if I see a frown on your face or hear a sound of displeasure. Bitches like you don't want soft guys," he said with a sneer. "Y'all want somebody who'll take control and dominate your asses. You'll probably start liking your new lifestyle after you get the hang of it," he said with confidence. "And if you get to the point where I can tell that you enjoy serving me and if you start loving the pain that I give you…hell, I just might keep your ass alive.

"But if you disobey me, you're going to have to suffer severe consequences. So pay close attention. When I say kneel, I want you to break it all the way down. When I say beg, you'd better sit on the back of your legs and give me your best imitation of a dog begging for a bone." Reed laughed.

"Begging for a bone…now that's funny. Yeah, I want you begging for *this* bone," he said as he crudely grabbed his crotch. "You belong to me now. I'm never letting you go, so if you want to enjoy life with me, don't disobey me," he calmly informed her. "This is it, Sensation," he said with a wave of his hand. "The only way you're leaving this house is in a body bag. Understand?"

Too rattled to think straight and too terrified of what he was insinuating to allow his words to really sink in, she nodded eagerly. She was at the mercy of a crazy man, but having a strong will to survive, Chanelle managed to stretch her dry, cracked lips into a happy smile. She'd have to play along with his bizarre game until she could figure out a way to escape.

"That's what I've been waiting for. Let me see that pretty smile again."

Though it hurt to move her chafed lips, Chanelle quickly complied and produced an even bigger smile.

Chapter 39

The furniture inside the airy, high-ceilinged room was minimal. There were two polyester travel chairs with armrests and drink holders, and a bookcase filled to capacity. The excess books were stacked haphazardly in various places on the floor. There was also a mattress, box spring, and an old wooden table.

There seemed to be hundreds of canvases set upon easels and propped against walls. Some of the canvasses displayed finished work while others were colored with just a few brush strokes.

Ammon had a two-room apartment. Two and a half if you counted the miniscule bathroom that Dayna had to visit the moment Ammon opened the door. His apartment was just a hovel when compared to Dayna and Reed's spacious home. She didn't mind; she'd be happy with Ammon anywhere—in a cave or in a hut made of thatch.

"Would you like a cup of herb tea?" he asked, taking off his suit jacket and slinging it on one of the travel chairs. He headed toward the small kitchen before Dayna could respond.

"Sure, why not?" she replied, wondering if she should trail behind and lend a hand or something.

"Do you have a preference?" he called.

"What do you have?"

"Whatever you'd like. I have it all," he boasted.

Curious to see his substantial tea assortment, she paced to the kitchen to take a peek. She expected tons of packaged boxes of Celestial Seasonings, but instead found numerous Ziploc baggies that were well stuffed with what looked like dried fruit, flower petals, and leaves. On the countertop, Ammon had placed two mugs.

"All you have to do to make an authentic cup of herb tea is boil some water and mix together some herbs," he explained with a smile that Dayna thought was adorable. "Now, if you like your tea sweet, I can throw in some dried fruit and dried flowers."

It sounded crazy, but Dayna was willing to trust Ammon and go along with the adventure. In appreciation of his gracious hospitality, she vowed to drink every drop. Even if the tea tasted disgusting, she'd guzzle it down as if were as delicious as Red Zinger, her all-time favorite.

"Go!" He shooed her with a good-natured wave of a hand. "Have a seat in one of my comfortable chairs," he said, laughing. "Or look around. As you can see, I'm a minimalist…I don't have much. But you seem to like my work, so go ahead; take a look at my personal art gallery."

Dayna reluctantly left the kitchen. She liked Ammon's

company. Perusing the numerous mounted canvasses, she found herself stuck on one of his oil paintings, a snapshot of urban life painted on a canvas. Happy children jumped through water that gushed from an opened fire hydrant. Mothers watched from a distance while sitting on their stoops. The scene seemed so real. Even the cracks in the painted sidewalk were so life-like, Dayna felt that if she touched it, she'd feel the deep grooves.

Ammon emerged from the kitchen carrying two steaming mugs. "I got creative and invented something just for you. "Here you go," he said, handing her the mug. "Take a sip. I named it Dayna's Delight."

"Dayna's Delight!" She echoed with glee. "You named it after me?" Ammon made her feel so special, she just couldn't stop smiling. *Ooo, I can't wait to tell Cecily about this!*

Being that he'd named the tea after her, Dayna was even more determined to pretend the tea was delectably delicious no matter how awful it tasted.

After blowing on the aromatic hot liquid, she took a small and reluctant sip. "Mmm!" she moaned loudly. "Ammon, this is *sooo* good!" And surprisingly, she wasn't telling a fib. Dayna's Delight tasted much better than her former favorite, Red Zinger. "What did you put in this?" she asked, taking a bigger sip.

"I brewed a blend of dried orange peel, dried cherry pieces, and rosehips. Oh, yeah, I added some secret spices." Ammon gave Dayna a sneaky smile.

ãããã

She made a mental note to share every aspect of the evening with Cecily. She'd describe with vivid clarity every detail of Ammon's painting of happy children; it was called "Hot Fun in the Summertime," she learned. But at some point between sipping tea and the discussion of his paintings, they ended up tangled together in his bed. At that point, Dayna's mind turned to mush and she realized she'd never be able to remember the order in which their intimate acts of love occurred.

His hand brushed her neck, giving her shivers as he slowly unzipped her dress. He kissed each shoulder and nipped at her neck, whispering, "You're more beautiful than I imagined." With the top of her dress dangling around her waist, Dayna pressed Ammon's hand against the hem, silently urging him to take the dress off.

He ignored her unspoken plea and unsnapped her rose-colored bra. He cupped each full breast and squeezed them ever so gently and then lowered his mouth to her nipple. Ammon sucked it with such tenderness, Dayna cried out as her frenzied fingers became entwined in his locked hair. He made love to the other breast, circling the areola with the tip of his tongue, licking the nipple until it became a hard dark pearl.

Tender stirrings made her cry out his name. "Ammon!" she said as she tried to squirm out of her dress. "Please, Ammon, take it off!"

"Hush!" he said in a firm whisper. "Stop, baby, we don't have to rush."

Dayna bit the inside of her bottom lip to contain herself, but quiet whimpers and moans escaped despite her desire to calm down. These acts of intimacy were brand-new to her. Neither Reed nor anyone else had ever touched her like this…and Ammon had only just begun.

He covered her face with kisses: her eyelids, her nose, her cheeks, and her chin. She wanted to open her mouth and scream. Didn't he realize that she was quietly losing her mind? He'd said not to rush, as if he planned to use his sweet lips to torture her all night.

She reached out to touch him; to pull him closer to her, but Ammon pinned her arms to her sides. "Don't move, Dayna. This is *your* night, baby. The only thing I want you to do is to open your heart and be willing to let me love you."

Love! Did he say love? Was he trying to make her have a nervous breakdown? *I'm already in love with you; I loved you on sight!* she screamed in her mind.

Ammon tugged her dress down and pulled it off and then lovingly smoothed his hands over her round hips and kissed each thigh. His touch felt like fire. Her body craved penetration, but Dayna forced herself to enjoy the gift of his touch.

Ammon stared at her nakedness. For the first time, Dayna felt free of inhibitions. She allowed herself to enjoy the feeling as his eyes explored her body. She felt glorified in her body's perfection as well as its imperfections. She did not flinch when his eyes lingered on breasts that were no longer perky or when his eyes glossed over forearms with muscles well hidden beneath flesh. She did not wince when he fixed his eyes upon the mound of her paunch. His loving gaze swept over thighs that were soft, thick, and womanly. Ammon's eyes seemed to adore every inch of her from her head down to her toes.

Turning her over, he massaged her shoulders, communicating his emotions with his strong touch. Long locks swept across her back, causing her to shudder. Then he licked a moist trail down her spine and kissed each buttock. He squeezed and kneaded her butt cheeks, and then ran his finger along the crack.

Next, Ammon created a small opening between her thighs and gently slipped his hand beneath her mons pubis, his middle finger searching for that hidden place. He didn't probe with his finger, he simply fondled her love button, giving Dayna one of the highest forms of pleasure…not stopping until his finger was wet…not stopping until tears fell from her eyes. Not stopping until Dayna grew limp with satisfaction.

After the divine love ritual, which didn't include intercourse, Ammon cradled Dayna in his arms, breathing in the scent of her hair, kissing the side of her face.

"Ammon, I feel guilty," she said, her eyes exploring his face.

"Don't."

"But—"

"Shh!" He held a finger to his lips.

"Why?"

"There's no reason to feel guilty."

"But...you weren't satisfied," she said and buried her face in his chest.

Ammon clipped Dayna's chin between his thumb and index finger and brought her hidden face into view. "I am satisfied. We shared something special, the beginning of new love being born. This kind of intimacy is sacred, don't you realize that? I guess you could call it sacred love."

Sacred Love! It was true; the experience was truly sacred. And one day soon they would experience their oneness with each other, joined together in healing sexual love.

Before sleep could claim her, she studied Ammon's beautiful face, trying to memorize every detail. In case it had all been just a vivid dream, she wanted to preserve the image of this man who would forever hold a place in her heart.

Chapter 40

"I'm thirsty," Chanelle finally found the nerve to say.

Reed bent down and roughly brushed his thumb across her dry, cracked lips. "Yeah, your lips are chapped." He yanked her hair. "Stand up. I can't have you scratching up my dick with those fucked-up lips."

Her legs were unsteady. After crawling around for hours, it was difficult to stand.

"Close your eyes; I have a present for you." She quickly obeyed. He turned away and got something out of a drawer that made a clanging sound.

"Okay, open your eyes, Sensation." As if he were gracing her with an expensive gift, he presented her with a pair of shiny handcuffs. "Hold out your wrists," he said cheerfully. Chanelle did as he said. She grimaced when she felt the tightness and heard the click as he locked the cuffs around her wrists.

Reed popped her upside her head. "Didn't I say I don't want to see a frown on your face?"

"I'm sorry."

"And?"

"I'm real sorry for frowning."

He drew back his arm and balled his fist. Chanelle jerked back so hard she fell against the chest of drawers. Reed doubled over in laughter.

"All right. Now let's try it again. Don't make me punch you," he warned. "You're sorry…whom?" Reed leaned toward her and cupped his ear.

"I'm sorry, Master," she replied enthusiastically.

"Much better."

She felt enormous relief at having provided the correct response.

Reed strode off, leaving Chanelle alone and handcuffed.

She looked longingly at the window. If she got a running start, she could hurl herself through the windowpane. Any cuts or other injuries sustained from the two-story fall couldn't be worse than the torturous acts this maniac had in mind.

However, before she could put her plan in motion, she heard his footsteps coming up the stairs. She was so afraid of him, just the sound of his footsteps made her eyes mist, and her lips quiver in fear. *Oh God, what am I going to do?*

Reed held a bowl of water carefully and placed it at Chanelle's feet. Then, changing his mind, he picked the bowl up and carried it to the other side of the room. He unlocked the handcuffs. "There's your water. Go get it," he said, pointing to the bowl.

Chanelle got down on her knees and crawled over to the bowl.

"Goddamn! You catch on quick," he said, as he gleefully walked behind her. "Look at that big pretty ass. Umph, umph, umph! I used to love to watch that ass when you crawled around onstage."

Chanelle's mind raced back to her stripping days. Back to when she was free. Crawling on stage like a panther had felt empowering; it was seductive and she was in control. But this...this groveling and crawling to get a drink of water was disgusting; it was a disgraceful and humiliating shame.

When she finally reached the bowl, she kneeled back on her haunches and cupped the bowl with her hands. She felt so weary and afraid of Reed's oppression, her hands shook as she held the bowl. Not wanting to lose one drop of the precious water, she concentrated on steadying her hands.

Reed kicked her in the ass—not too hard, but hard enough to cause her to lurch forward and spill half the water on the floor. "Put that bowl down and lap it up."

She placed the bowl down. Humiliated, she lowered her head and began lapping the water. She was quickly losing her identity and starting to feel like a real dog.

"Good girl." He patted her head. "I should call you Fido."

Too thirsty to feel insulted by the suggestion of being called by a dog's name, Chanelle licked around the bottom of the bowl, trying to get every bit of moisture.

"All right, that's enough," Reed said as he grabbed the

hair on the crown of her head and yanked her away from the bowl. Still holding her hair, he scrutinized her lips and then tested the texture with the back of his hand. "Damn! Your lips are still hard as a damn Brillo pad. I'm gonna have to use some Vaseline to soften them up." He groped his penis. "Seeing you crawling and lapping up that water got my dick hard." He pulled her hair hard until she rose to her knees; he pushed her face and held it against the stiffness beneath his pants. "See what I mean?" His penis pulsated like a heartbeat against her face.

"I can't leave you alone. You have to come with me while I get the stuff." He led her into the bathroom where he smeared petroleum jelly on her lips and then promptly marched her back into the bedroom.

"I've been waiting a long time for this," Reed said as he unzipped his pants. "It wouldn't be wise to disappoint me," he warned. He grabbed his dick and thumped her on the side of her face. "Come on; get on it!"

Feeling more degraded than she thought humanly possible, Chanelle took him inside her mouth.

"Mmm, yeah, baby. Work those lips. Start earning some of that money I paid you," he said as she gave him head.

Chanelle worked her lips, her tongue, her jaws, and her throat, determined to give the best blowjob of her life.

❧❧❧

After the blowjob, Reed wanted sexual intercourse. He took her downstairs and sexed her in a dozen different positions, violated her for hours, yet he still was unsatisfied and kept coming back for more. Chanelle's vaginal lips were beet red, swollen, and sore.

Reed bragged that drinking liquid ginseng made him as virile as an eighteen-year-old.

Now, after drinking another bottle of the golden elixir, he demanded Chanelle do a handstand.

She gave him a look of disbelief. Then, remembering his threat, she instantly fixed her face and assumed a blank expression. To her relief, he didn't strike her; he merely snarled and pushed her. "Get up and do your stage routine. Work that ass the way you do onstage."

Fearing his intentions, Chanelle did as she was told but tried to do a handstand facing Reed. "Turn the fuck around, bitch; you don't do it like that. Your ass should be facing me, not the wall."

Obediently, Chanelle turned around and did what she was told.

"You better not fall; I'm warning you," Reed muttered as he tried to get in the right position to enter her from behind. It was impossible to penetrate with her standing on her hands without support. "Get up against the wall," he yelled in frustration. He pointed to a wall on the other side of the living room.

She crawled to the appointed place and waited for further instruction. "Do a handstand, bitch. Damn! Stand up against the wall!"

She complied. Reed got behind her and began brushing his penis up and down the crack of her ass.

She trembled in fear. Never, ever had she allowed anyone to fuck her in the ass. The very thought of such a violation caused her anus to nervously contract. Reed spread her cheeks and slathered cold lubricant inside the sensitive area. Anticipating excruciating pain, Chanelle bit down on her lip and waited.

He held on to her ankles and slowly entered. Anal penetration was humiliating and hurt like hell. And standing upside-down during the abusive act increased the pain.

"Let me see that ass clap!" he demanded, slapping her backside as he worked his penis in and out of the virgin territory.

She tried to contract the muscles in her buttocks, but under the circumstances, it was painful and difficult. Tears formed in her eyes. She silently cried.

Later, after he allowed her to shower, Reed told Chanelle to join him back downstairs. He insisted that she sit at his feet—like a dog—while he watched TV. Bone tired from every horrible aspect of her ordeal, she drifted off to sleep.

Reed shook her awake, stomped into the kitchen, and came back carrying a metal spatula.

"Please don't," she whined as he waved the cooking utensil. Reed shook his head. She whimpered but didn't struggle as he turned her over his lap. *Thwack! Thwack! Thwack!* He counted each blow. The third hit cut into her ass. Wiping the blood from the spatula onto her back, he asked, "Did you ask me if you could go the fuck to sleep? Do you find me boring?"

Chanelle knew Reed would kill her if she cried; so she held back tears of pain and started talking. "No, Master; I'm not bored. It won't happen again. Please don't hit me anymore."

With Chanelle lying across his lap, Reed whispered in her ear. "You know my dick gets real hard when you talk like that. Why are you talking so sexy? Don't tell me you want some more of this good dick?" He rubbed his crotch and gave her a lewd crooked smile.

She was in a quandary as to how she should reply; she couldn't endure any more penetration. But having good common sense and knowing the words this monster wanted to hear, Chanelle replied in a docile tone, "Yes, Master. I want some more of your good dick."

"Damn, you're a horny bitch." He pushed her off his lap. "Not right now, I'll give it to you later. I have to make a quick run to South Street. I want to buy some of those freaky sex gadgets. Let's see…what do we need?" He stroked his chin thoughtfully and then brightened. "Oh yeah, we'll need a leash, a collar, and something that'll cause some pain. Something like nipple pinchers, a whip... those sorts of things. You know what I mean?"

"Yes, Master," she whispered mournfully as she recovered from being thrown onto the floor. She steadied herself into a seated position on the floor, but remembering that dogs don't sit up like people, she scrambled to her hands and knees.

Reed glanced at her. A perturbed look crossed his face. "Kneel," he commanded. But before Chanelle could respond, he changed his mind. "No...fuck kneeling. Beg, bitch."

Chanelle blinked rapidly and changed her position. She sat on her haunches, allowing both wrists to hang limp. Her tongue lolled out and hung over her bottom lip. For good measure, she panted just like a dog.

Reed smacked her in the face with the spatula. "Stop blowing your funky breath in my face; I didn't tell you to do all that," he roared, threatening her with a wave of the spatula.

"I'm sorry, Master. I'm so very sorry, Master. And I can't wait for you to get back and discipline me with your new devices."

She was playing along but she'd be damned if she was going to stick around and wait for him to come back with a bag filled with some weapons of torture.

Satisfied with her response, Reed marched her back upstairs, blindfolded and gagged her, and retied her to the bed posts.

Feeling utterly helpless, Chanelle realized with certainty that Reed would kill her before he'd set her free. It was her darkest hour and she knew it would take a miracle for her to survive this ordeal.

When Chanelle heard the front door close and then the sound of the car backing out of the driveway, she began to fervently pray for a miracle.

Chapter 41

She'd only spent a few weeks in jail and wouldn't have had to stay for that amount of time if she hadn't been hit with an old prostitution-related bench warrant. It was cool, though. She needed the break—to chill, clean out her system, and get her weight up.

Out of jail for two days, Buttercup needed a place to rest her head. Trying to get into a city homeless shelter was a bitch. She knew the drill. They ran you ragged, making you sign up at the main office that was located on Ridge Avenue in North Philly. If she expected to get a bed, she had to go to the office to get her name processed in the computer. After all that aggravation, the next step would be to trek to the Women's Shelter downtown on Broad Street. Once she arrived at the Women's Shelter, there was a strong possibility that her name still wouldn't be in the computer. And if the downtown Women's Shelter was too crowded, she'd have to hoof it all the way back to West Philly to wait in line at another shelter on Forty-Second and Parrish. It was a shame the way they ran people all over town for just a cot and one damn hot meal.

Before she could even begin to start the long journey, Buttercup had to get lit! There was no way she could stand in any of those long-ass lines with a bunch of funky-ass people unless she was high as a kite. But getting high required money, so there she sat in the front seat of a police squad car in Fairmount Park—the headlights turned off, the car hidden behind trees.

She spit the bitter liquid out of the passenger window and wiped her mouth with a Burger King napkin she found tucked in a crevice between the seat and the door.

Despite the fact that cops were always locking her ass up and making her give them blowjobs at half-price and sometimes for free, at least one of them was good for something. "So, did you get me that information?" she asked the officer, whom she had just finished servicing.

He lifted his butt from the seat to zip up his pants. "Yeah, I got it; here you go," he said and gave her a piece of paper. "All right, come on now…I gotta get back to work. Where do you want to be dropped off?"

She looked at the paper, then looked at the cop hopefully. "Can you take me up there?"

"Now you know that's out of my jurisdiction; I can't drive you that far," the cop complained.

"All right, how far can you take me?"

"I can take you as far as Fifty-Fifth and Pine. I gotta get back to the station," he replied with undisguised irritation.

"That's going in the opposite direction," she said, matching his tone. "Just let me out at that A-Plus gas station over on Thirty-Eighth and Girard."

The cop pulled out of the darkness and cruised onto the street. He swung into the parking lot of the brightly lit service station.

Buttercup got out, slammed the door, and walked around to the driver's side. "Since you won't give me a ride, can you at least give me a tip?"

"Damn, you're a pest," the cop grumbled. Begrudgingly, he gave her a ten-dollar bill and roared out of the lot. He made a sharp left turn and then turned on the lights. The siren blared as he sped off in the direction of Fifty-Fifth and Pine.

Buttercup successfully hitched a ride but the guy who picked her up insisted on getting a handjob for his trouble. It seemed everybody wanted something; good Samaritans seemed to be a thing of the past.

The driver took her to her destination—a quiet tree-lined street. The soft lighting of a lamppost illuminated the piece of paper with the address she was looking for.

The house was dark, no parked car or truck. No people roaming around; no sign of life. Good. That's the way she liked it. Money was tighter than tight and her best bet was to get inside the house she was casing. There was a lot of money in there; she just had to figure out a way to break in.

She walked around the back and used her shoe to tap the basement window and then wiggled her thin body inside.

She tiptoed around the dark basement and found the stairs easily. Breaking and entering was not a new activity for her, but she felt an adrenaline rush because this time it was personal. She intended to take back something that rightfully belonged to her.

Careful not to turn on a light, but wishing she'd had the sense to ask the cop for a flashlight, she crept around the kitchen, then the dining and living rooms. Where do people usually keep their money? She stopped pacing. Standing still helped her think. Upstairs! The money would definitely be upstairs in a bedroom, hidden in a bureau drawer. Excited, she quietly climbed the stairs. Yeah, most people stashed their dough in their bedrooms, she decided as she counted the rooms in the hushed, dark hallway.

She heard a rustling sound coming from one of the bedrooms and almost peed on herself. She should have cussed that punk cop out for not accompanying her. He had talked some shit about not being able to do anything without a search warrant. Shit, from her experiences with cops, they always did whatever the fuck they wanted— with or without a damn search warrant.

The rustling sound grew louder and Buttercup headed for the stairs, and then changed her mind. *Fuck it…I'm out!* But along with the rustling, she heard something else that made her freeze. Her legs ceased to move; her heart clenched up and refused to beat.

"Help!" someone cried from one of the rooms. *Help? Who the fuck is that?* Buttercup asked herself. *Damn, it's just my luck to run up into some fucked-up bullshit!*

Terrified, but not having the heart to turn away from the tortured voice, she opened the door and with much hesitation, she clicked on the light.

She let out a small scream when she saw the tied-up girl. Electrical tape covered the girl's mouth. There was a ragged opening in the center; the girl had obviously chewed through the tape.

Buttercup didn't go near the ravaged girl; she was too afraid. If the girl had bitten through that tape, she might be starved and crazy enough to bite Buttercup as well. Leaving the girl sniffling and whimpering, Buttercup found a phone in another bedroom. She supposed there were still some good Samaritans out there. But she'd never have imagined herself playing that role. Life was sure strange. Smiling proudly, she lifted the receiver and dialed 9-1-1.

❧❧❧

Fuckin' cops didn't appreciate nothing! She'd helped them catch that bastard perpetrator but they still wouldn't leave her alone. She'd been answering their endless stream of questions for what seemed like hours.

The bastards came right out and asked if she'd had sex-for-pay with the man, trying to trick her into saying something that would land her back in jail. But Buttercup was no fool. She concocted a story about being held hostage, too. And since she knew firsthand about Reed's penchant for beating on women, she laid it on thick. With tears streaming, she told the officers, "He tied me up to the bed, duct-taped me, and tried to tear up my private parts."

"What?" asked an incredulous female officer who, judging by her expression, felt personally offended.

"He told me he was going to fuck me until my pussy lips started bleeding."

"And did that happen?" a male officer asked, appalled and unable to keep a straight face. He scratched his head and scrunched up his face as he regarded Buttercup with horrified curiosity.

"What?" Buttercup asked.

"Did he…you know…cause your womanly parts to bleed?"

"Hell no! Once he started talking about putting his mark on me—"

"His mark?" the officers asked in unison.

"Yeah, he said he was going to keep me tied up and fuck me until my pussy was all torn up and raw. He said he'd do it all day and all night if necessary. Said he wouldn't stop until my coochie looked raggedy and well fucked."

The officers shared a look of revulsion.

"He said my stuff is too pretty," Buttercup said with pride.

The female officer rubbed her forehead wearily. "And did he make these same remarks to Chanelle Lawson?"

"He had me tied up downstairs; she was upstairs. Like I said, I don't know what he was doing with her; you have to talk to her if you want her side of the story. Now, can I please leave?"

"Not just yet. We have a few more questions."

"Damn, y'all done had me up in here long enough. Shit, I need a lawyer."

An hour later, an important-looking attorney that she could never have afforded came to her rescue and put a stop to the questioning.

The expensively attired attorney, who spoke in an authoritative tone, was on point. The cops didn't have a case against Buttercup and finally had to let her go.

Outside the police station, the news media descended upon her, sticking microphones in her face. "How's it feel to be a hero?" someone called. "Did you know Chanelle Lawson before you two were held hostage? How do you feel now that you're free?" another asked.

"Don't say a word to these vultures," the lawyer advised

her. "I've already arranged an exclusive with one of the tabloids. Chanelle Lawson refuses to talk about the ordeal, so they're willing to pay twice the amount for your story. You can pretty much write your own check."

Buttercup smiled. Yeah, most people saw her as a worthless crackhead. But this crackhead had enough sense to memorize her so-called *boyfriend's* license plate. The cop had paid her only ten dollars for a blowjob, but she'd gotten him to run boyfriend's license plate and give her his home address. Now, she was going to get paid!

It didn't matter that she conveniently pretended to have been held hostage. What people didn't know surely couldn't hurt them.

Besides, after all the bullshit that bastard had put her through, she deserved to get some revenge. Not only had he literally fucked her over, pretended to be her boy-friend, stole her grandma's money, but the muthafucker also had the nerve to use a fake-ass name.

She wondered if there was another can of money left in her great-grandmother's house. Since she was about to strike it rich, she didn't have to snoop around in the abandoned house, but she had plenty of addicted friends who could use the money. No one understood or cared about people with addictions; they were despised and persecuted. So Buttercup decided she would try to help her friends stay high by putting the word out that there was possibly a large sum of money stashed somewhere in her great-grandmother's house.

Feeling like a philanthropist, she fell in step with her attorney as he approached his limo. The driver got out and opened the door for Buttercup.

"We're going to put you up at the Marriott," the attorney informed her. "Is that all right?"

"Fabulous," she responded. Staying at the Marriott and ordering room service and having her drugs delivered was a lifestyle she could get used to.

Chapter 42

There were rumors that the abductor had not only held Chanelle Lawson hostage, but another woman as well, a drug-addicted hooker. News reporters wanted verification—they wanted to get the scoop. The hospital staff carefully shielded Chanelle from the media. "She's not making any statements, leave her alone!" The head nurse rolled her eyes and slammed down the phone.

Balloons and flowers filled the hospital room. Cash donations folded into get well cards poured in from well-meaning strangers from throughout the country who had heard the news that Chanelle Lawson had survived living in a torture chamber for three days.

"You have a visitor; she says she's a friend," a nurse said, peeking her head inside Chanelle's room.

"Who?" Chanelle asked suspiciously. She didn't have any real friends.

"Saleema Sparks. She said you know her as Hershey."

Chanelle paused to think about it. "Okay, she can come in."

Hershey rushed into the room with a bouquet of flowers, smiling though her eyes could not conceal that she was deeply troubled and concerned. She leaned over and gave Chanelle a kiss on the cheek. "I'm so sorry, Chanelle. Thank God you're all right. I know you probably don't want to talk about it, but I'm curious…how'd you get out of that mess alive?"

For a moment, Chanelle was quiet, and then she sighed and said, "I prayed for a miracle and God answered my prayer."

"I feel so responsible…"

Chanelle shifted her position and pushed herself up a little higher. "Why? You didn't have anything to do with that situation. I'm the one who trusted a man because he seemed nice and had an attractive face…" Chanelle gulped and didn't finish the sentence. The memory of her encounter with Reed Reynolds would be etched in her mind forever, so why talk about something she'd be trying to forget for the rest of her life?

"I know," Hershey said, patting Chanelle's hand. "I feel bad that I didn't take you under my wing and school you. Girl, I knew you were green. If I had got inside your head and made sure you realized that in this crazy world there ain't hardly a soul you can trust, you wouldn't have never got all caught up in that mess." Wearing a sad expression, Hershey swallowed and shook her head.

"I have to take the responsibility for that, Hershey. I don't know why you're trippin'."

Hershey's eyes filled with tears. Chanelle was shocked.

She thought Hershey had ice water in her veins. She found it hard to believe she was capable of crying.

With the tables turned, Chanelle rubbed Hershey's back as she released a floodgate of tears. "Most people think I'm just a hard-core madam, but I'm in the business because I have a lot of responsibilities. I'm raising my best friend's daughter because she's all messed up... in a psychiatric hospital. The place she used to be in didn't really take care of her right, so I moved her to a real nice place out in Horsham, Pennsylvania. It's costing me an arm and a leg. That's part of the reason I gotta stay on my hustle."

"I know," Chanelle soothed. "Don't worry, you're gonna be blessed for what you're doing."

"You don't understand," Hershey said, sniffling and wiping away tears. "When I realized you were diggin' Marc Tarsia hard, I should have been up front and told you the truth. But instead I told you that lie about his bachelor party—"

"Marc didn't get married?"

"No."

"Then why'd you tell me that? I was really feelin' him; I was falling in love."

"I know. That's why I wanted you to think he was getting married. I was trying to protect you because I knew you were falling hard for Marc."

Chanelle gave Hershey a blank look.

"Marc has a pattern of getting involved with working girls," Hershey explained. "He gets some kind of freakish kick out of making women think he's going to take them out of the life. He starts out by inviting them to go sailing, but never comes through. It's nothing but a game to him; he does it just for kicks."

Chanelle was quiet while the information sank in.

"I thought if I told you that he was getting married, you would get mad and toughen up like me. I didn't think you'd be so hurt—quit the business and run right into the arms of a maniac."

"Well, I'm over Marc now," Chanelle said defensively. "Believe me, after the ordeal I just survived, I'm just gonna do *me*. I'm not trying to get involved in another dangerous love affair. I probably won't look at a man in a romantic way until I'm at least twenty-five or damn near thirty," Chanelle said with a sardonic chuckle.

"You know, you remind me a lot of my best friend, Terelle. You look a lot like her, too. She wasn't as lucky as you; she really got messed up." Hershey let out a long, sad sigh. "When you quit working for me, you said you were gonna go legit and start saving money. Didn't you say you wanted to get out of Philly and start all over again?"

"Uh-huh. I haven't changed my mind; I'm still leaving."

"Where're you going?"

"I don't know. Wanna hear something strange? You've been talking about not trusting people and I understand where you're coming from, but people who don't even know me have sent me their good wishes and have donated money. Now, I can hire a lawyer and change my name, go to school, and start all over again. And just like I believe in miracles, I believe that most people have good hearts."

Hershey was briefly pensive, then she reached into her purse. "Speaking of donations, I brought a little something to let you know I care."

"Aw, Hershey…you didn't have to…"

Hershey kissed Chanelle on the cheek. "Yes, I did," she said. "And by the way, can I ask you a favor?"

"Of course."

"You say you believe in miracles, so would you pray for a miracle for my best friend Terelle? She could sure use one."

Chanelle smiled and nodded. "I'm gonna pray real hard for your friend."

"Thanks." Hershey got up to leave. "Take care of yourself."

"I plan to take real good care of myself," Chanelle said and meant it with all her heart.

Chapter 43

Mother's Day. Searching for the warmth of Ammon, Dayna stretched out her arm. His side of the bed was empty. "Ammon," she whispered sleepily. No answer.

Forcing herself to become alert, she sat up, rubbed her eyes and glanced at the bedside clock. Seven-thirty. "Ammon," she called out louder, unable to keep the sound of alarm from creeping into her voice.

She called his name again. This time there was an agitated lilt to her tone. Still no answer. Where could he be this early on a Sunday morning? It wasn't that Dayna felt she had to keep tabs on Ammon; she just needed to know he was okay.

Life with Ammon was a wonderful dream, periodically disrupted by her own fear. That fear now pulled her thoughts back to the day Reed was sentenced to a twenty-year prison term.

The memory of his chilling last threats caused her to shudder. As Reed was being led away in handcuffs, he looked at Dayna and shouted: "It's not over, Dayna; you're still my wife. You must be crazy if you think I'm gonna let you run off into the sunset and cheat on me with that sandal-wearing artist. They haven't made prison bars strong enough to keep me away from you. Trust me; it's just a matter of time before I get out of here and reclaim you. Your adulterous boyfriend better watch his back," he threatened. "They got me on these bullshit charges, so if they take me down again…it's going to be for murder." Reed laughed and the sound of his sinister laughter still echoed in Dayna's mind.

Dayna had thought Reed to be a sociopath. He was. But he was also diagnosed as a sexual sadist. She was deeply worried and constantly plagued by the inescapable fear that Reed would find a way to break out of prison and kidnap her and murder Ammon.

To this day, she was still legally married to Reed. He refused to sign the divorce papers, and unfortunately, she would have to remain married to Reed for at least another year.

The elegant dream home she'd shared with Reed, now considered the House of Horrors, was still on the market, unsold. It appeared no one, and certainly not she, wanted to live in a house that had been the site of such a heinous crime.

A note propped against the door of the microwave filled her with instant relief:

I didn't forget brunch. I'm hard at work at the studio trying

to finish an important project. I'll be home around ten. Love,
Ammon

She breathed a sigh of relief and kissed the note. Oh, how she loved that man.

Ammon, now a successful and financially independent artist, used his former apartment as his studio. Together, he and Dayna lived in a cozy little one-story house that had a hovering weeping willow tree and was encircled by a picket fence.

With her fear of Reed pushed to the recesses of her mind, feeling cheerful now, Dayna filled the teapot with water. Humming softly, she drifted to the cabinet and reached for a bag of dried herbs and began blending together ingredients to brew her favorite tea.

❧❧❧

"Hey baby; I'm home," Ammon yelled.

"I'm in the bedroom," Dayna caroled, as she gave herself a final look in the mirror. She checked the time. "Ammon, hurry up; you have to get dressed. Our reservation is for eleven o'clock and you know what a stickler my mother is about being on time."

Wearing a paint-spattered T-shirt, Ammon came into the bedroom and flopped down on the bed. Specks of paint dotted his hands and fingers. He didn't seem to be in a hurry to shower and change.

Dayna gave him a sidelong look, which she hoped

would encourage him to get moving. He didn't budge.

"She found the perfect match in her new boyfriend," Dayna continued, deciding to ignore Ammon's resistance to getting dressed. "He's worse than my mother when it comes to punctuality. They're probably both standing in her doorway right now—arms folded, tapping their feet," Dayna said with a chuckle. Ammon smiled, but didn't seem to find the comment funny. It certainly didn't encourage him to start getting ready for brunch.

"Ammon," Dayna admonished. "Get up. Any second, the phone's going to ring and I'm letting you explain why we still haven't left."

"Okay. Let me rest a few minutes; I've been working since four o' clock this morning."

"Four o'clock! What were you working on at that hour of the morning? I can't believe I slept so peacefully without you lying next to me. How come you never mentioned having to work on a special project?"

"Must have slipped my mind," he said casually.

Dayna swatted his leg. "Come on, Ammon; start getting dressed." She used a whiny voice to get him moving along.

"All right." He rose lazily. "Oh, I just remembered something," he said, sounding suddenly enthused.

"What?"

"It's in the living room." He grasped her hand. "There's something I want to show you."

Dayna followed an energetic Ammon. With lumbering

movements, however, she could barely keep up his pace.

In the living room was a covered canvas, which she found odd since Ammon hardly ever brought commissioned work home. She usually visited his studio to see his work. With her curious face tilted and resting on her palm, Dayna waited anxiously for Ammon to show her the finished painting.

He removed the cover and Dayna gasped, closed her eyes, and placed both hands on her stomach. Finding it difficult to breathe she began to pant. Ammon rushed to her side. "What's wrong, baby? Are you all right? Do you want to sit down?"

Speechless, she shook her head and whimpered, "Thank you," as she pointed to the painting.

The painting reminded Dayna of Ammon's mural "Family" but with a different twist. In this painting, the man kissed the woman's neck; his arms were wrapped around her. The woman's eyes were downcast as she looked lovingly at her man's hands, which rested upon her swollen belly.

Ammon walked behind Dayna and embraced her from behind. Rubbing her pregnant stomach, he whispered in her ear, "Happy Mother's Day, baby. Do you like your present?"

"I love it," she said, weeping. "It's you and me."

"And our unborn child," Ammon added, rocking her while standing.

"What's the title of the painting?"

Ammon smiled. He gave Dayna a kiss and said, "It's called 'Sacred Love.'"

Never had she known such happiness, never had she felt so honored and respected—never had she felt so complete. Every day with Ammon was a joyous celebration. The experience of their oneness was truly sacred love.

AUTHOR BIO

Allison Hobbs was raised in suburban Philadelphia. After high school she worked for several years in the music industry as a singer, songwriter, and studio background vocalist. She eventually attended Temple University and earned a Bachelor of Science degree. She is the national bestselling author of *Pandora's Box, Insatiable, Double Dippin'*, *The Enchantress* and the upcoming *A Bona Fide Gold Digger*. Hobbs currently resides in Philadelphia. Visit her at www.allisonhobbs.com and www.myspace.com/allisonhobbs or email her at pb@allisonhobbs.com